"Nate, I'm so sorry. I shouldn't have—"

"Don't."

His sharp command startled her into silence. Why was he so angry with her?

His jaw tensed and he raked his fingers through his hair with an angry, jerky thrust. "Don't apologize. You didn't do anything wrong."

Was he just being polite, trying to spare her feelings? "I don't understand."

He took a deep, defeated-sounding breath. "You think I'm a hero. I'm not."

That again. "You're being too modest. You—"

But he wouldn't let her finish. "Verity, I don't deserve hero worship. Not from you, not from anyone. I treasure every moment of our time together this afternoon, more than you will ever know. But you don't know—"

Seeing the dread in his expression, she wasn't really sure she wanted to hear what he had to say. "If it's something you'd rather not talk about, don't feel you need to tell me."

His smile had more grimace than humor to it. "Too late. I need to tell you this for myself as well as for you. There's something you don't know about me, about what I've done."

Winnie Griggs is the multipublished, award-winning author of historical (and occasionally contemporary) romances that focus on Small Towns, Big Hearts, Amazing Grace. She is also a list maker and a lover of dragonflies and holds an advanced degree in the art of procrastination. Winnie loves to hear from readers—you can connect with her on Facebook at facebook.com/winniegriggs.author or email her at winnie@winniegriggs.com.

Books by Winnie Griggs

Love Inspired Historical

Texas Grooms

Handpicked Husband
The Bride Next Door
A Family for Christmas
Lone Star Heiress
Her Holiday Family
Second Chance Hero

Visit the Author Profile page at Harlequin.com for more titles

WINNIE GRIGGS

Second Chance Hero

HARLEQUIN® LOVE INSPIRED® HISTORICAL

Recycling programs for this product may not exist in your area.

 LOVE INSPIRED BOOKS

ISBN-13: 978-0-373-28311-8

Second Chance Hero

www.Harlequin.com

Printed in U.S.A.

For God has not given us a spirit of timidity;
but of power, and of love, and of a sound mind.
—2 Timothy 1:7

With sincere thanks to my generous friends who are always ready to brainstorm with me— Connie, Amy, Christopher, Dustin, Renee, Beth and Lenora. And to my fabulous editor Melissa Endlich, whose suggestions are always aimed at making my work tighter and stronger.

Chapter One

Turnabout, Texas
April 1897

Verity Leggett took firmer hold of her daughter's hand as they approached the street crossing. There wasn't much in the way of carriage or horse traffic this time of morning, but she always preferred to err on the side of caution, especially where Joy was concerned.

Suddenly Joy stopped in her tracks and pointed to her right. "Look, Mama, a dog."

Verity stared suspiciously at the hound slinking out of an alley two blocks away. She was glad they weren't headed in that direction. Joy loved animals with all the indiscriminate abandon her five-year-old heart could summon. She definitely hadn't learned the value of caution yet.

"I see him." Verity hitched the handle of the hatbox she carried a little closer to her elbow. "But Miss Hazel's dress shop is this way. And don't forget, you can play with Buttons when we get there."

Distracted by thoughts of the cat who resided in

the dress shop, Joy faced forward again, cradling her doll, Lulu, in the crook of her arm, and gave a little hop-skip. "I brought a piece of yarn for Buttons to play with."

"I'm sure Buttons will be quite pleased." Verity knew her droll tone was lost on her daughter, but that was okay. It was just so good to see how well Joy was thriving since they'd moved to Turnabout a year ago.

As Verity guided her daughter onto Second Street, her gaze slid past the closed doors of the apothecary and the saddle shop to focus on the last building on the block. Good—the dress shop was already open. She gave the hatbox a little swing and grinned in anticipation of Hazel's reaction to her latest millinery creation. It was just the sort of flamboyant frippery her friend liked.

The new sign Hazel had recently hung over her shop door was an example of just how far her friend would take her love of the dramatic. It was elaborate in shape, brick red in color, and was emblazoned in fancy gold lettering that proclaimed the establishment to be Hazel's Fashion Emporium. Her friend was quite put out that folks in town still referred to her business as simply "the dress shop."

Then, almost as if drawn to it, her gaze moved to the closed door of the shop next to Hazel's. The window bore the name Cooper's Saddle, Tack & Supply in crisp white letters. Mr. Cooper, the owner, had moved to Turnabout just a couple of weeks ago and had opened his shop on Monday. She hadn't officially met him yet—only seen him from a distance in church and around town. Not that she was in any hurry to get to know him better. After all, she was twenty-four years old and a widow. Hardly someone who would be looking to form attachments of that sort.

And even if she had been looking for such a thing, Mr. Cooper was not at *all* the type of man she'd be attracted to. There was a guarded air about him that, even from a distance, made her think he wasn't all he seemed, that he held something tightly leashed inside himself. Perhaps it was just her imagination, but it was enough to put her guard up. Some women might be attracted to men who seemed just a little bit dangerous or adventurous, but she preferred someone who was dependable and reliable, someone like her late husband, Arthur.

Still, something about the man tugged at her imagination…

The door to the saddle shop opened as if on cue, and her pulse kicked up a notch. But to her surprise, instead of Mr. Cooper, a small brown dog padded out. The animal looked around, then sat on its haunches next to the doorway, for all the world as if it were guarding the place.

Surely that animal didn't belong to Mr. Cooper? She would have pictured him with a large hunting dog—not this small, cuddly-looking pet that reminded her of a child's stuffed bear.

Joy, who was chattering to her doll, Lulu, about Buttons, hadn't noticed the animal yet. Verity braced herself for the gleeful clamor that would come whenever her daughter *did* notice.

A heartbeat later Mr. Cooper himself stepped out, broom in hand, and Verity paused the merest fraction between one step and the next. There was no denying that there was a presence about the man, much more impactful up close than from a distance. It wasn't his size—he couldn't be more than a couple of inches taller than she was, maybe five foot nine. Nor did he seem to be actively trying to command attention. In fact just the opposite. But there was a hardness about him, an air of stoicism and confidence—or was it a kind of self-containment?—that was hard to ignore.

Then he bent to scratch the dog behind the ears, and her impression of him shifted. His closed expression softened to something resembling exasperated affection, and the dog responded with tail-wagging exuberance. His brown hair, worn a bit longer than normally seen around here, was nearly as dark as his dog's coat and it had the slightest of waves to it.

Mr. Cooper straightened, obviously ready to sweep the walk in front of his shop, and only then noticed the two of them approaching. His expression closed again and he paused to let them pass.

It seemed she was going to meet the newcomer now, whether she wanted to or not—at least enough to exchange greetings. His gaze might be impassive, but still Verity's nerves jangled at being the focus of it. She tamped that feeling down, but before she could offer a greeting, Joy spotted the dog.

"Oh, look at the little doggie, Mama. Isn't he cute?"

Verity nodded, studiously *not* looking Mr. Cooper's way. "Yes, he is."

Joy, however, seemed to have no qualms about meeting Mr. Cooper's eyes. "Is he your doggie, Mister?" she asked brightly.

The man's expression eased into a slight smile. "He is. His name is Beans."

Verity blinked. What an odd name to give a dog.

Even odder still that such a fanciful name had come from such a decidedly *un*fanciful-seeming man.

"Can I pet him?" Joy asked.

Verity, worried about allowing her daughter to approach a strange animal, stepped in before Mr. Cooper could respond. "Stop pestering Mr. Cooper—it's not polite. We need—"

"It's no bother." His voice had a husky, gravelly quality to it. But it wasn't unpleasant. In fact she rather liked the sound of it.

"Beans won't hurt the child," he said. Then he turned back to Joy and gave her another smile. "If your mother allows it, Beans and I don't mind."

Joy looked up at Verity. "Can I, Mama, please?"

"*May* I," Verity corrected. She glanced at the dog. The animal appeared friendly enough, so she gave a reluctant nod. "Very well, but just a quick, gentle pat. We need to get along to Miss Hazel's shop."

Smiling brightly, Joy rushed over to the dog and knelt down to stroke its head and talk nonsense to it for a minute. The dog accepted the attention with a happy wag of its tail. A moment later it had its two front paws planted on Joy's knees and was trying to bathe her face with his tongue.

Verity made a small involuntary move to intervene, and then the sound of Joy's giggles stopped her. She supposed there was no real harm in letting her daughter have fun with the animal for a few minutes.

Instead, she forced herself to look away from Joy and face the dog's owner. Up close, Mr. Cooper was even more interesting. There was an ever-so-slight dimple in his chin, but it in no way took away from his firm jawline or the chiseled planes of his face. It was those piercing blue-gray eyes, however, that drew her in, made her want to learn more about him. Combine that with his guarded air, and he had a definite presence about him. He wasn't exactly what you'd call handsome—his features were too irregular for that. No, not handsome, but arresting.

Yes, most definitely arresting.

Then she realized he was waiting for her to say something. "I hope you don't mind," she said with what she hoped was a neighborly smile. "Joy has such a love for animals, it's impossible for her to pass one by without stopping to pet it."

"Beans seems to be enjoying the attention," he said noncommittally. Then he glanced toward Joy. "My sister was the same way."

She noticed something momentarily cloud his expression, but it was gone by the time he turned back to her. Then she realized he'd used the word *was*. She'd passed away then. Was his loss recent?

Verity decided to change the subject. "It's nice to see someone making use of the old boot shop."

He nodded. "It's working out well for what I need."

Definitely not much of a conversationalist. She tried again. "How are you liking Turnabout so far?"

"The folks here are neighborly and it seems like a good place to set down roots."

Is that what he wanted to do—set down roots? Stability and responsibility were certainly fine traits to aspire to. But did that mean he'd been a drifter before he came here?

"I'm pleased to hear it." Then, remembering that poignant mention of his sister, her smile warmed. "And if you're looking to leave your past behind you," she said softly, "and find a new place to belong, then you've come to the right place."

At the flash of surprise in his eyes, she realized just how presumptuous that must have sounded. Embarrassed, she quickly turned to Joy and held her hand out. "Come along, pumpkin. Time to tell the dog goodbye. Thank Mr. Cooper and let's be on our way."

Joy obediently turned to Beans's owner. "Thank you, Mr. Cooper. Beans is a nice doggie." She held out her doll. "And Lulu likes him, too."

Risking a glance his way, Verity saw that he was giving her daughter a broad smile, apparently choosing to ignore her own ill-conceived remarks of a moment ago.

"You're welcome," he said, executing a half bow. "Both of you. Anytime."

Verity decided he should smile more often—it transformed his face, making him appear much more approachable. But perhaps he reserved his smiles for puppies and children.

As if to punctuate that thought, he turned back to her, his expression once more merely polite. Then he nodded and took firmer hold of his broom.

Intrigued by these contradictory glimpses of the man, and still embarrassed by her earlier words, Verity put a hand on Joy's shoulder and gently nudged her toward Hazel's shop.

And tried not to think too hard about the fact that she'd like to see one of those warmer smiles directed her way.

Nate Cooper swept the sidewalk in front of his shop, his thoughts focused on the mother and daughter who'd just walked away.

He glanced down and noticed Beans watching them, as well. The animal's tail was still wagging, but much slower now. "You like that little girl, don't you, boy?"

Beans looked up as if he understood the question, and Nate paused long enough to give him a quick scratch behind the ears. "Well, don't worry," he said as he straightened. "I'm pretty sure she likes you, as well."

The little girl—Joy, her mother had called her—had certainly been taken with his four-legged companion. Her giggles had been sweet proof of that.

For just a heartbeat, she'd reminded him of Susanna. Joy's physical resemblance to his younger sister was only superficial—honey-colored hair and a button nose—but it was the way the child had responded to Beans that had tugged at him. Susanna had loved animals with that same wholeheartedness, especially dogs.

It was surprising how, after all these years, little reminders like that could hit him in the gut with such force.

As he pushed the broom, his thoughts shifted from the child to her mother. There were definitely no bittersweet memories to ambush him when thinking of her. Quite the opposite.

This wasn't the first time he'd noticed her since his move to Turnabout. She was a member of the small choir at the local church. Both times he'd attended the service there, he'd taken notice of her. Not at first, though. The drab widow's weeds she wore and her dark hair had made her a shadow that the eye easily skipped past.

But all that changed the moment she began to sing.

Her face took on such a luminously serene yet passionate glow, as if she truly felt every word, every note she sang. And even from where he sat he could see a fire in her large green eyes that drew him. He hadn't been able to take his gaze off of her until the preacher began his sermon.

There'd been none of that fire in her today, though. In fact, the way she'd reacted when her daughter approached his little bit of a dog, she'd seemed nervous and something of a handwringer. Did that enchanting spark come through only when she sang?

Still, knowing it was there, he was intrigued enough to want to unearth it. And just now he'd found he liked her speaking voice too, a difficult-to-describe mix of genteel lady and country girl. There was something else he'd noticed as well, something that hadn't been apparent until he'd seen her up close just now. Right below the left corner of her mouth was the faintest of small scars. It didn't detract from her appearance. In fact, if anything it added an element of interest to her otherwise merely pleasant features. It also made him want to find out how she'd gotten it.

But it was when she'd relaxed enough to show him a genuine smile just now that she'd really caught his attention. The words that had accompanied her smile, however, had startled him. It was almost as if she'd understood his private yearnings.

Had she really meant what she said, or was it just some sort of polite bit of verbiage she would have said to any newcomer? And if she knew what sort of past he was trying to leave behind him, would she still have uttered those words?

She'd obviously known his name, but he had no idea

what hers was. And since she hadn't offered, he hadn't felt it appropriate to ask.

But now he wondered—should he have asked? There'd been a time when he would have known how to carry on a polite conversation, but his social skills had grown rusty with disuse.

If he was ever going to fit in here, though, he'd need to relearn.

"I think the sidewalk is clean enough."

Nate looked up to see Adam Barr standing there, an amused half smile on his face. Adam was the closest thing Nate had to a friend these days, and was the person to whom he owed his current toehold on stability.

Nate returned the smile. "Just enjoying the morning sunshine."

Adam nodded and Nate knew without any exchange of words that his friend understood his meaning.

Nate leaned against the broom. "And what is the town's esteemed banker doing on this side of the street? Checking up on me?" He was only half joking. The bank, where Adam had his office, was a block and a half in the other direction.

"Not at all." Adam nodded toward the apothecary. "Reggie asked me to stop by Flaherty's for her."

Nate frowned. Reggie, Adam's wife, was expecting their third child. "She's not taken ill I hope."

Adam shook his head. "No, nothing like that. It's for Patricia. She's developed a rash and Reggie asked me to pick up some ointment for it." Beans had joined them now and was sniffing at Adam's boots. The man stooped down to absently scratch the animal behind the ears. "So how *is* business?"

Nate shrugged. "Slow. I sold a bridle Monday and

yesterday Ed Strickland brought in a harness for me to mend." He tightened his hold on the broom handle. "But it's only my third day so I didn't expect a rush of business just yet." But it would need to pick up soon if he was going to pay his bills.

Adam nodded toward the display window. "I imagine that's getting you some interest."

Nate glanced at the item Adam was referring to and felt a small tug of pride. It was a saddle—one of the few possessions he'd brought with him to Turnabout. He'd made it himself and spent a lot of time and effort on it. The display piece was a visible testament to his skill as a saddler. "I've had a few inquiries, but nothing serious yet."

"I predict it will catch just the right eye soon." Then Adam glanced ahead. "Looks like Mr. Flaherty is opening his doors, so I'll let you get back to your sweeping." And with a nod, Adam headed for the apothecary.

Nate brushed the broom over the sidewalk one last time, his thoughts still with his friend. When Adam had invited him to move here to Turnabout, he'd described the town as a good place for fresh starts, something he'd known Nate was seeking. Nate had now seen firsthand just how well things had worked out for Adam. His friend, who hailed from Philadelphia, had truly made a life for himself in this town. He'd married a local woman and now had two children with a third on the way. He also had a position as manager of the local bank and had become an accepted, even prominent, member of this community. All that in spite of having spent six years in prison. Of course, not everyone here knew that part of his past.

Nate, whose own past was similar to Adam's, both in where he'd come from and where he'd been, passionately wanted that kind of future for himself. At least the being accepted and belonging part.

It wasn't that he didn't want the family part too—he absolutely did. It was just that he knew it was better—for everyone—if he didn't pursue that dream.

For one thing, he had no luck whatsoever in relationships. More often than not, he ended up hurting the very people he cared most about.

For another, he could never pursue a serious relationship with a woman without letting her know what he'd done. And what woman would want to marry a man with a past like his? Especially not a certain widow whose face popped into his head at the thought. No, it was best all the way around if he just settled for a comfortable, neighborly relationship with the folks around here.

After all, what more could a man who'd robbed a bank and then spent nine years in prison paying for it expect?

Chapter Two

"I can't wait to see the latest of your fabulous creations."

Verity firmly pushed aside thoughts of the very interesting Mr. Cooper as she smiled at her friend Hazel's extravagant compliment. "I'm not sure about fabulous, but I do hope you like it." She glanced toward Joy, who sat on the floor playing with Buttons. Maybe someday, when they had a house of their own, she could get Joy the pet she so passionately wanted. In the meantime, perhaps Aunt Betty and Uncle Grover wouldn't mind a caged pet, like a sweet little songbird...

"Oh, my..."

Her friend's delighted exclamation pulled Verity's thoughts back to the present.

Hazel lifted Verity's current millinery creation out of the hatbox and studied it, her eyes gratifyingly alight with admiration. "I do believe this is your best one yet. It's absolutely exquisite." Then she shook her head in mock confusion. "Who would guess that your restrained demeanor hides a woman with such a stylish flair?"

Verity drew up at that. "I'm a widow, remember. My *restrained demeanor*, as you call it, is not only appropriate but expected."

Hazel seemed unimpressed by her reasoning. "You've been widowed over a year now, so it's okay to put off wearing such dreary colors all the time. And we both know that before you were even married you dressed much more conservatively than the rest of us."

Verity knew her friend meant well, but the words still stung. As if her mourning for Arthur would automatically end based on a date on a calendar. Besides, she had already added some color to her wardrobe. True, she still wore black skirts, but her shirtwaists contained gray or lavender or even some dark green. In fact, her Sunday best was the only solid-black dress she still wore, and she'd even added a bit of gray to the collar and cuffs of that one. It was only proper that, as a widow, she didn't try to wear bright colors or frills.

As for the rest, with that scar on her face, she'd never been one of the "pretty girls," and she'd long since come to terms with that.

Verity gave her friend an exasperated look. "Not all of us are as comfortable with flamboyant airs and drama as you are."

This shop was proof of that. Color and furbelows were everywhere. Besides the dress forms that displayed examples of her work, there were bolts of fabrics in every shade imaginable, from pastels to deep jewel tones, both solids and prints, spools of lace and cord and ribbons, trimmings such as feathers and beads and medallions, fashion plates displayed artfully around the store—and all arranged in a manner to catch the eye and entice one to come close to admire and touch and perhaps purchase.

Verity loved it here, loved how it made her feel, as if she was inside a fantastical daydream where nothing harsh could intrude.

But she was just a visitor here—it wasn't *her* world. "Which is a shame."

For a startled moment Verity thought her friend had read her thoughts. Then she realized Hazel was merely responding to her last statement.

Hazel's grin had an I-know-best twist to it. "I think a little flamboyancy and drama in your life is just what you need."

Verity relaxed and returned her grin. "That's what I have you in my life for. And why I create these hats." One of the things she'd missed most about Turnabout when she'd married Arthur and moved so far away was her friendship with Hazel. They'd kept in touch with the occasional letter, but being able to spend time together was so much better.

When Verity had moved back to Turnabout after Arthur's death last year, she and Hazel had picked up where they'd left off.

Joy's giggles drew her attention and she glanced in that direction. The girl was jiggling her bit of yarn in front of Buttons. Hazel's cat was trying to bat at it with one of her front paws, much to Joy's delight.

Verity turned back to see Hazel rotating the hat this way and that, trying to view it from all angles. Wetting her lips and affecting a casual expression, Verity gave in to the urge to do a little probing. "Have you met your new neighbor yet?"

"You mean Mr. Cooper?" Hazel glanced out the

door, as if she could see around the corner to his shop. "Just casually. He seems rather mysterious, don't you think, just showing up here out of the blue?" Her eyes sparkled with saucy speculation. "I know he's a friend of Adam Barr's, but still, one can't help but wonder what his story is. Especially when he looks right at you with those striking eyes."

Verity popped her hand on her hip in mock outrage. "Hazel Theresa Andrews, I thought you were sweet on the sheriff. Has another man finally caught your fancy?"

Hazel tossed her head. "I'm getting tired of waiting for Ward Gleason to take notice of me. It certainly won't hurt anything to let him know I have options." Then she narrowed her eyes. "Why do you ask? Do you have *your* eye on Mr. Cooper?"

Seeing the speculation in her friend's expression, Verity tilted her chin up defensively. "Don't be silly. I don't even know the man."

"He didn't happen to be outside his store when you walked by just now, did he?"

Hazel was too perceptive by half. "He was. And yes, we chatted for a moment. But only because Joy wanted to pet his dog. You know she can't pass by an animal without wanting to play with it."

"So you *did* meet him."

"Not exactly." She waved a hand. "I mean, no introductions were exchanged. But saying hello was the neighborly thing to do." Verity mentally cringed when she heard the defensive note creep into her voice.

And of course Hazel pounced right on it. "Well, now, isn't this an interesting turn of events. Our meek-as-a-lamb, practical-as-prunes Verity is interested in the very rugged and far-from-meek-looking Mr. Cooper."

"Don't be silly," she said, drawing herself up even straighter. "I have no interest in the man beyond a natural curiosity."

"Of course you don't." But from the knowing smile on Hazel's lips, Verity could tell her friend didn't believe her protests. It was time to steer this conversation in a different direction.

"Thanks for letting Joy play with Buttons," she said. "She looks forward to it whenever I tell her I'm headed over here."

To Verity's relief, Hazel accepted the change of subject as she carried the hat to the nearby cheval glass. "Buttons enjoys it, too," her friend said absently as she placed the hat on her head at a sassy angle. Then she preened, turning and tilting her head different ways to admire the effect. "Oh, I love it, especially the flirty way the brim is folded. If it wasn't yellow I'd consider keeping it for myself." She glanced over her shoulder at Verity. "Yellow never was my color."

Verity disagreed. With Hazel's vivacious red-gold hair and sparkling green eyes, there was very little that didn't look good on her. But she kept her opinion to herself.

Hazel removed the hat and turned back around. "Now, you on the other hand, with that gorgeous mahogany-colored hair and your fair complexion, would look stunning in this."

"Not particularly suitable mourning attire," Verity said drily.

Hazel sighed dramatically. "I've already said my piece on *that* subject. But I can tell your mind is made up." Then she shrugged. "Ah, well, it'll look nice in the window next to that lavender dress with the scrumptious lace."

Verity fidgeted with her sleeve. "I do wish you'd let me pay you something for displaying my hats in your shop."

"Well, I won't, so let's hear no more about it." Hazel patted a few stray hairs back in place before moving away from the mirror. "And don't think it's because I'm feeling altruistic. I'm getting something out of it, too. My sales have definitely gone up since your hats went on display next to my dresses."

Verity had been thinking lately that she'd like to open a millinery shop of her own one day, and Hazel's words gave her an added nudge in that direction. Despite Uncle Grover's and Aunt Betty's assertions that they liked having her and Joy stay with them, she couldn't—wouldn't—live on their charity forever. It had been fifteen months since that awful day Arthur was killed. It was time for her to move on with her life, to decide what kind of future she wanted for herself and Joy.

If she could start her own business and make a go of it, she might just be able to afford to have a home of her own again. But there was so much risk involved in such an undertaking, risks she wasn't sure she could afford to take. It definitely wasn't a step to take lightly. For one thing she'd have to save up more money before she could even get started. And what if she failed? Besides, the one time she'd mentioned it to Uncle Grover, he'd counseled her about all the pitfalls she could face and she'd gotten the impression he didn't think it was something she should even attempt.

Still, every time she allowed herself to dream about the future she wanted for herself and Joy, the yearning to take more control of her life grew.

"Have you heard about the plans for the Founders' Day celebration?"

Verity pushed away her daydreams and focused on Hazel's question. "You mean there's going to be more to it than the town picnic this year?"

"A *lot* more. Ever since Mayor Sanders realized this is the seventy-fifth anniversary of Turnabout's founding, he's wanted to do something special, which to him means something bigger and flashier."

That was Mayor Sanders, all right. Some things about this town never changed.

"He's talking about a grand festival," Hazel continued, "sort of like a county fair, with games, contests, food, performances. He's even talking about bringing in a traveling circus or an acting troupe."

Verity listened with only half an ear as Hazel recounted the discussion from yesterday's town council meeting. Instead, her thoughts drifted back to Mr. Cooper.

Hazel was wrong. She wasn't taken with the man. Well, not exactly. She was merely curious about him. When she looked into his intense eyes, she still got the sense of something controlled but dangerous. Yet seeing him with that little lapdog had contradicted that impression. Showing kindness to a small animal and speaking of putting down roots seemed to indicate a man who was compassionate and responsible.

Which was the real man? Or was it possible he could be a combination of both?

The sound of a dog barking outside made her think

again of the small dog itself. Beans—what a whimsical name for the animal.

Perhaps someday—there was that nebulous *someday* again—if she could find a similar lapdog, one that she knew was well behaved, she could get it for Joy.

Verity glanced over her shoulder to check on her daughter again, but neither the five-year-old nor the cat was in the same spot any longer. She turned fully around. "Joy?" Where had the girl gotten off to?

Hazel paused midsentence and glanced quickly around the shop. "She probably followed Buttons to one of his hiding places. Check behind the counter."

"Joy!" Verity said the name louder this time, using her no-nonsense, answer-me-now voice. She knew it was probably an overreaction, but she couldn't help herself. Her late husband's violent death had given her a terrible lesson on how tragedy could strike in the blink of an eye. And she'd found herself wanting to hold tighter and tighter to her daughter ever since.

When there was still no response, Verity's focus sharpened. If Joy was just behind the counter, why wasn't she answering? "Joy, this isn't a game. Come out this minute."

Still no answer. Could she have gone upstairs? Verity had half turned in that direction when Hazel spoke up, halting her in her tracks.

"She's out on the sidewalk."

Verity spun around and headed for the door. Why hadn't she kept a closer eye on Joy?

A warning shout sounded just as she stepped outside, closely followed by a gasp from Hazel.

She watched in horror as her daughter, intent on chasing Buttons, darted in front of an oncoming wagon. Verity raced forward screaming Joy's name. The child turned, then froze as she saw the horse bearing down on her.

Verity stumbled and realized with shattering clarity that she would never reach Joy in time.

Chapter Three

For an agonizing heartbeat, as the wagon bore down on her daughter, time froze. Verity felt every irregularity in the pebble that bit into her palm, could taste the tang of blood from where she'd bit the inside of her cheek when she fell to the ground, could see the dust motes hanging in the air before her.

Please, Jesus. Please, Jesus. Please, Jesus.

She wasn't sure whether she was uttering the frantic prayer aloud or if it was just shrieking through her thoughts.

From somewhere a woman screamed, but all sounds, save for the wagon's relentless rumbling progress, seemed to come from a great distance.

Verity spotted the moment the wagon driver spied Joy and tried to turn his horses.

And still Joy didn't move.

Then, from out of nowhere, Mr. Cooper shot past her, and time sped up with a whoosh. He dived toward Joy, reaching her a heart-stopping split second before the horse's hooves would have trampled the child, and pushing her out of the way.

Without remembering having moved, Verity was suddenly kneeling in the road with her weeping daughter clutched tightly against her. Her heart thudded painfully against her chest and her breath came in near gasps. She'd come so close to losing her precious baby. She could still feel the stab of keening desolation that pierced her the moment she'd realized she couldn't get to Joy in time. This time the prayer she sent up was one of thanksgiving.

"Mama, you're squeezing too tight." Joy's querulous complaint ended on a hiccup.

Verity had to fight down the hysterical bubble of laughter that wanted to leap from her throat. Instead she loosened her hold and pushed back just enough to examine her daughter, brushing aside a tendril of Joy's hair with fingers that trembled uncontrollably. "Don't you *ever* scare Mommy like that again."

Joy shook her head, then hiccupped again as her tears stopped.

Verity was vaguely aware that Hazel stood at her elbow and that a crowd had gathered, but her attention remained focused on reassuring herself that Joy really was okay.

Fortunately, her daughter appeared more scared and confused than hurt. The stains and smears on her pinafore were dirt, not blood.

"I'm so sorry."

Verity looked up into the pale, worried face of Nestor James, the wagon driver.

"Please tell me your little girl's okay," he continued as he crushed his hat in his hands. "I didn't see her 'til I was practically on top of her."

"It's not your fault, Mr. James." Though her voice

was still shaky, now that Verity knew Joy was okay she could be reasonable. "I should have kept closer watch over her. And it appears Joy isn't hurt—just shaken up. Thanks to Mr. Cooper."

She looked around for the man who'd saved her daughter.

And only then realized he hadn't fared as well as Joy.

He was sitting up, his movements slow and stiff. There was a darkening bruise on his forehead, he held his left arm stiffly and his sleeve was ripped and stained with blood and dirt.

Sheriff Gleason had bent down to lend him a hand up.

Verity immediately intervened. "Don't get up yet, Mr. Cooper. Not until I've had a look at you." There was no telling how badly he might be injured.

He gave her a startled look, which she ignored. Instead she turned to Sheriff Gleason. "Keep an eye on him, please." Then she turned back to Joy. "Do you hurt anywhere, pumpkin?"

Joy bent her right arm and lifted it for inspection. "I hurted my elbow. And Lulu got smushed."

Quickly noting that Joy's elbow was merely scraped, Verity bent down and gave it a kiss. "There, is that better?"

Joy nodded, swiping at the dirt and tears on her face with her other sleeve. Then she handed the doll up to her mother. Verity obediently gave the doll a kiss, as well. "There. You should both feel better once you've washed up a bit."

Then she gave her daughter a stern look. "Now, I

want you to stay close to Miss Hazel while I check on Mr. Cooper."

"Yes, ma'am."

Hazel took Joy's hand and gave Verity a nod.

Inhaling a fortifying breath, Verity turned to check on the condition of the man to whom she owed so much.

Nate Cooper watched the woman's sudden transformation with fascination. A moment ago she'd been understandably shaky, emotional, on the verge of hysteria even, over what had nearly happened to her daughter.

He would have thought that the sight of his sorry state would have pushed her even further toward hysteria. Instead, she seemed composed and even decisive. Which was something of a relief. He'd rather deal with an oncoming wagon all over again than with an overly emotional woman.

But what had she meant by *have a look at you*? Did she fancy herself a doctor? He'd seen the kiss-it-and-make-it-better approach she'd used with her daughter and the doll—not exactly by-the-book medicine. Though, come to think on it, he wouldn't be particularly averse if she wanted to try that method with him...

He quickly pushed that entirely inappropriate thought aside as the woman in question knelt down beside him.

"Before I do anything else," she said softly, "I want to tell you how unbelievably brave what you just did was, and to let you know I'm so much more than grateful. You not only saved my daughter just now, but me, as well."

The woman's moss-green eyes glowed with a gratitude that verged on hero worship. That shook him much more than the accident with the wagon had. He hadn't been on the receiving end of such a look since he'd lost his sister nearly a decade ago, and he wasn't quite sure what to make of it. But hero worship was something he didn't want.

Or deserve.

He'd just been at the right place at the right time—nothing more. He'd seen Beans bark at the cat and send it running across the road. He'd then seen the child follow the feline. It had been pure instinct to go after her—nothing heroic about it.

"I'll be okay," he said brusquely, waving the woman away with his right hand. "You should see to your daughter."

The woman ignored his suggestion and began rolling up her sleeves. "Joy is fine, thanks to you. And that gash on your arm definitely needs some attention."

Without waiting for a response from him, she glanced up at the crowd milling around them. "Someone get me a pail of water to clean this up. And I'll need some clean rags, as well."

To his surprise, several individuals from the crowd nodded and rushed off to do her bidding. Then she turned to Sheriff Gleason. "Do you have a pocket-knife I can borrow?"

The lawman never hesitated. He pulled out his knife, opened it for her and handed it over.

Nate raised a hand. "Now, hold on." These folks might trust the woman, but he wasn't ready to let her cut on him. "What do you intend to do with that thing?"

Her brow went up and there was an amused twist

to her lips. "Don't worry, I'm not planning to operate on you. Yet." He was only partly reassured by her dry tone.

She took the knife and, with a quick movement, sliced his already ripped shirt all the way to the cuff.

He tried one more time to wrest control from the stubborn woman. "See, it's just a cut. I'll be okay. If it makes you feel better I'll go see the doctor." He tried to push himself up, but a sharp pain shot through his left ankle and he winced involuntarily.

"You are *not* okay." She put a firm hand on his right shoulder. "Don't move until I have a look at you." Her expression softened slightly. "Don't worry, I do have some medical training."

That would explain her air of authority. But was she serious? "You're a doctor?"

"Not exactly. But the town's doctor is my uncle and my late husband was a physician, as well. So you see, I've worked with doctors most of my life. I know what to do."

The "not exactly doctor" turned to the dressmaker, who still held the little girl's hand. "Would you mind taking Joy back to your shop until I've finished here?"

"Of course." Miss Andrews smiled down at the little girl. "Come on, sweetie, let's get you and Lulu cleaned up and then we'll see if we can find a cookie to snack on."

The woman's gaze lingered on her daughter as the two walked away. But a moment later a young man set the requested pail of water at her feet and she turned to smile up at him. "Thank you, Calvin. Now would you mind running over to the clinic and letting my uncle know he'll have a patient shortly?"

"Yes, ma'am." And with that the young man was off again.

Finally she turned back to him. "Since I'm about to tend to your injuries," she said with a caretaker's smile, "I should probably introduce myself. I'm Mrs. Verity Leggett."

Nate gave a short nod. "Mrs. Leggett. I'm Nate Cooper."

"Now that we've gotten the pleasantries out of the way, let's get this arm cleaned up, shall we, so we can see what we're dealing with?"

He still wasn't comfortable with the idea of being examined by a female doctor, no matter how pretty or confident she was. It seemed vaguely ungentlemanly to put her through such unpleasantness. "There's no need to trouble yourself, Mrs. Leggett. I can get myself over to the doctor—"

She didn't let him finish. "I agree that my uncle should see you. And he will—just as soon as I make sure we have this cleaned up and the bleeding has stopped."

She dipped a cloth in the water and then gently dabbed at the gash, cleaning away the dirt and blood with her right hand while she supported his arm with her left. Her touch was gentle but sure, and not at all unpleasant.

As Mrs. Leggett bent over him, he could smell the faint scent of honeysuckle on her, could see the glint of sunlight tease out touches of auburn in her mahogany hair. The feel of her hand supporting his arm as she gently cleaned the cut was warm and strong in a uniquely feminine kind of way.

As she bent closer to study her progress, that stray

image of her kissing her daughter's injury popped up in his mind again. Would she—

He abruptly pulled his thoughts back from that dangerous cliff. His reaction to her was a testament to how long it had been since he'd felt the gentle ministrations of a woman, nothing more. And he was certain she wouldn't welcome any indications that he felt anything other than gratitude.

When Mrs. Leggett had the cut cleaned to her satisfaction, she leaned back and studied it. "You're definitely going to need stitches, but I don't believe you've cut anything vital." She looked up then and met his gaze with a reassuring smile. "The bleeding has slowed, but I'm going to wrap it tight to make certain it doesn't start flowing again before we get you to the clinic."

When she had put action to words, she met his gaze again. "Now, your left leg seemed to be giving you problems when you tried to get up. Where does it hurt?"

So she'd picked up on that. "It's my ankle, but I'm sure it'll be fine in just a bit."

She scooted over and took his booted foot in her hands, again disregarding the niceties of social behavior. Her gentle probing had him gritting his teeth, but he did his best to not show any outward signs of pain.

She gently set the foot back down. "It's definitely swollen. I think we'll leave the boot on until Uncle Grover is ready to examine it. But you shouldn't be walking on it for now." Then she met his eyes. "Are you hurt anywhere else?"

His head pounded, his shoulder and ankle throbbed

and he was starting to feel light-headed. Nothing a little rest wouldn't cure. "No."

Her raised eyebrow told him she wasn't convinced, but she didn't press. Instead she gave his good arm a light pat. "Don't worry, we're going to take very good care of you."

Despite his reservations, he had to admit he liked the sound of that.

Mrs. Leggett made as if to stand and the sheriff was at her elbow, lending her a hand.

She smiled up at the lawman. "Thank you, Sheriff. Would you find some men to help carry Mr. Cooper over to the clinic? I'll go on ahead to help my uncle get things ready."

The sheriff tipped his hat. "Yes, ma'am."

Carry him? "That won't be necessary. I just need a little help getting up."

She gave him a don't-be-ridiculous look. "You won't be doing any walking on that ankle, at least not until Uncle Grover takes a look at it."

The woman wasn't shy about giving orders. "Well, I certainly don't intend to let myself be carried through town like a sack of flour. I'd rather hobble. If I could borrow a shoulder to use as support—"

"Your hurt ankle is on the same side as your hurt arm so it would be inadvisable to put any strain on it."

She even *talked* like a doctor.

Before he could protest again, the man who'd been driving the wagon stepped forward. "I can take him to your uncle's clinic in the back of my wagon, if you like?"

Nate clamped down an uncharitable stab of annoyance that the man's words were directed at Mrs. Leggett rather than him.

But the doctor's niece nodded, as if she, too, thought it was her decision to make. "Thank you, Mr. James, that will work nicely. I'll leave this in your and Sheriff Gleason's very capable hands." And with another reassuring but rather condescending smile for him, Mrs. Leggett turned and walked into the dress shop. A moment later she stepped out again with her daughter held on her hip. With the little girl's head snuggled against her shoulder, she marched down the sidewalk.

His eyes followed her progress until she turned a corner and disappeared from view. He still couldn't quite get over her transformation into a coolheaded, would-be doctor. When she'd stopped in front of his store on her way to the dress shop, he'd gotten the impression that she was more diffident than decisive. But just now, she hadn't had the least bit of hesitation about taking charge and issuing orders. And she also hadn't been the least bit put off by either the blood, ugly gash or the fact that she'd had to kneel in the middle of the dusty street to minister to him.

Now that she'd tended to him, she'd changed back into the concerned mother again.

The movement of the wagon pulled his thoughts away from the puzzle Mrs. Leggett presented and onto more immediate matters. He watched as the men maneuvered the vehicle right up beside him, then braced himself to stand. His left side had taken the brunt of the blow. Both his shoulder and ribs felt as if they were on fire, and the gash she'd taken such pains to clean and wrap protested any time he attempted to move his arm. His ankle was the most problematic, though.

She hadn't really needed to warn him not to place any weight on it—the offending joint was doing a thorough job of that all by itself.

But as long as nothing was broken, he should be able to deal with the discomfort, even if it meant using crutches to get around. After all, he didn't need the use of his legs to do his job. And he certainly couldn't afford for this to keep him out of commission for long. He was still in the process of getting his fledgling business established.

Not that he regretted his actions. Better *he* get hurt than something happen to that little girl.

Sheriff Gleason bent down. "I think it best you shove your pride aside for now and allow us to help you into that wagon. Mrs. Leggett isn't going to be happy if I let you put weight on that ankle of yours." He grinned. "And right now I'm more worried about her druthers than I am yours."

Nate nodded. Being helped into a wagon might not be the most dignified way to board, but it was a good sight better than getting carried through town.

The sheriff nodded toward one of the other men. "Jeff, lend me a hand here." The two men positioned themselves on either side of Nate, then helped him up. The action shot a bolt of pain down his left side, and he had to clamp down hard not to let loose with a string of expletives. He'd spent too much time away from the company of God-fearing folk—he was having to learn how to act in polite company all over again.

The sheriff climbed in beside him, presumably to keep him from falling out, then called to Nestor to get moving.

Nate gritted his teeth throughout the jarring, interminable-seeming ride to the clinic. Perhaps he *would* take it easy today. The workday would probably be half over before the doctor was finished with him, anyway.

When they finally arrived at the clinic, Nate was guiltily relieved to see Mrs. Leggett and an older man who was presumably her uncle step outside with a stretcher—he would have had trouble taking more than a few steps on his own. Mrs. Leggett had changed into a clean dress and wore a crisp white apron over it.

"Mr. Cooper, this is my uncle, Dr. Grover Pratt," she said as soon as she was close enough to speak to him. "Uncle Grover, this is Mr. Cooper, the man who saved Joy's life."

Nate shifted. All this excessive gratitude was making him uncomfortable.

"Hello, young man. Let me add my thanks to that of my niece. That was a very brave thing you did, saving our Joy."

"I'm just glad I was in a position to help her, sir."

Sheriff Gleason clamped him on his uninjured shoulder. "Don't let his modesty fool you, Doc. I saw the whole thing. Mr. Cooper here is a real hero."

Dr. Pratt nodded. "Let's start showing our appreciation by getting him inside, where he'll be more comfortable."

Sheriff Gleason and the wagon driver took the ends of the stretcher and Nate maneuvered himself onto it with a minimum of help. Mrs. Leggett stayed beside him as the men transported him into the clinic. Her hand rested lightly on his good arm, as if she wanted to make certain he didn't fall off. The feel of her hand on him was…comforting. Then she looked down and gave him a reassuring smile. Almost as if she truly cared about him.

Was this all part of her job as the doctor's assistant?

Stupid question—of course it was.

Once the men had deposited him on the padded table in the examining room, they took their leave. Nate sat on the edge of the narrow but sturdy table with his legs dangling over the side. By refusing to lie down, he felt marginally more in control of the situation.

To his surprise, Mrs. Leggett didn't follow the men out. Surely she didn't plan to assist in the actual examination?

"I have strict instructions to take extra special care of you." Dr. Pratt cast a smile his niece's way. "So let's get to it."

The doctor began to lay out some of his implements. "Verity, please help Mr. Cooper remove his shirt."

Apparently she *was* going to stay. And participate. He wasn't quite sure how he felt about that.

But she didn't seem the least bit disconcerted by her uncle's request. Her expression remained pleasant but detached and her movements were businesslike as she approached him. Still...

"That's okay, I can manage," he said as he quickly started working the buttons with his right hand.

"Don't be silly." From her tone, she could be speaking to a wayward child. "This is part of my job. Besides, your arm is hurt and it's best you don't move it more than necessary until the doctor can take a look at it."

By this time Nate had managed to free all of the buttons, but he let her help him ease the already-ruined shirt off his arms and shoulders. As he did so, he was very conscious of the old scars she would see on his torso. What would she think?

But it wasn't until she'd laid the garment aside and turned back to him that he noticed any sort of reaction. Unlike the recoil or emasculating pity he'd expected, however, it was a wince and flash of guilt that she quickly suppressed.

Glancing down, he saw the ugly bruise that had formed on his left side, no doubt from his contact with the wagon. Had she not noticed anything else?

Once more wearing that businesslike, doctor's-helper demeanor, she quickly moved around to remove the arm bandage she'd applied earlier. Her touch was every bit as sure and impersonal as before.

Once done, she stepped away and allowed her uncle to take her place.

"Well, Mr. Cooper, let's take a look, shall we?"

Nate nodded. "Please call me Nate. And your niece didn't seem to think it was too serious."

Dr. Pratt smiled. "Verity's got a good eye, but why don't you let me have a look, anyway?"

As Dr. Pratt performed his examination, he took his time and made a point of letting Nate know what he was doing and why. It was all very different from the treatment he'd grown accustomed to the past nine years.

Even though Mrs. Leggett did her best to remain unobtrusive, Nate found himself very aware of her presence. Her movements were deft and sure, and she seemed to anticipate her uncle's requests so that very few words were spoken between them.

Verity—that was a rather old-fashioned name, but somehow it suited her. And her daughter was named

Joy. Both named for virtues. The jaded part of him wondered if they found the names a burden to live up to. Not the little girl, of course, at least not yet. But the mother?

After cleaning the wound and studying it, the doctor looked up to meet Nate's gaze. "You're going to need stitches, but I don't see any reason why this cut shouldn't heal completely with no lasting damage, other than a scar, as long as you take it easy the next few days."

That was a relief. He could deal with one more scar. It would be difficult, though, to do his work without full use of his arm.

The doctor moved on to examine Nate's shoulder and side. Nate did his best to bear the probing stoically and not show any signs of discomfort. Mainly because he didn't want to make Mrs. Leggett feel any guiltier than she obviously already did.

But a part of him admitted that he didn't want to display weakness in front of her, either.

Finally, Dr. Pratt straightened. "Well, your shoulder and ribs are bruised but not broken. That knot on your head is of some concern, but so far you aren't exhibiting any signs of a concussion. Now I'm going to take care of suturing your arm before we take a look at your ankle."

Nate nodded. "Whatever you say."

Dr. Pratt gave him a considering look. "I think this will go better if you lie down on the table."

Without a word, Nate swiveled and swung his legs up on the table, then lay back. The doctor offered him a strip of leather to bite down on, but Nate shook his head. This wasn't his first time to get stitched up, so he knew what to expect.

Mrs. Leggett, who had quietly laid out the necessary implements, stood beside her uncle as he applied the stitches, ready to assist as needed.

Nate kept his gaze fixed on the ceiling as the doctor went to work, refusing to utter so much as a whimper. But apparently he wasn't as impassive as he would have liked, because about halfway through the procedure, Mrs. Leggett moved next to him and applied a cool cloth to his brow. Surprised by the action, he left off staring at the ceiling long enough to meet her gaze. She gave him an approving, sympathetic smile that somehow eased the pain of the procedure. A moment later she had slipped back into her less personal, bedside demeanor and returned to her uncle's side.

When at last Dr. Pratt was done, he straightened. "You can sit up now if you like," he told Nate.

Nate had to admit, if only to himself, that it hadn't ended any too soon. It had taken all he had not to cry out a time or two. Only the fear that he would embarrass himself in front of Mrs. Leggett had kept him from doing so.

The doctor glanced toward his niece as he helped Nate sit up. "Verity, would you take care of wrapping his arm for me?"

"Of course." She reached into a cabinet and pulled out a roll of gauzy-looking cloth.

As she had out in the street earlier, she used her left hand to hold his arm with a gentle firmness while she wrapped the bandage around it with her right hand. She kept her eyes focused on her work so he was free to study her at will.

Trying not to think too much about the warmth of her hand on his, he found himself fascinated by the lone wispy curl of hair that had escaped her otherwise tightly controlled hairstyle. It swayed and danced with her every movement, an incongruously playful counterpoint to her businesslike demeanor.

His fingers actually itched with the desire to reach up and touch it, to let it curl around his finger and see if it felt as impossibly soft as it looked.

Startled once again by the direction his thoughts had taken, he forced himself to look away and found Dr. Pratt watching him thoughtfully. He suddenly felt like a schoolboy caught in some mischief.

A moment later, Mrs. Leggett was done and she stepped back and gave him a smile. "There. How's that? Not too tight I hope."

"It's fine, thank you." Not that he would have complained even if it hadn't been.

Dr. Pratt moved closer. "Now let's have a look at that ankle." The older man studied it a moment without touching him, then looked back up. "My recommendation is that we cut the boot off. Otherwise, you're going to find this much more than uncomfortable. And if your foot is broken it could cause even more damage." He spread his hands. "But the choice is yours."

Nate frowned. He didn't have the funds to spend on new footwear right now. And he was no stranger to pain. "Let's give removing it whole a try first."

"Very well. If you change your mind once I get started, though, you just have to say the word." He turned to his niece. "Verity, please stand behind Mr. Cooper so he has something to lean back against if he needs to."

With a nod, she did as her uncle asked, positioning herself at his back and gripping the edge of the table on either side of him.

And he was honest enough with himself to admit he liked the feel of having her all around him. But, knowing she wouldn't feel the same, he refused to take advantage of the situation.

He'd remain upright, no matter the cost.

With that in mind, this time he accepted the offer of a leather strap to bite down on.

Chapter Four

Verity could tell Mr. Cooper was doing his best to avoid leaning against her. She saw his knuckles whiten as his grip on the table edge tightened, saw his muscles tauten to unbelievable levels, saw the sweat bead on the back of his neck. This couldn't be good for that freshly stitched gash.

That reminder of his bandaged arm made her fingers tingle again. When she'd wrapped his arm earlier, she'd found it surprisingly difficult to maintain the polite detachment that usually came so easily to her. Instead she'd been keenly aware of the warmth of his skin, the sound of his breathing and the feel of his gaze on her.

That last had rattled her more than anything else. Why had he been staring at her with such intensity. What was he thinking? Did he believe it unladylike for a woman to do this sort of work? Or maybe he'd noticed her scar and was fascinated the way some folk were by such imperfections.

Uncle Grover asked him again if he'd prefer to have

the boot cut off, but Mr. Cooper shook his head. Probably gritting his teeth too hard to speak, stubborn man.

A few excruciatingly long minutes later, he let out a single grunt of pain as her uncle managed to finally wrench the boot free. It was only then, as he reflexively sagged with relief, that he allowed himself to lean back against her.

She stood completely still, supporting his solid torso for the three heartbeats it took for realization to hit him. She knew the second it happened. He suddenly stiffened and then jerked upright again. Without turning, he tossed a mumbled apology over his shoulder. Was he embarrassed at what he might consider a show of weakness?

He removed the leather strip he'd been biting on and set it on the table beside him. Verity couldn't help but notice how deep an impression his teeth had made.

She moved around to assist her uncle and winced at how red and swollen his ankle was. As her uncle went about his examination, she kept an eye on the patient. Mr. Cooper bore it stoically, but she saw the muscles in his jaw tighten each time her uncle put the least bit of pressure on the injury.

At last her uncle straightened. "Well, the good news is you have a sprain, not a break."

"And the bad news?"

"You're going to need to stay off of it for a while."

Mr. Cooper frowned. That was obviously not what he'd wanted to hear. "How long?"

"If you want that ankle to heal properly I strongly suggest that you stay off of it for at least a week."

Mr. Cooper raked a hand through his hair. "But it's nothing that will keep me from my work?"

Uncle Grover gave him a severe look. "Only if you work sitting down."

"I do. And I suppose I can use a cane to get around."

"Crutches would be better. But with your bruised shoulder and the fresh stitches I've just applied to your arm, neither will be advisable for the next few days."

Verity saw the rebellion in Mr. Cooper's eyes. Then she realized that, like Hazel, he probably lived above his shop. Stairs would be very difficult, if not impossible, for him to navigate in his condition.

"What do you expect me to do in the meantime, just lie about?" His tone was short and clipped. "I have a business to run." Then, as if he realized he'd been abrupt, his expression lost some of its hard edge. "I'm sorry. None of this is your fault."

Verity disagreed. This was *all* her fault—he'd gotten injured because she hadn't kept a close watch on her daughter. "Perhaps I can assist you in some way," she offered. "I'm sure Uncle Grover can spare me for a few days."

Before her uncle could confirm what she'd said, Mr. Cooper spoke up. "I appreciate the offer, ma'am, but I don't think that will be necessary. I'll figure a way to work it out."

Was he just being polite? Or was it that he wasn't interested in having her around?

"You two can work that out later." Uncle Grover's stern look was aimed at them both. "For now, I would suggest Mr. Cooper stay here at the clinic, where we can keep him under observation."

"I don't think—"

Her uncle raised a hand. "If it's money you're worried about, don't." He met Mr. Cooper's gaze with an earnest, direct look. "You were injured helping my great-niece—there will be no charge for anything related to your injuries."

"That's very kind of you. But—"

How did he expect to go anywhere without help? "The only place you're going is to our infirmary." She could see another protest forming on his lips so she tried again. "You need to listen to my uncle. With that knot on your head, someone should keep an eye on you, at least for the next twenty-four hours, and since you live alone, this is the best place for you. Besides, I believe you live in an apartment above your shop, is that correct?"

"Yes, but—"

Uncle Grover joined the debate. "Even if you *could* make that climb to the second floor—" his tone made it clear that was doubtful "—it's not something you should be doing right now, not in your condition."

Verity saw Mr. Cooper's jaw tighten at the phrase "in your condition."

"If need be I can bunk downstairs in the shop for a few days."

"Young man, now you're just being stubborn."

"Besides," Verity added, "we have a nice comfortable bed right through there." She waved to a door in the far wall.

"It's just a sprained ankle. I'm not some sickly bed patient."

So his irritation stemmed from a bit of male pride. "Of course you're not. We just want to make certain we take good care of you. Besides, meals are provided, and I promise you Aunt Betty's cooking is something to look forward to. She has a pot of chicken and dumplings on the stove for lunch today."

Without giving their patient a chance to argue further, Uncle Grover turned to Verity and nodded to one of the cabinets. "Please fetch Mr. Cooper something more comfortable to wear while I prepare a draught for him. Then you'll need to step out so he can change."

"There's nothing wrong with the clothes I have on."

Was the man going to fight them every step of the way?

"I was being polite," Uncle Grover said. "Your shirt is now rags and the rest of your clothing is the worse for wear and, not to put too fine a point on it, filthy. For the sake of your health, and my niece's and wife's sensibilities, you need to change. There's a clean nightshirt we keep here just for such circumstances."

Verity hid a grin. Uncle Grover wasn't averse to using a bit of blackmail to get his way, especially when he felt it was for his patient's own good.

She placed a clean nightshirt on the table beside Mr. Cooper, then collected the soiled bandages and his discarded shirt and moved to the door. "I'll take care of these and let Aunt Betty know we'll have an occupant in the infirmary."

Uncle Grover nodded absently. "Thank you, my dear."

With a breezy smile for the still-glaring Mr. Cooper, she sailed out the door and closed it behind her.

She had to admit, she was pleased by the idea that Mr. Cooper would be under their roof a bit longer. It would give her an opportunity to get to know him better. Because she felt that the two of them were linked now in some intangible but very real way.

Partly because he'd saved her daughter's life.

And partly because she felt that little tug of attraction whenever she was around him.

Nate swallowed down the unpleasant-tasting draught Dr. Pratt handed him without a word, but refused the man's offer to help him change clothes. After the doctor made his exit, Nate frowned at the oversize nightshirt. This day had certainly taken an unexpected turn. It wasn't a very auspicious milestone on the road to his fresh start.

Then again, it hadn't been all bad. Getting to know Mrs. Leggett better certainly hadn't been an unpleasant experience. Of course, she seemed to think of him as either a patient or hero, neither of which sat well with him.

Best not to think on how he wanted her to think of him, though. With a huff of frustration, he snatched up the nightshirt.

Nate had barely finished changing when he heard a light tap on the door. Had the doctor forgotten something? But when he bade the person enter, it turned out to be Dr. Pratt's niece, rather than the doctor himself.

Verity entered the room and gave him an approving smile. Then she moved purposefully across the room. "Now let me get you settled into the clinic's guest room."

"Guest room, is it? I feel as if I was coerced rather than invited to stay there." He watched her, admiring her efficient movements.

"Oh, come now, it's not such a hardship to stay with us here, is it?"

How did he answer that? "I know you're doing what

you think best." He offered her a half grin. "And *guest room* does sound friendlier than *infirmary*."

His answer seemed to satisfy her, but she dropped the subject. Instead she waved a hand toward a door across from the one through which she'd entered. "Our clinic *guest* room has comfortable beds for long-term patients. Fortunately, it's not in use right now so you'll have it all to yourself." She pulled a wheeled chair out from a corner of the room and pushed it over to him.

Ah, well, he supposed a conveyance that allowed him to sit up was preferable to that stretcher again.

She stood beside the examination table, obviously prepared to assist him.

"Where's your uncle?"

"He was called out to tend to another patient. Don't worry, I can get you situated." She moved closer to the examination table. "Just place a hand on my shoulder for support."

He didn't much relish the idea of treating her like a support post, but it didn't look as if he had much choice. "Thank you." He placed a hand on her shoulder, finding it both firm and soft at the same time. And then he caught the faint scent of honeysuckle again—it was all he could do not to inhale deeply.

Perhaps accepting her help wasn't such a bad thing after all.

He carefully slipped from the table, using her shoulder for balance more than support, then slid into the chair.

As soon as she saw that he was settled in, she moved behind the chair and set it in motion. "Don't worry, we'll see that you're made as comfortable as possible."

"I don't doubt that, but my shop—"

"Taken care of. I already asked Sheriff Gleason to have someone keep an eye on it so no one will be bothering it. If you'll let me know where you keep your key, I can go by a little later and lock it up for you."

The woman was nothing if not efficient. "But that doesn't take care of my dog."

"Oh, my." He heard the dismay in her voice. "I hadn't thought of that." Then, as they crossed into the other room, "Of course we must see to your dog." There was a short pause where he could almost feel the wheels turning in her mind. "I suppose I'll just have to bring him here until you're well enough to go home."

From the way she said that, he could tell she wasn't particularly happy about it. Did she blame Beans for the accident? "Perhaps I should just go home after all."

"Nonsense. Joy has been after me for ages to get her a pet. You wouldn't want to deny her this taste of what it would be like, would you?"

Before he could respond, she moved on. "I don't imagine you could do much work for the next day or two, anyway. And for that I'm truly sorry. It's a poor reward for your valiant rescue."

He wished she'd quit bringing up terms like *rescue* and *hero*. She was right about his condition, though. He certainly didn't want to put out shoddy work by doing things one-handed. Nevertheless, it was frustrating to have to shut down his shop right now.

But he was suddenly feeling lethargic. Was it a delayed effect of his injuries? "Perhaps, just for today then. As to your question about the key, I keep it next to the till during the day."

Mrs. Leggett parked the chair next to one of two comfortable-looking beds. She turned down the coverlet, then straightened and faced him again. "Now let me help you into bed."

He nodded. While he was certain he could accomplish the task on his own, he found himself not quite so reluctant to accept her help this time.

She placed a hand around his waist as he stood, then helped him ease over to the bed. Once he'd swung his legs into the bed, she fussily arranged the light coverlet over him.

"There now." She stepped back. "That draught Uncle Grover gave you should help ease your pain and also help you to sleep, which is the best thing for you right now. We'll talk again when you wake up."

A sleeping draught? No wonder his lids were feeling heavy.

She pointed to a cord that hung in easy reach of the bed. "If you need anything, pull that cord. It'll ring a bell in the house and one of us will be right in to see what you need."

He tried to watch as she bustled about the room, but his eyelids were getting heavier. She pulled the curtains closed, cocooning the room in shadow. He lost sight of her for a moment, then suddenly she was there bending over him. "One last question. I'm afraid your trousers and shirt are in a sorry state. Would you like me to get you a fresh change of clothes when I fetch your dog?"

Were they really talking about his clothing now? "I suppose. They're in the wardrobe in my bedchamber."

She smoothed the covers over his chest one more time, and the gesture brought him back to a time when his family had been intact and his world had been pleasant and uncomplicated.

"Sleep now," she said softly. "We'll talk again when you wake up."

So he did.

Verity softly closed the door behind her. Mr. Cooper was a true hero in her book—literally a godsend to her and Joy. She was only sorry he'd paid such a steep price for his quick action and bravery. If only there was something she could do to make certain his business didn't suffer for his absence.

She headed for the kitchen, where she found Joy and Aunt Betty preparing lunch. Verity still felt the need to reassure herself that her baby was okay.

Aunt Betty looked up. "How's our patient doing?"

"He's settled in the infirmary." Verity moved to stand behind Joy's chair and placed a hand lightly on the girl's shoulder. "Hopefully he'll sleep for a few hours."

Her aunt nodded. "Poor man. Sleep's the best thing for him."

"Before he fell asleep, he reminded me that he has a dog." Joy's head went up at the mention of the animal. "I assured him I'd see to it while he's laid up." She gave her aunt a diffident look. "I can check on it several times during the day, of course. But I was wondering what you would think about my bringing the animal here instead. I know Uncle Grover doesn't like house pets, but it's a small dog, so it shouldn't be much trouble."

Her aunt hesitated for just a moment, then spoke. "Of course you should bring it here. I'm sure your uncle will agree, it's the least we can do for the man who saved our little Joy."

"Thank you." Relieved, Verity rushed to reassure her aunt. "And don't worry, I'll make sure the animal doesn't get in your or Uncle Grover's way."

Aunt Betty gave her a gently chiding look. "Verity dear, this is your and Joy's home now, too. You must learn to treat it as such."

Only it wasn't, not really. Verity felt that longing again to have a house of her very own. If only she could open a millinery shop with some assurance it wouldn't fail.

Joy, who was practically squirming in her seat, looked up. "Are you really going to get Beans?"

Verity smiled at the hopeful expression on her daughter's face. "I am. Would you like to come with me?"

Joy immediately slid from her chair. "Yes, ma'am."

As she and Joy headed out a few minutes later, Verity found herself moving with a bounce in her step. She tried to tell herself that it was just an eagerness to get this errand taken care of, but she knew better. Was it wrong of her to be so intrigued by the idea of getting a peek at Mr. Cooper's lodgings?

Then she pulled her shoulders back. Of course not. It was nothing more than a natural urge to learn more about the man who'd saved her daughter's life.

Or at least that's what she told herself.

Chapter Five

Obviously excited by the idea of seeing Beans again, Joy chattered all the way to Mr. Cooper's place. Fortunately, most of her comments were directed to her doll, Lulu, and didn't require a response from Verity. She kept firm hold of her daughter's hand the whole time, but her mind kept drifting to thoughts of what Mr. Cooper's place might look like and if it would provide new insights into the man himself.

When they arrived, Verity spotted Calvin Hendricks seated on the bench that sat between the apothecary and the saddle shop. Calvin was a local youth who was fast approaching adulthood. Apparently he'd been the one tapped by Sheriff Gleason to keep an eye on Mr. Cooper's shop.

"Hi there, Miz Leggett." Calvin stood, then turned to her daughter. "And hello, Joy. I sure am glad to see you walking around and looking good as new."

"Mr. Cooper saved me," Joy said, as if it was momentous news. Which, as far as Verity was concerned, it was.

"That he did. And it was right heroic of him, too." Calvin turned back to Verity. "How's he doing?"

"He's got some painful bruises, a gash on his arm and a sprained ankle, but thankfully nothing that won't heal. Uncle Grover stitched him up and he's resting at the clinic." She waved toward the saddle shop. "I'm here to fetch his dog and a change of clothes, and to get his key so we can lock the place up."

Calvin nodded. "Anything I can help with?"

"Thank you, but no. It shouldn't take me more than a few minutes."

"Well, if you change your mind, I'll be right out here." And the youth sat back down on the bench, as if to demonstrate he wasn't going anywhere.

Verity opened the shop door and stepped inside. She and Joy were immediately greeted by a yipping ball of excited dog. Joy stooped down to greet the animal and quickly had her face washed in doggie kisses.

Verity carefully closed the door behind them, unwilling to risk Beans running out and Joy following him in a repeat of the earlier mishap.

Deciding to tackle the matter of clothing first, she headed toward the stairs at the back of the shop. She slowly crossed the room, studying her surroundings with keen interest. The place had a definite masculine feel—all leather and wood and metal.

Harnesses and leather straps of various lengths and widths hung from pegs on the wall to her right. There was a worktable to her left. A selection of tools, most of which she didn't recognize, were displayed there. They were neatly arranged and organized, though his system wasn't immediately obvious. She imagined him working here, wearing the heavy canvas apron that hung on a peg behind the table, his head bent over his work, his strong, callused hands wielding those strange tools, his arresting blue eyes focused on his work.

The smell of leather hung heavy in the room, so strong she could almost taste it. Under that scent, she could also detect the aroma of oil and just a faint tang of metal.

Only when she reached the bottom of the stairs did Verity realize her daughter hadn't followed her. Appalled by her lack of attention so soon after Joy's accident, she spun around. "Come along," she said, holding out her hand. "We need to fetch something from Mr. Cooper's room upstairs."

Joy's lower lip pushed out in something suspiciously like a pout. "But I want to stay down here and play with Beans."

"Beans can come with us."

Her daughter's expression cleared. "Okay." She stood and waved to the dog. "Come on, Beans."

The dog obediently trotted at her heels, then bounded up the stairs with her.

The staircase led up to a landing that had an open sitting room straight ahead and a kitchen to the right. The rooms were stark, with only a bare minimum of furniture. Perhaps Mr. Cooper just hadn't had the time, or the funds, to do much more. But surely he would have brought some personal possessions with him, from his former home.

There was a door off to her left that she assumed led to his bedchamber. "Joy, you and Beans can play right over there. I won't be but a minute."

She marched to the door, then hesitated before opening it. It suddenly seemed invasive to enter his private space, even if she did have his permission. Which was silly. She was only going to fetch him a change of clothing and then leave. And she did have his permission to be here, after all.

Verity opened the door and stepped inside. A quick glance around showed a neatly made bed, a wooden chair and a small bedside table. On the opposite wall was a trunk and the wardrobe. Everything looked as if it had seen better days.

She noticed a picture on the bedside table, and her curiosity got the best of her. She went closer and discovered it was the image of a young woman. She was quite lovely, in a delicate, fragile sort of way. Her clothes were fine quality, her heart-shaped face very sweet and delicate. She had an ethereal quality to her and seemed to be everything Verity was not. Was this the kind of woman Mr. Cooper admired?

Who was she? She was obviously someone who meant a great deal to him as it was the only picture, the only personal item really, in the room. A family member? A sweetheart? And where was she now?

Verity straightened abruptly and turned away. What was she doing? She had no right to snoop into Mr. Cooper's personal life. He'd given her permission to take care of some necessities for him, not snoop into things that were none of her business. She marched to the wardrobe, grabbed a clean shirt and pair of trousers, then headed back out.

"Come along, Joy, time to go."

As she descended the stairs she thought how different his clothing smelled from what Arthur's had. Where her husband's had smelled of antiseptic, soap and cigars, Mr. Cooper's smelled of leather, of course, but also soap and something faintly woodsy.

She decided that she liked it.

Nate woke from his nap to see flowers floating in front of his eyes. What in the world—

Was he still dreaming?

"Do you like them?"

The flowers, which he now saw were in a glass jar, floated to the side and the little girl holding them finally came into view.

"Well, hello there, Joy. Does your mother know you're in here?"

"I just wanted to give you these," she said, not answering his question. She held the flowers out toward him a little more. "Do you like them?" she asked again.

"They're lovely."

Apparently this was the correct response, because her face split with a grin. "They're for you. From me and Lulu." She proudly held them out to him.

"Why, thank you. But who's Lulu?"

The child held out her doll. "My dolly."

He looked the doll in the "eyes." "Very nice to meet you, Lulu." Then he turned back to Joy. "The flowers are nice, but may I ask why you are giving me such a nice gift?"

"You rescued me and Lulu. You're a hero."

There was that word again. "It was my pleasure. But little girls really shouldn't play in the street."

"That's what Mama told me, too." Her tone wasn't particularly penitent. "But I wasn't really playing in the street. I was trying to catch Buttons."

"Buttons?"

"That's Miss Hazel's cat. He likes to have me chase him."

Nate let the girl's interpretation of the cat's motives stand. But he had a feeling Mrs. Leggett was going to have her hands full raising this one. "I see. But you still shouldn't have gone out in the street."

Joy pursed her lips in a stubborn line. Then she smiled. "I'll put your flowers right here on the table where you can see them whenever you want to." She put words to action, then came back to stand beside him. "Everyone is saying you're a hero. What's a hero?"

Now, how was he supposed to answer that? "First of all, I'm not a hero. I was just the first one to get to you. But to answer your question, a hero is a person who does something for other people who need help, without worrying about what it might cost him."

"Oh." She pondered that for a while then waved toward his bandaged arm. "Does it hurt a lot?"

He was touched by the worried look in her eyes. "I've had worse."

She hugged her doll to her chest. "It's my fault, isn't it?"

Another tricky question. He studied her woefully guilty expression, wondering how best to answer her. But before he could say anything, Joy spoke again.

"I'm sorry. And Lulu's sorry, too."

He smiled. "Apology accepted."

She brightened and changed the subject. "Beans is in the kitchen with Aunt Betty. We gave him some of the scraps from lunch. Me and Mama brought him here so he could be close to you. Do you want me to go get him for you?"

"Not right now—"

The door opened behind the little girl, and Mrs. Leggett came in carrying a tray. He sat up straighter, his stomach reacting to the delectable aromas with a rude rumble.

Mrs. Leggett, however, was staring at her daughter rather than him. "Joy, what are you doing in here?"

Her daughter looked at her as if that was a particularly silly question and waved toward the makeshift posy. "I brought Mr. Cooper some flowers, see? You said we should always thank people who do nice things for us."

He saw the woman struggle with whether or not to chastise the girl. "True," she said, finally. "But bothering Mr. Cooper is not a good way to thank him. I hope you didn't wake him from his nap."

"She wasn't bothering me," Nate said quickly. "I woke up on my own. But it was nice to have such a pretty face to wake up to."

And nicer still to have Mrs. Leggett's smiling presence here with him. Even if that smile was currently directed at her daughter.

Verity smiled as Joy preened at Mr. Cooper's compliment. He was a much more thoughtful man than she'd first assumed. She set down her tray and turned back to Joy. "We'll discuss this later. Why don't you go check on Beans?"

"Yes, ma'am." Before heading for the door, Joy turned back to the patient. "Thank you again for saving my life, Mr. Cooper. And I think you're wrong. You really *are* a hero." And with those words she skipped out of the room.

Once Joy disappeared out the door, Verity turned

to her daughter's rescuer and shook her head. "I'm afraid Joy is much too impulsive. I hope she wasn't bothering you."

"Not at all." He sat up straighter and she hurried to his side, setting the tray down and plumping pillows behind him. All part of being a nurse.

He inhaled deeply. "Whatever you brought in with you smells wonderful."

"It's that bowl of my aunt Betty's chicken and dumplings I promised you. I thought you might be ready for something to eat."

He smiled and she liked the way it softened his entire face. "You thought correctly."

Verity lifted a napkin from the tray and handed it to him, then carefully set the tray on his lap. "How's this?"

"Fine, thank you."

Then, as she took the spoon, he frowned. "There's no need for you to wait on me."

"Are you sure?" She'd been rather looking forward to feeding him. "I know your arm and shoulder are injured."

"Just on my left side. My right arm is fine."

"Very well." She surrendered the spoon reluctantly. But for some reason she wasn't quite ready to leave. After all, she needed to keep an eye on him to gauge his condition.

"I locked up your shop when I fetched Beans," she said. Then she waved a hand to the small dresser across from his bed. "Your change of clothes is in the upper drawer and the key is on top."

"Thank you." He scooped up another spoonful of

the chicken and dumplings, his gaze never leaving hers. "How long did I sleep?"

"About four hours. It's after one o'clock."

He grimaced and she hurried to reassure him.

"No, that's a good thing. You needed the rest. It helps you to heal faster." He didn't appear convinced, so she changed the subject. "How does your leg feel?"

"Better."

Not a very descriptive answer. "Uncle Grover should be in shortly to change the dressing on your arm and also have another look at your other injuries."

"Perhaps then he'll see that I can manage well enough to go home."

Why was he in such a hurry to leave them? There certainly wasn't anyone at his place to rush home to. Instead of responding to his comment, however, she crossed the room to open the curtains. "Let's let a little more light in here, shall we?"

When she returned to his side, she lifted the tray with the now empty bowl and smiled down at him. "Would you like some more?"

"Not now, thank you. But please relay my compliments to your aunt. That was very good, especially compared to my own cooking."

Was he dismissing her? Perhaps he wanted to rest some more. "Is there anything else I can get for you?"

He seemed to hesitate a moment, then raised a brow in question. "Something to read perhaps?"

That was unexpected. "Of course. What sort of books do you like?"

"What do you have on hand?"

"I'm afraid Uncle Grover's library consists mostly of medical tomes and journals. I believe Aunt Betty has some books of poetry and some devotionals. I have a volume of poetry, some Shakespeare, Dickens and a few of Mr. Twain's novels. And of course some children's stories for Joy. Oh, and I think I also still have a copy of yesterday's *Turnabout Gazette* if you haven't seen it." She waved a hand. "If none of that is of interest, I'd be glad to find you something at Abigail's library. Just let me know what sorts of books appeal to you."

"I've read Shakespeare and Dickens. Perhaps I'll try Twain. And I believe I will take a look at the *Gazette*."

Apparently he was well educated. Now that she thought on it, there was a certain refinement that crept into his speech from time to time. It embarrassed her that she'd made so many wrong assumptions about this man. She should know better than to jump to judgments.

"I'll fetch the book and newspaper for you as soon as I put away these dishes. Can I do anything else for you?"

After his *No, thank you* response, Verity made her exit and slowly headed toward the parlor, where most of the family's books were located. Her thoughts, though, were on Mr. Cooper rather than her errand.

There was still a faint air of something less than welcoming simmering below the surface in this man, a feeling of standoffishness. But for some reason it didn't scare her away—in fact it had just the opposite effect. She was beginning to see him as a brave, honorable, well-educated person who just needed someone to teach him to trust enough to open up.

If he had a wilder side to him, well, he seemed to

have it well controlled. And that was a sign of maturity and responsibility, wasn't it?

The sound of a tap at the door pulled Nate from his reading. One thing he could say for this place, they respected a person's privacy. Which, after his time in prison, was another thing he'd never take for granted again.

He sat up straighter. "Come in."

Mrs. Leggett stuck her head in the doorway. "You have a visitor, but if you'd prefer to rest I can ask him to come back at another time."

There was only one person here in Turnabout who would be visiting him. "Not at all. Show him in."

She gave him an assessing look, as if gauging his condition, then nodded and withdrew.

Sure enough, Adam Barr strolled through the open door a few minutes later.

"Hope I'm not disturbing you," his friend said, "but Dr. Pratt said you're up for visitors."

Nate waved Adam to a chair near the bed. "Actually, other than being a bit banged up, I'm fine. I'd be back home if it was up to me, but Dr. Pratt practically strong-armed me into staying."

"He cares about his patients," Adam said. Then he grinned. "Are the ladies of the house smothering you with kindness?"

Smothering wasn't exactly the word he'd use, but he let it stand. "It's a definite change from what I've been used to."

"A little female attention is never a bad thing." Then Adam leaned back. "I hear you've become something of a town hero as of this morning."

Nate grimaced. "I just happened to be in the right place at the right time. You and I both know there's nothing heroic about me."

Adam frowned. "I know nothing of the sort. In fact, I have good reason to believe otherwise." He stroked the faded scar on his cheek, a reminder to both of them of how they'd met—in a prison fight.

When Adam had entered prison all those years ago, Nate had already been there six months. That first day, a couple of the more hardened inmates had cornered the new arrival as he exited the food line and Nate had weighed in to even the odds. The two had been friends ever since.

"That was just me looking for a fight—nothing more."

"That's not how I saw it." Adam crossed his arms and gave Nate a drawn-brow look. "Besides, I spent time in prison, too. Do you think that makes me less capable of acting heroically?"

Nate gave a sharp, dismissive wave. "You didn't belong there. I did."

That was one reason, besides his own selfish desire to be free of his past mistakes, that he couldn't reveal to the townsfolk that he'd spent time in prison. Because, since folks knew that he and Adam were already acquainted, any confession on his part might cause speculation about Adam's own past.

"You had your reasons for what you did." Adam shrugged. "But be that as it may, you served your time, so your debt is paid. And everyone deserves a second chance."

He *had* come to Turnabout looking for a fresh start, a place to begin again without the anchor of his past to weigh him down. Knowing that his friend believed in him allowed him to have faith that he might be able to pull it off.

He just wished he felt as if he deserved this second chance. He knew the Good Lord had forgiven him long ago, but he was still having trouble forgiving himself.

Then Adam changed the subject. "So how long do you plan to lie around here lollygagging?"

"Assuming Dr. Pratt doesn't tie me to my bed, I'm heading back to my place in the morning."

"Well, I wouldn't be in too big a hurry. I hear Mrs. Pratt is quite a cook."

"You've heard correctly. I've already sampled her chicken and dumplings and it has my own cooking beat by a mile." Then he turned serious. "Which reminds me, would you mind letting Mrs. Ortolon know I may not be able to help her at the boardinghouse for the next several days?" He touched the bandage on his arm. "I definitely won't be swinging an ax anytime soon." He'd been doing odd jobs at the boardinghouse in the evenings for meals and pocket change to help him get by until his business was better established.

"I'm sure she already knows, but I'll stop by when I leave here."

"Thanks." Nate brushed at a bit of lint on his coverlet. "Mrs. Leggett—she's a widow, I take it."

"She is. Her husband died a little over a year ago. She and Joy moved back here shortly after it happened."

Some time had passed, then. Of course, he knew from his own experience that one never totally "got over" the death of a loved one. "So she wasn't living here when he passed away." He hoped she'd had friends, people she could lean on, around her.

Adam shook his head then shifted in his seat. "There's something you should probably know if you're going to be around Mrs. Leggett much—her husband's passing wasn't peaceful. He died of a gunshot."

Nate froze for a moment as that sunk in. That must have been horrific for her. Had she witnessed it? Had Joy?

Then Adam cleared his throat and gave him a look that had a touch of sympathy in it. "It happened during a bank robbery."

Nate dropped back against his pillow as all the implications of that news thundered down around him like a rockslide.

Chapter Six

After Adam had gone, Nate retrieved his book, but he didn't open it immediately.

Adam's revelation changed everything. He couldn't stay here, couldn't trespass on this family's hospitality any longer than he already had, couldn't bear to have Mrs. Leggett look at him with that admiration and gratitude, not knowing what he now knew.

Injured ankle or no, he'd make it back to his place. He just wished he'd thought to ask Adam to bring a wagon around to transport him.

Deciding to test his mobility, Nate threw off the bedcovers and stood, putting all his weight on his good leg.

Before he could try taking a step, there was another tap at the door. He clenched his jaw and sat back down on the bed, but left both feet on the floor. It might not be Mrs. Leggett. It could be Dr. Pratt or even Adam, returning to say something he'd forgotten earlier. "Come in."

But, of course, it *was* Mrs. Leggett. She halted just

inside the doorway and frowned at him. "What are you doing up?"

His frustration and guilt spilled out before he could stop them. "For goodness' sake—I have a sprained ankle, not a bullet in my chest."

Her recoil brought him up short. None of this was her fault. "I'm sorry, I'm just tired of being treated like an invalid."

She recovered quickly. "Of course. But you *do* know that you have to take it easy if you want to heal properly, don't you?"

"I do. But I don't take well to mollycoddling. In fact, I can get absolutely churlish. Which is why I should head on back to my place now."

That set her back again. "Nonsense. We've already agreed that you should spend the night here. Nothing's changed."

Oh, but it had. In fact, *everything* had changed. "I know what I said earlier. But now that I've had my rest, I'm thinking clearer and I believe it's better if I go on home." He shifted, feeling at a distinct disadvantage dressed in this ridiculous nightshirt.

She crossed her arm like a schoolmarm confronting an unreasonable child. "Uncle Grover, as an experienced physician, would certainly know better than you how to deal with your injuries. And he has stated that it's important for someone to keep an eye on you for at least twenty-four hours."

He shrugged. "I'm sure I'll be fine." Then, before she could throw another argument at him, he added, "You may consider me foolhardy if you wish, but regardless of you or your uncle's warnings, I plan to head home as soon as you leave so I can get dressed."

He held her gaze, refusing to back down, hoping she'd give in to his determination. If she only knew the truth about him, she'd be showing him to the door rather than trying to convince him to stay.

Finally, the authoritative frown slipped from her expression and a furrow of uncertainty creased her brow in its place. "I see. You obviously feel quite strongly on the matter." She slid a stray tendril of hair behind her ear. "Have we done something to offend you? Made you feel unwelcome or uncomfortable in some way?"

"No, of course not."

"Then I don't understand. Why the sudden change of attitude and the rush to be gone from here?"

What could he say? That he was no longer comfortable here not because of anything they'd done but because of what *he'd* done, because of the kind of man he was? If he said that, he'd have to give her the whole sordid story, and this wasn't the time or place for that. If he was lucky, that time would never come. "I just don't want to be a bother," he said feebly. Then he waved a hand in near surrender. "If you're certain it won't put you or the doctor out…"

Her smile returned, as if he'd just given her a wonderful gift. "That's settled, then—we'll have no more talk of your leaving today." She became businesslike again. "Shall I help you get settled back in the bed?"

Nate shook his head, doing his best to not put her out more than he had to. "I'm tired of being a slugabed. I think I'll get dressed and sit up for a while."

He saw the objection form on her lips, but then she seemed to think better of it. "As long as you don't wear yourself out, I don't see any harm in that." She crossed the room to retrieve his change of clothing.

As she brought it over to him, she took a quick look around the room. "If you're going to be sitting up for a while, the most comfortable option may be to use the wheeled chair. I can put a pillow at your back to make it more comfortable."

"Whatever you think best." He might as well capitulate completely.

She wheeled the chair next to him, then retrieved a pillow from the spare bed and plumped it up against the back of the chair. Then she turned back to him with one fist planted on her hip. "I would tell you not to take advantage of the added mobility this chair gives you," she said, her tone dry, "but I know I'd probably be wasting my breath. So instead I'll tell you to be careful you don't put any strain on that left arm of yours."

Was that actually a hint of amusement in her eyes? Surely the straitlaced widow wasn't teasing him.

"Do you need help with anything else?" she asked.

"I think I can manage."

"Very well." She waved toward the bell pull. "Just remember to give that a tug if you find you do need something."

As he watched her leave, he decided that what he most needed was to get away from here as soon as possible.

Otherwise, his resolve to keep his distance from the intriguing—and now altogether off-limits—Mrs. Leggett was going to be very sorely tested.

As Verity closed the infirmary door, her smile faded. What was going on with Mr. Cooper? Why had he been so insistent that he needed to go home? It had almost seemed like he was fleeing from something.

Did he truly prefer to be alone? That was such a heartbreaking thought.

Well, someone needed to show him the joy that could come with being an active part of a welcoming community. This town had certainly welcomed her back with open arms when Arthur had been killed. No, more than welcomed her, they had shown her love and compassion, praying for her and with her, letting her know she was not alone in her grief.

Of course she'd spent most of her growing-up years here in Uncle Grover's home, had been one of them, so to speak. But she had seen these folks offer that same warm welcome to strangers who needed a place to start afresh. Like Mr. Tucker and those ten orphan children who'd arrived here last year. He'd actually ended up married to the local widow Eileen Pierce and together they'd adopted all ten children.

Yes, sir, this town was a good place to make a new life for oneself, if one really wanted it.

Then again, perhaps that was the problem. Did he prefer to be left alone?

She shook her head. That was a foolish thought. Some people were forced by circumstances to cut themselves off from the world, but no one *preferred* to be alone. Even if a person thought that was what he wanted, he just needed to be shown the joys of having friends and neighbors who cared.

Well, if that's what Mr. Cooper needed, it was the least she could do for the man who had saved her daughter's life.

She smiled, her mind spinning with ideas of how she might accomplish that.

* * *

Sometime later that afternoon, Nate was roused from a light doze by a soft knock on the door. Sitting up straighter in the chair and hoping there were no traces of sleep remaining on his face, he bade the visitor enter.

It was Mrs. Leggett again. "How are you doing?" she asked. "Tired of sitting up yet?" No doubt it was part of her job here to check in on the patients occasionally.

He grimaced. "Actually, I'm much more tired of this forced inactivity. The book is good, but I'd prefer to be up and about."

"We can't have that, but would a change of scene help? While Uncle Grover doesn't want you to put any weight on that foot just yet, I could wheel you into the parlor or out on the porch if you'd like." A saucy note of challenge lit her eyes. "I could even sit down to a game of chess with you, if you play. But I have to warn you, I often beat Uncle Grover when we play."

Despite his intention to remain aloof, Nate found himself responding to this teasing side of her. "I haven't played chess in quite a while, but I've never been one to back down from a challenge."

Within a few minutes she had wheeled him into the parlor and up to a small table. Then she pulled the game board out from a cupboard and took a seat across from him.

Mrs. Leggett proved to be a thoughtful, strategic player. But she also liked to chat as she contemplated her moves. "Joy is enjoying having Beans here."

"I'm glad."

She moved one of her pawns, then leaned back to

wait on his countermove. "If you don't mind my saying so, he seems like a rather odd choice of pet for a man such as yourself."

He shrugged. "Actually, Beans chose me."

"What do you mean?"

He made his move, then sat back. "I spent a few days in Kansas City on my way here. One day this ridiculously small mutt showed up outside the hotel where I was staying. It was obvious the animal had had a hard time of it." It had been raining and the dog was wet, dirty, scratched up and obviously starving.

"I stumbled on him at a weak moment and made the mistake of feeding him a few scraps." Nate shrugged. "He started following me around and I couldn't find anyone who'd lay claim to him. When he followed me to the train depot, I took him with me on impulse."

The truth was, the mutt reminded him of a dog his sister had adopted when she was a kid. And that's where the name had come from, as well. Because of her pet's dark brown coat, Susanna had named it Coffee Bean, but it had quickly been shortened to Beans.

Nate shook off that memory and focused on Mrs. Leggett again as she moved a pawn. "I guess you could say both Beans and I came here looking for a fresh start."

That drew a speculative look from her. Had he revealed too much?

He made a quick move on the chessboard, then changed the subject. "Joy is certainly an exuberant child."

Mrs. Leggett's expression took on a wry twist. "She is definitely a handful. Her lack of fear scares me sometimes."

There was that hint of timidity again. "Most children are born fearless. They have to be taught to fear. Surely you don't want your daughter to be fear*ful*."

Her posture turned defensive. "A little bit of caution wouldn't go amiss."

He didn't let that go unchallenged. "As long as it doesn't turn into excessive timidity."

She frowned at that, obviously disagreeing with his sentiment. But she didn't comment. Instead, she changed the subject. "Did you have a nice visit with Mr. Barr?"

Nice? That was much too soft and feminine a term to suit him. "Adam was just checking in on me."

"Do you mind if I ask how you and Mr. Barr know each other?"

Nate hesitated. How did he answer that question without revealing too much about his, and for that matter Adam's, secrets?

Verity saw the hesitation on his face. Was there some private matter there she'd inadvertently intruded on? How could she take the question back without making it worse?

Before Verity could figure that out, he spoke up.

"I've known Adam for a number of years." His gaze was focused on the chessboard rather than her. "We've maintained a correspondence since he's moved here. His letters made Turnabout sound so appealing that when I was ready to relocate I decided to try it here."

She realized he hadn't exactly answered her question. But she ignored that and moved on. "And where is home?"

"I was born and raised in Plattisburg, Pennsylvania."

"Do you still have family there?"

His jaw tightened. "No, they're all gone now. That's why I decided to try a change of scenery."

Verity's heart went out to him at that admission. She'd lost people in her life as well, but there'd always been other family members around to help her through the rough time. Mr. Cooper was definitely a man in need of a community.

But she'd pressed him enough for one sitting.

And apparently he thought so, too, because he changed the subject. He waved a hand toward the piano at the other end of the room. "That looks like a fine instrument. Do you play?"

She shook her head. "No, that belonged to my mother, who got it from her mother. I'm afraid I never learned to play. Joy's started to show some interest, though, so I'm hoping when she's a little older I can find someone to teach her."

"Actually, she's not too young to start now."

She looked at him with renewed interest. "It sounds like you know something on that subject yourself."

He gave her a little half smile that seemed to hide some other emotion. "I used to play, but it's been years."

She glanced back at the piano before meeting his gaze again. "I'm not sure if it's still in tune, but if you'd like to play while you're here, please feel free. It would actually be nice to hear it get some use again."

He lifted his left arm. "Aren't you worried about my using this arm too much?"

"Aren't there pieces written to be played with one hand only?"

He raised a brow. "Is that another challenge, Mrs. Leggett?"

She saw the amused twist of his lips, and something inside her nudged her toward a capricious response. Lifting her rook, she placed her fingertips to the area above her heart and schooled her features into a shocked expression. "Dear me, Mr. Cooper, I would never extend such a *taxing* physical challenge to an incapacitated patient." And with a sweet smile for him, she set her rook back down on the board. "Check."

He gave her a full-blown smile at that and inclined his head in acknowledgment. "Touché." Shifting in his chair, he focused back on the board.

The game went on for another twenty minutes, and the conversation turned to more impersonal topics as they continued their game. But her thoughts kept drifting back to his unexpected reaction to her question about Adam Barr. She knew both he and Mr. Barr were from Pennsylvania, but had no idea how they'd ended up here in Turnabout. Was Mr. Cooper hiding something to protect his friend?

Or himself?

Verity eventually lost the game, but she didn't mind. While she had enough of a competitive streak to enjoy winning, she also enjoyed just playing the game with a likable competitor. And Mr. Cooper was definitely likable. Even though he was undeniably guarded, the occasional peeks she caught of his self-deprecating attitude, his dry humor and his confident intelligence were quite an appealing combination.

She had just stood to put the game away when a bell

sounded. She gave Mr. Cooper an apologetic smile. "That means we have a visitor at the clinic. I should check in to see if Uncle Grover needs me for anything. Would you like me to wheel you back to the infirmary or would you prefer to stay here?"

"I'll stay here, if you don't mind."

It was the answer she'd expected. "Of course. Make yourself at home." She crossed the room and grabbed a large wooden box.

"This is Aunt Betty's stereopticon," she said as she set it on the table in front of him. "I'm sure she wouldn't mind if you took a look at it."

With that, she hurried away to check in with Uncle Grover.

Nate knew he was in trouble. Mrs. Leggett was becoming more than just an interesting woman to him. She was bright, kind, composed. And, when she let herself relax, had an unexpected sense of humor. Granted, he didn't have a lot of experience with women—he'd gone to prison at nineteen and before that, well, before that there had been other priorities in his life.

But he knew enough to know this woman was special.

And she was still very much off-limits to him.

Chapter Seven

Verity hurried up the walk. Uncle Grover had sent her to the apothecary shop to pick something up for him and she'd decided to stop by the library while she was out to pick up a book for Mr. Cooper. Her uncle was no doubt wondering what had taken her so long.

She delivered the packet to her uncle, chatted with him for a few minutes about how the Simmons boy was doing since his splint had been removed yesterday, then she glanced toward the far door.

"Has Mr. Cooper returned to the infirmary yet?"

Her uncle looked up distractedly. "I haven't seen him come through. As far as I know he's still in the parlor, where you left him."

Verity moved toward the door that connected the clinic to the house. "I suppose I should check on him then. He might be ready to get some rest."

Her uncle nodded and turned to the bookcase behind him, obviously searching for a particular tome.

As Verity stepped inside the house, she heard someone playing the piano. Had Mr. Cooper decided to try it one-handed after all?

She quietly moved to the open parlor door and paused on the threshold. Sure enough, Mr. Cooper sat in front of the piano, playing with his good hand. He wasn't using sheet music so he must be playing from memory.

He sat in profile to her, so she could see his expression as he played. There was a look of intense concentration tinged with frustration—no doubt because he was forced to play one-handed. Even so, he was doing a remarkable job.

When he was finished with the piece, he sat perfectly still, his hand still resting on the keys, his head down.

"That was lovely," she said softly.

His head jerked up and around to face her, and for a moment she saw an unexpected vulnerability there. Then he straightened and gave her a crooked smile. That vulnerability—if it had been there at all—was gone. "You must be tone deaf if you call that lovely," he said drily.

Relieved that he'd decided to take her intrusion without rancor, she smiled and stepped into the room. "Actually, my ear for music is said to be pretty good."

"Just because you sing in the choir…"

So he'd noticed that, had he? For some reason that cheered her. "Actually, I'm the choir director. So yes, I think that makes me somewhat qualified to judge." She remembered the book she carried and held it out to him. "Here, I picked this up at the library for you."

She saw a flicker of surprise in his eyes before he reached out to take it from her.

"Thank you." He studied the cover. "*Ranch Life and the Hunting-Trail* by Theodore Roosevelt."

She couldn't tell from his expression how he felt about it. "Have you already read it?"

"No."

"It's a new arrival to Abigail's library. I thought it looked intriguing."

"And so it does." He held it up. "Thanks again. I look forward to reading this."

Joy skipped into the room just then, Beans at her heels. As soon as the dog caught sight of Mr. Cooper, he bounded over to his side and put his paws up on the man's good leg.

Verity's gaze focused on the way Mr. Cooper absently reached down to scratch Beans's head. There was something to be said about a man who cared for his dog.

And a man whose dog cared so enthusiastically for him.

Joy turned to Verity. "Aunt Betty says to tell you that supper will be ready soon. And that she hopes Mr. Cooper is up to joining us at the table."

Joy turned to Mr. Cooper and stepped closer. "I hope you're feeling better."

"I am, Joy, thank you. And those pretty flowers you brought sure did brighten up my room."

Okay, there was another point in Mr. Cooper's favor—he was going out of his way to be nice to her daughter.

Joy smiled. "So I helped?"

"You most certainly did."

Joy stooped to pet Beans, but she kept her gaze on Mr. Cooper. "Was that you playing the piano a while ago?"

"It was."

Her expression turned wistful. "Mama says I can learn one day, too."

Her daughter's words drew Verity up short. Why hadn't she ever heard that longing note in Joy's voice when they discussed piano lessons before? Was that new? Or had Verity not been paying close enough attention?

She decided she'd talk to Zella, the church pianist, after the service on Sunday about giving Joy lessons.

Nate looked around the supper table with the sinking feeling that he was fighting a losing battle. As soon as he'd learned the circumstances of Mrs. Leggett's husband's death, he'd known he had to pull back and not try to forge anything more than a polite, neighborly relationship with this family.

Yet here he was, seated with them, eating their food, sharing their hospitality.

Once they'd settled in their seats at the table and Dr. Pratt had said the blessing, Mrs. Pratt reached for the bowl of peas that sat to her left. "Allow me to serve your plate, Mr. Cooper. You shouldn't be straining that arm of yours this soon."

"Thank you, ma'am." Everything about the doctor's wife seemed soft—her voice, her appearance, her temperament.

Dr. Pratt accepted the biscuit plate from his niece. "Well, young man, other than your accident this morning, I hope you're enjoying your move to Turnabout."

"Yes, sir. This seems to be every bit as fine a place as Adam assured me it would be."

"You mean Adam Barr?"

"Yes, sir. He wrote me several letters extolling the virtues of Turnabout."

"Adam is a fine young man. Despite being from back east, he's become an important and well-liked member of our community."

Nate wondered if the same would be able to be said of him someday.

Mrs. Leggett spoke up. "Turnabout is growing. When I returned last year after a seven-year absence, I was surprised by the changes."

She'd returned after a bank robber killed her husband, Nate reminded himself. Which meant she would be understandably unsympathetic to anyone who had ever robbed a bank.

He turned from her to Mrs. Pratt, hoping his guilty feelings didn't show. "This is a fine meal, ma'am. I appreciate your sharing it with me."

"You're quite welcome. It's always a pleasure to cook for someone who appreciates the effort." She reached for her glass. "I assume that was you I heard playing the piano earlier."

"Yes, ma'am. I hope you don't mind."

"Not at all. It was nice to have music in the house." She gave him a warm, motherly smile. "You're quite talented."

"Thank you." Yes, he was definitely getting in deep with these folks.

All through the rest of the meal the family made it a point to include him in the conversation and make him feel a welcome addition to the gathering.

When they pushed back from the table, Mrs. Pratt held a hand up to forestall her niece. "Let me take care of the dishes, dear. And Joy can help me. You should take care of our guest."

Nate tried to protest. "That's all right. I don't want to be—"

But the doctor's wife wouldn't let him finish. "Nonsense. You're a guest in our home and I pride myself on my hospitality."

Nate doubted she offered all residents of the infirmary this kind of treatment, but he couldn't continue protesting without running the risk of repaying her kindness by seeming churlish or ungrateful.

Mrs. Leggett moved behind him and took the handles of his wheelchair. "No point in arguing. Aunt Betty may look like a softie, but she normally gets her way." She steered him out of the dining room. "I know you've been cooped up indoors most of the day. If you like, I can wheel you out on the porch for a breath of fresh air."

He should refuse. "I'd like that."

In short order she had wheeled him out the front door. She parked his chair near the door then moved to stand by the rail, looking out over the front lawn.

Dusk had settled in and Nate saw the twinkle of a few fireflies in the distance.

He shifted in the chair. "Don't feel like you need to keep me company. I'm perfectly fine here on my own, and I promise not to tell your aunt if you want to slip away and take care of something else."

"I don't mind." She kept her back to him. "It's nice out here this time of day."

There was another long silence. Then she turned to face him. "So why leather working?"

"What do you mean?"

"You're obviously very well educated. You play the piano like someone who has practiced extensively. That doesn't sound like someone who would turn to making bridles and saddles for a living."

I do it because it was the work I was given while in prison. But he didn't say that. "Are you saying someone who works with his hands can't be well educated?"

"No, of course not. It just seemed a curious combination."

"There is something satisfying about the work I do, something artistic and creative."

She nodded. "Sort of like the hats I make."

"You make hats? For sale?" Somehow that seemed out of character.

"Yes. That's why I was at the dress shop this morning."

"So you don't have your own shop?"

"Oh, no. Not yet, anyway. I just make them when the mood strikes me, and Hazel sells them in her shop for me."

What kind of headgear did she fashion? Sober bonnets like that black affair she wore most every day? Surely there wasn't that big a market for such dull headgear.

Then he had another thought. "You said *not yet, anyway.* What's stopping you?"

She seemed a little taken aback by his question, so he raised a brow in challenge. "I figure, since you quizzed me this afternoon, I would return the favor."

She relaxed and smiled. "I suppose fair is fair. But there's nothing particularly interesting about my answer. I said not yet because I'm not ready."

"I assume this is something you really want, not just an idle dream."

"Oh, yes. I want to be able to fend for myself and Joy, to not have to take advantage of the charity of Aunt Betty and Uncle Grover forever."

Had she given up on the idea of remarrying someday? "Well, then, what are you *really* waiting for?"

She gave him a puzzled frown. "You make it sound like it's something I could do at the snap of a finger. Starting up a business takes planning and forethought. Which you should know since you've just opened one yourself." She rubbed her hands along her upper arms. "But I'm sure it'll happen someday. And for now, I'm happy to muddle along doing three or four a month to sell at Hazel's shop."

He couldn't really picture her as a "muddle along" kind of person. But he'd let that slide.

Maybe he'd check out the dress shop window next time he passed by to see what sort of hats she created— it might tell him a little more about the kind of person she was. He suddenly had a stray thought of what she might look like in a different kind of dress, one that was a lively color with more flattering lines. One that didn't remind everyone who looked at her that she was a widow.

He stiffened as he realized what direction his thoughts had taken. "If you'll excuse me, I think I'll go back to my room now."

Her expression immediately shifted to one of concern. "Of course. You must be tired after the day you've had."

He grimaced. "It seems I've already done my fair share of resting today. But I wouldn't mind lying down and I'd like to dig into that book you brought me from the library." And the sooner he was away from Mrs. Leggett's company, the better.

For both of them.

Verity pulled the pins from her hair as she sat in front of her vanity. She lifted the silver-handled brush she'd inherited from her mother and pulled it through the thick tangle of her hair.

What a day today had been. She'd finally met the town's newest resident, Joy had come within a hair-breadth of getting seriously hurt, and Mr. Cooper had moved into the infirmary.

Such a good man. And modest, too. He seemed actually uncomfortable with accepting their gratitude for what he'd done.

Well, he had it whether he wanted it or not. And she'd make it her mission to see that everyone knew what a fine, brave man he was.

She paused and bowed her head.

Heavenly Father, thank You for seeing my daughter safely through her near miss today, and thank You for sending Mr. Cooper into our lives. I think perhaps You sent him to us for a reason and I hope that You will find a way to use me to help him in some way. Help me to always be open to whatever direction and work You have in store for me. Amen.

She turned down her lamp and crawled into bed, already looking forward to what tomorrow would bring.

Nate stretched, pleased to note that the twinge of pain in his right arm seemed less noticeable today than yesterday. He leaned back and studied the harness he'd been working on.

Not bad, considering he was moving slower than normal. Dr. Pratt had consented to allow him to return home this morning only after he'd promised to come back to the clinic tomorrow so his injuries could be checked. He wondered idly if Mrs. Leggett would be there.

Okay, maybe not so idly.

She hadn't seemed very happy that he was ready to return home. And he had to confess that he'd been more than a little pleased by that.

Nate glanced around his shop, trying to imagine how Mrs. Leggett had looked wandering through here yesterday, amid his very masculine wares and tools. Stranger yet, imagining her upstairs, moving through his quarters to find him a clean change of clothes.

What had she thought of his place, of how spare and impersonal it was? Had she been all business, quickly taking care of her task at hand and getting out? Or had she lingered, studying his things?

How would he have handled it if the situation had been reversed?

He glanced up as someone walked past his open door. It was Mrs. Leggett and her aunt. He watched as they passed by, tracking their progress across the large shop window. At the last minute, Mrs. Leggett glanced inside and gave him a warm smile when their glances met.

Was her primary emotion toward him gratitude? That wasn't what he wanted.

Nate leaned down and absently scratched Beans behind the ears. What *did* he want?

He'd thought he knew when he arrived here. But maybe it was changing.

An elderly gentleman stepped through the door just then, pulling Nate's thoughts back to the present.

"Now that we've finished with old business, let's move on to a discussion of the upcoming Founders' Day Festival." Regina—otherwise known as Reggie—Barr, head of the Ladies Auxiliary, looked around the room with an expectant smile.

Verity shifted in her seat. She was having trouble focusing on the discussions going on around her. The meeting was running longer than normal and she was anxious to get back home and check on Joy. It wasn't that she didn't trust Uncle Grover to watch her daughter, but she didn't want the girl to be a bother to him. Besides, she still hadn't quite gotten over the scare of Joy's near accident yesterday.

Verity let the discussion swirl around her, lending only half an ear to talk of prizes, games, competitions, music, parades, fireworks and goodness only knew what else.

The idea of the festival seemed a bit frivolous to her. But if these folks wanted to get excited about it, then she saw no real harm in it. Besides, it would be something Joy would have fun participating in.

Verity's mind turned to Mr. Cooper. He had spent the morning reassuring Uncle Grover that he was quite capable of taking care of himself. He'd seemed inordinately eager to leave them. Was it merely because he wanted to be back among his own things? Or was there another reason?

Realizing her thoughts had drifted into inappropriate territory, Verity sat up straighter and tried to pick up the thread of the discussion.

"Thank you, Daisy. Now for the next item on the list, Janell Whitman has volunteered to work with the schoolchildren to prepare a short play for our entertainment during the festival. She'd like to have a volunteer to help her."

Verity thought about volunteering, but Abigail Fulton, one of the younger members of the Ladies Auxiliary, immediately raised her hand.

Reggie pointed her pencil toward the young girl. "Thank you, Abigail."

Hazel raised a hand and spoke up without waiting to be recognized. "Let me know if you want costumes for the children—it'll be my contribution to the festival."

Janell gave her a broad smile. "That would be wonderful. I'll come by your shop tomorrow and we can discuss it."

Reggie looked down at her list. "All right, I think that was the final item on our agenda. Anyone have anything else we need to discuss?"

The meeting broke up shortly after that.

As they stood, Aunt Betty touched Verity's arm. "Don't wait on me, dear. I want to chat with Daisy about helping her with the refreshments for the festival."

Verity nodded and moved toward the door. Her thoughts turned almost at once from the Founders' Day Festival to Mr. Cooper. How was he faring now that he was back at his own place? Perhaps she should stop in and check on him.

As a concerned medical assistant, of course.

So lost in thought was she that she jumped slightly when Hazel came up and linked arms with her.

"Sorry if I spooked you," her friend said. "I just wanted to ask how Joy is doing today."

"She's doing fine, much better than Mr. Cooper."

"Ah, yes, the hero of yesterday's drama. I hear he spent the night at the clinic."

"Yes. Uncle Grover wanted to keep an eye on him for the first twenty-four hours."

"And was he a good patient?"

Verity ignored her friend's arch tone and answered the question as stated. "Other than not liking to be, as he put it, mollycoddled, he was fine." She brushed at a piece of lint on her skirt. "He moved back to his place this morning."

"Do I detect a note of disappointment?"

"Disapproval would be more accurate. He should have stayed under my uncle's care a little longer. But he does have a stubborn streak."

Hazel grinned, then changed the subject. "By the way, your hat sold already. Stop in and I'll pay you. And that means I'll be ready for your next creation whenever you can get it to me."

Verity nodded. "I already have a design in mind. I should have something ready for you in the next couple of days."

They chatted about fashion and the upcoming festival the rest of the way to the dress shop.

Verity exited the shop feeling the satisfactory weight of extra coins in her purse. Hopefully it would be enough for the first few piano lessons for Joy. Her steps slowed as she approached the saddle shop. Yes, she definitely should check in on Mr. Cooper to make certain he was doing okay.

Mind made up, she stepped forward purposefully. The little bell over his door jingled as she entered. Beans, who'd been soaking up the warmth in a puddle of sunshine, bounded to his feet and raced over to greet her. But it was Mr. Cooper she watched, even as she stooped to scratch the dog. Was he glad to see her?

He'd looked up at the sound of the bell, but his expression had closed off as soon as he saw her. Now he set down his work and leaned back. "Excuse me if I don't stand." His tone was self-deprecating as he motioned to the crutch behind him. "Is there something I can do for you?"

She gave Beans a final pat and straightened. "I've just come from Hazel's and thought I'd stop in and check on you." Was he not glad to see her? "How are you feeling?" she finished feebly.

"I'm managing."

"Is there anything I can do for you? I'd be glad to prepare some meals for you or take care of some of your housecleaning. After all, it's my fault you're in this fix."

"Mrs. Leggett, please stop trying to take the blame for my accident. It just happened—it was nobody's fault."

"There you go, being modest again. You really should learn how to take a compliment."

He didn't say anything to that—just continued to watch her in that uncomfortably unreadable way.

"You're staying off of that foot, I hope."

He spread his hands. "As you can see."

"And the stairs?"

"Only when absolutely necessary."

Before she could quiz him further, the shop door opened. She turned to see Cletus Keeter, a farmer from just east of town, entering with a harness in hand.

"Well, hi there, Mrs. Leggett. I heard about what happened to Joy yesterday. I hope she's okay."

"Hello, Mr. Keeter. Yes, Joy is just fine, thanks to Mr. Cooper here." She nodded to both men. "Well, I'll leave you two gentlemen to your business. Good day, Mr. Cooper, Mr. Keeter."

Mr. Cooper nodded, still not softening his politely businesslike demeanor.

As she stepped out on the sidewalk, Verity realized that, now that he was on his own again, it seemed it was going to be more difficult than she'd thought to break through Mr. Cooper's reserve. But she wasn't the least bit daunted. If there was a way to get past his guard, she was determined to find it.

Some things were just worth fighting for.

Chapter Eight

"Verity, do you have a moment?"

Verity, who'd arrived at the mercantile only a few minutes ago, paused in her shopping to find Janell Whitman approaching her. "Of course."

"As mentioned at the Ladies Auxiliary meeting yesterday, Abigail and I will be putting together a little program with the children as part of the Founders' Day celebration."

Verity nodded. "I'm looking forward to seeing them perform."

"I was thinking that perhaps we'd do a play based on the story of the founding of the town. Mr. Parker and Mr. Fulton have agreed to write the play for us."

"That will be fun."

"But the number of parts will naturally be limited and I'd like to make certain all of the children have a way to be involved."

Verity had always thought the town was blessed to have a teacher like Janell Whitman, one who really cared about the children. "I agree that we don't want anyone to feel left out. How can I help?"

"I thought one option would be to form a choir with the remaining children and have them put on a musical performance, as well."

Verity felt a little stirring of excitement as she began to see how the teacher was looking to involve her.

"The problem is," Janell continued, "both Abigail and I will be fully involved with the play. And of course neither of us have your talent when it comes to music. So we were wondering if you'd be willing to take that on."

"Of course." The chance to form a children's choir, even a temporary one, was something she would very much enjoy doing.

"Zella has already agreed to play the piano for you and lend a hand with directing the children as needed."

"She'll be a good help." Zella was the church pianist, and a more patient woman didn't exist. She'd be quite good with the children. "How many students would be involved?"

"I'm thinking seven from my group and Mr. Parker thinks about five from the older students in his group."

A dozen, then. But then she had another thought. "One more question. Would you object to having a few of the younger children join this little choir?"

Janell smiled. "Such as Joy, you mean? Of course not, as long as you're willing to work with them."

"What kind of program did you have in mind?"

"Nothing too elaborate. I was thinking two or three simple songs with an uplifting theme. But this will be your project and I'm sure whatever you decide to do will be fine."

Already Verity's mind was brimming with ideas. "All right. As soon as you get me the names of the children involved we'll schedule the first practice. In the meantime, I'll speak to the parents of some of the other younger children to see if any of them are interested in participating. And I'll speak to Zella after choir practice tomorrow about any ideas she might have."

Janell smiled. "Looks like you're definitely the right person for the job. I'll leave it all in your very capable hands." And with a wave, the schoolteacher moved on.

Verity finished her shopping while mentally making a list of things she could do while waiting for the names of the participating children. She could visit the parents of some of the children Joy's age to see if she could recruit a few more choir members. Eileen Tucker would be her first stop—Molly and Joey Tucker were Joy's best friends.

She could also talk to Hazel. The dressmaker had already volunteered to provide costumes for the children who were in the play. Perhaps she could also talk her friend into doing some short, simple, smock-like choir robes for the children's choir.

Yes, she'd go by Hazel's first. And since it coincidentally just happened to be right next to the saddle shop, perhaps she'd stop in and check on Mr. Cooper while she was at it.

Nate looked up from his workbench to see Adam striding into the shop. Truth to tell, he was glad of the interruption. Nice to have something to think about besides the way he'd been less than gracious with Mrs. Leggett.

He leaned back. "Here to get a harness repaired?"

"Just visiting."

Was Adam checking up on him? Was he worried

about Nate's ability to repay his loan? Then Nate pushed that thought aside. He owed his friend more trust than that. He nodded toward a nearby chair. "Have a seat."

Adam looked around as he sat. "I don't see your crutch. Don't tell me your foot's healed already?"

"Not completely." Nate reached behind him and grabbed the walking stick he'd fashioned from a strong, straight branch and some scraps of leather. "I'm using this instead."

"How's the arm?"

"Much better." Nate rolled his shoulder to prove his point.

"Glad to hear it. Because I've come to ask you a favor."

Now, that was unexpected, but he welcomed the chance to repay, at least in part, the debt he owed his friend. "Name it."

"Zella Ford, our church pianist, has had a family emergency and has to go out of town to attend to it. She may be gone for a month or more."

Uh-oh, he didn't like the direction this was taking.

"If I remember correctly, you play the piano, don't you?"

Nate nodded.

"Good. Then I'd like you to consider taking her place during the interim."

Nate stared at his friend, trying to figure out what was behind this. Was this some misguided scheme to get him more involved in the community? "Why me? I mean, isn't there someone else here in town who plays piano and would be better suited?"

"Mrs. Peavy, our housekeeper, normally steps in on the rare occasions when Zella can't attend services."

"Well, then—"

"Mrs. Peavy is a generous woman and when Reverend Harper spoke to her about the situation, she agreed to step in. But she's been having flares of rheumatism in her hands lately and I'd like to spare her any extra use of them if I can. Besides, with Reggie expecting again, I'd like to selfishly keep her focus on our household."

"I see." Nate nodded, remembering what he owed Adam. "I suppose, when you put it like that, I can't say no."

"Good. The choir practices for an hour every Saturday at four o'clock."

"I understand Mrs. Leggett is the choir director."

"She doesn't care to be called that, but yes, the choir looks to her to lead their practices. And she usually works with Reverend Harper to make the hymn selections." He studied Nate. "That won't be a problem, will it?"

"No, of course not." It seemed the more he resolved to keep his distance from the widow, the more circumstances conspired to throw them together. But he'd already given his word. And there was no reason he couldn't handle this in a businesslike manner.

"Good. Because there is one other thing. Reverend Harper says Mrs. Leggett will also be working with some of the local children to put on a musical performance for the Founders' Day Festival. She'll need you to work with her on that, as well."

"Does she know that I'm taking Mrs. Ford's place?"

"I haven't said anything to her, or anyone else for

that matter. I wanted to make sure you would agree first." He gave Nate that probing look again. "There's no reason *she* should object, is there?"

"None that I'm aware of." He grimaced. "In fact, she still considers me a hero."

Adam relaxed as the light of understanding dawned in his expression. "I see. Well, there's nothing wrong with that."

Nate answered with a scowl. Then changed the subject. "I assume there is sheet music. Back when I had access to a piano, the pieces I played were classical rather than from hymn books."

"I'm sure there is, but you'll have to ask Mrs. Leggett about that." Adam stood. "I'll let Reverend Harper and Mrs. Peavy know the good news."

"And Mrs. Leggett?"

"I'll leave that up to you. Remember, choir practice is tomorrow at four o'clock at the church."

As Adam left, Nate wondered if Mrs. Leggett would welcome the news or not. With his luck, she'd see this as one more aspect of him being a hero.

He groaned and decided it was time to take Beans for a walk.

Every Saturday, at three o'clock, Verity and four of her friends from the choir met at the Blue Bottle Sweet Shop and Tea Parlor for tea before they went to choir practice. It had become a ritual of sorts for the five of them.

Besides herself, there was Hazel, and Janell Whitman, Reverend Harper's daughter Constance, and Abigail Fulton, the young woman behind Abigail's Subscription Library.

Constance Harper was the last to arrive this Saturday, and she didn't immediately take her seat. Instead she stood facing them with barely suppressed excitement. She was obviously bursting with news of some sort. "I have an announcement."

Verity smiled. "Whatever it is, it looks like good news."

Constance nodded. "Yes. Well, both good and bad. I'm afraid this is the last Saturday tea I will be attending with you ladies for quite some time." Then she grimaced. "That's obviously not the good-news part."

"Well, I should say not!" Abigail gave her friend a pouty frown. "The good news better be mighty good to make up for that bad news."

Constance coyly took her seat. "Oh, it is."

From the smile on the girl's face, Verity had no doubt that something wonderful had happened.

"Well," Abigail said impatiently, "don't keep us waiting."

"The reason I won't be here is that I'm going to pharmacy school in New York."

There was an immediate chorus of congratulations, followed by a stream of questions.

Finally Constance held up both hands, palms out. "Thanks, everyone. I will miss all of you, of course, but this is such a great opportunity. Mr. Flaherty has taught me a lot since I've been working for him at the apothecary shop, but he says there's more to be learned and he wants me to be ready to take over the business when he retires in a few years. So he's sending me to a pharmacy school. He's even offered to pay for my classes."

"Oh, Constance, that's wonderful."

"It sounds as if Mr. Flaherty sees something very promising in you. You should be proud."

"You must stop by the fashion emporium so we can chat about New York. I can let you know what to expect." Hazel had family in New York and spent a few weeks there every summer.

As their tea was delivered, Janell, who was seated next to Verity, turned to her. "How are your plans for the children's choir coming?"

"Very well. I've been in contact with the mothers of several younger children. In addition to Joy I have three other younger children recruited."

Janell smiled and shook her head. "You're a brave woman."

Verity returned her grin. "It'll be fun." Then she sobered. "I heard Zella is going to be unavailable to play the piano for us. I'll miss her, but Mrs. Peavy will do fine, I'm sure."

"Oh, haven't you heard?" Constance chimed in from Janell's other side. "Mrs. Peavy isn't taking Zella's place this time. Mr. Cooper is."

Surprised by that little tidbit of news, Verity sat up straighter. How interesting that they were going to be thrown together yet again. Did Mr. Cooper know about the children's choir yet? She hoped that wasn't going to be a problem for him.

"Well, now, isn't that an interesting development." Hazel's voice had a definite what-have-we-here edge to it. "Who would have imagined a man like him could play piano?"

Verity shot her friend an annoyed look. What did she mean *a man like him*? "He's actually quite talented."

"Is he, now?" Hazel was looking at her with a mix of amusement and speculation.

"He practiced on the piano in our parlor while he was staying at the clinic."

To Verity's relief, Eve, the proprietress, arrived with a tray of sweets just then, and once they all had their refreshments, the conversation turned to other topics.

But Verity knew Hazel wasn't ready to let it drop entirely. Sure enough, when they left the Blue Bottle to head for the church, Hazel linked arms with her and nudged her with a shoulder. "So why didn't you tell me Mr. Cooper serenaded you with the piano while he was at the infirmary?"

"Because he didn't serenade me. He didn't even know I was listening until he finished playing the piece."

"Still, apparently he did more than lie in bed and recuperate while he was there. Tell me, is he as interesting as he seems? Did the two of you have some nice, long, get-to-know-you-better conversations?"

Verity drew her shoulders back in exasperation. "Hazel, really, he was a patient in the clinic, not a suitor."

"Not yet, anyway."

Verity gave her friend a stern look. "I know that look in your eye. Promise me you won't try to do any matchmaking."

Hazel sniffed and tilted her chin at a haughty angle. "You're just no fun at all sometimes."

"Promise me."

"Oh, very well." She good-naturedly changed the subject to a discussion about the proposal for a big fireworks display to close out the festival this year.

As Verity entered the church a few minutes later, she felt her pulse quicken in anticipation. Would he already be here? Had he volunteered to take Zella's place or had he been pressed into service? How would he feel about taking direction from her?

She gave her head a mental shake. Her thoughts were heading into territory it would be best to avoid. It was a good thing Hazel couldn't read her mind.

Mr. Cooper was already seated at the piano. He hadn't yet noticed her entrance, so she had time to study him.

He was thumbing through a hymnal, his expression unreadable. No one had approached him, but she wasn't surprised. It was that invisible wall he had erected around himself. Was he even aware he was doing it?

Well, making him feel a welcome part of the choir would be a good start. She marched down the aisle and went straight to the piano. "Mr. Cooper, thank you so much for agreeing to step in for Zella, especially on such short notice."

She turned to the gathered choir members. "Most of you have probably already heard about Zella having to go out of town to see to her brother for a while. We're very lucky to have Mr. Cooper to fill in for her. I've already had the pleasure of hearing him play the piano, and I can assure you he is quite talented."

Then she turned back to him. "Have you met everyone here?"

When he indicated he hadn't, she went around the group, introducing them one at a time. By the time the introductions were done, the last of the choir members had arrived and Verity was ready to begin the practice session.

Nate was impressed with Mrs. Leggett's leadership qualities. Just as when she took charge of his care right after the accident, she was firm but not bossy, and quick to lend a hand or lend praise where needed.

She had apparently spoken with Reverend Harper earlier about the scripture his sermon would be based on and chose songs that would complement his message. Some of the hymns were unfamiliar to him and he stumbled a bit the first time he played them. But she was as patient and gracious with him as she was with the rest of the choir.

By the time practice was over, he was confident he could play the hymns for the service tomorrow without any trouble.

The choir members began to slowly disperse, leaving in chatty groups of three or four. He saw the dressmaker, Miss Andrews, speak to Mrs. Leggett for a moment, but the widow waved her on and turned in his direction. Was she going to inquire after his health again?

"Thank you again for stepping in today. Your time and talent were greatly appreciated."

"I don't mind. I actually enjoy playing the piano."

"It shows in your playing." She hesitated a moment, then continued. "I don't know if anyone mentioned this to you or not, but I'm going to be working with a group of children to form a choir and present a program at the Founders' Day Festival. Zella was planning to help me, but now that she's unavailable—"

"You need another pianist. Yes, I'm aware, and I'm happy to step in."

Her relieved smile softened her features. "Oh, thank you. And I promise you won't regret it. Children are such a joy to work with."

Not ready to see her go yet, he asked the first question that popped into his head. "Do you know yet what kind of program you want to teach them?"

"I have some ideas, but I'm open to other suggestions if you have some to offer."

"Why don't you tell me what you're thinking first and I'll see if it sparks any ideas." He slid over on the piano bench. "But first, have a seat. You're making me feel most ungentlemanly."

She complied, coming around the piano to perch on the opposite end of the bench from him.

He listened to her plans, asking questions and making suggestions. But all the time, a part of him was also aware of her nearness, her contagious enthusiasm.

If it was going to be like this whenever they were together, he was in trouble. He would just have to make certain that they were together only when the choir—either the adult or children's version—were with them. No more of these one-on-one sessions.

"I plan to have practice sessions every Tuesday and Thursday afternoon right after school between now and the festival," she said. "Will that be a problem for you?"

"I can work with that."

"This first Tuesday I will mainly be evaluating the children individually to see where they are musically, and to see how well they can understand and follow directions. I won't necessarily need the piano for that, so I suppose if you don't want to come—"

"You're going to have over a dozen kids to work with. You'll need some help. I'll be here."

"I was hoping you'd say that." She stood. "Well, I should be getting home so I can check on Joy. Aunt Betty loves her, but that little darling of mine can be a handful sometimes." She moved away from the bench. "I'll see you at the service tomorrow."

He stood, as well. "I'll walk you out." He reached for his cane. As they walked toward the door, she easily matched her steps to his without comment. But when they stepped outside, she paused and turned to him.

"Do you need any assistance with the steps?"

Did she think him such an invalid? "I can manage."

His tone had come out sharper than he'd intended and he saw her brow go up. "Sorry," he said, "I'm just used to taking care of myself."

She gave him an understanding smile. "Well, you're amongst friends now. There's no shame in asking for or accepting help."

Amongst friends—he liked the sound of that. But could he truly consider himself their friend so long as he kept his history from them?

Sunday morning, Verity took her place with the rest of the choir at the front of the church. Mr. Cooper was already in place at the piano. Was he nervous? If so, he didn't show it.

The church bell rang, signaling to the latecomers and dawdlers that it was time to come inside and find their seats. Taking his cue as smoothly as Zella ever had, Mr. Cooper began playing an instrumental piece.

It wasn't a melody Verity was familiar with, and he seemed to be playing it from memory. There was no hesitation or stumbling. It was lovely.

Later, when the service was over, she approached Mr. Cooper with a smile. She had to wait her turn to speak to him, however, as several members of the congregation came up to compliment him on his playing and thank him for standing in for Zella. It did her heart good to see him receiving such warm acceptance from the folks here—perhaps now he wouldn't feel the need to keep himself so aloof.

When at last he was alone, she stepped up. "It seems as if I'm not the only one who thinks your playing is exceptional."

He shrugged as he put away the sheet music. "I'm glad the folks in the congregation enjoyed it."

"Aunt Betty asked me to invite you for lunch."

He reached for his cane. "That is very kind of your aunt, but I've already made other plans." He glanced toward the Barrs, and Adam's wife, Reggie, gave him a small wave.

"Oh, I see." She'd been prepared to counter his I-don't-want-to-be-any-trouble arguments but hadn't even considered that he might have other plans. She also hadn't been prepared for the stab of disappointment. "Well, enjoy your meal."

She turned, but before she could move away, Joy skipped up to them.

"Hello, Mr. Cooper."

He gave her a smile. "Hello, Joy. How are you today?"

She noticed that his cool reserve seemed to melt away when speaking to her daughter.

"I'm fine, thank you," Joy responded. "I like your piano playing."

"Thank you."

"How is Beans doing?"

"He's doing just fine. Thank you for asking." Then he leaned in, as if to relay a confidence. "But I do think he misses seeing you."

Joy nodded solemnly. "I miss him, too." Then she gave Nate a this-just-occurred-to-me look. "Maybe I should visit him."

"Joy!" Verity chided. "It's not polite to invite yourself over to someone else's home."

Her daughter widened her eyes innocently. "But he said Beans misses me. And I miss him, too." The child's tone implied that that was reason enough.

Mr. Cooper intervened. "I tell you what. I plan to take Beans for a walk over toward the schoolyard this afternoon. Would you like to come with us?"

"Can I, Mama?"

"May I," she corrected absently. Was he issuing the invitation more because he felt obligated or was it because he really wanted to? "Oh, pumpkin, I don't know—"

"You are invited, too, of course."

She looked from Mr. Cooper's impassive face to Joy's pleading one and nodded. "Very well." If nothing else, this would be a step along the path to getting Mr. Cooper out and about more.

Then she gave her daughter a no-nonsense look. "But only if you take your nap after lunch."

"I will, I promise."

Verity turned back to Mr. Cooper. "What time do you plan to take Beans for his walk?"

"Shall we plan to meet in the schoolyard around three o'clock?"

With a nod, Verity took Joy's hand and turned toward the door. She was happy they'd agreed to see each other later, but there was something about the way he'd issued the invitation, something in his tone and carefully schooled expression that made her wonder if he was regretting the invitation even as he was issuing it.

When they stepped outside, she informed Aunt Betty that they would not have a guest for lunch after all, then let Joy go with her and Uncle Grover while she turned to look for Hazel.

She spotted her friend across the churchyard speaking to Belva Ortolon. Belva was relatively new to Turnabout. She'd moved here about four months ago to help her aunt Eunice with the running of the boardinghouse.

When Verity approached, Belva gave her a smile of greeting. "Oh, hi, Verity. I was just telling Hazel how much I enjoyed the music this morning, and she tells me you picked out the hymns."

"I did." Verity liked the girl. There was an artlessness about her, an almost tomboyish quality that she found quite engaging.

Belva nodded approval. "'What a Friend We Have in Jesus' is a favorite of mine, so thank you for selecting it."

Before Verity could respond, Belva looked past her and straightened. "Oh, there's Mr. Cooper. I need to speak to him about something."

Surprised, Verity watched Belva approach Mr. Cooper and engage him in animated conversation. The girl seemed to know him rather well. Then Verity corrected herself—not girl, woman. She thought of Belva as a girl because of her youthful demeanor. But in truth she was a young woman of nineteen or twenty. By the time she herself had been that age she'd had a husband and daughter of her own.

Belva's aunt joined the pair just then and, together, the three of them made their way out of the church-yard. It occurred to Verity that Mr. Cooper hadn't actually *said* his lunch plans were with the Barrs. Could he be taking his meal at the boardinghouse with the Ortolon ladies instead?

Not that it was any of her business if he was.

"Mr. Cooper did a fine job playing the piano this morning."

Verity turned back around to see Hazel eyeing her with an amused glint in her eye.

"That he did." She fiddled absently with the tie on her bonnet. "He's starting to feel more comfortable with life here in Turnabout, don't you think?"

Hazel nodded. "How could he help *but* like it here?" She cut her eyes toward the man in question, then back to Verity. "And he apparently likes certain people here quite well." For a moment Verity thought she was referring to Belva. Then Hazel clarified, "I noticed how he watched you during the service this morning."

Verity waved a hand dismissively. "It's only because I'm choir director. He was taking his cues from me."

Hazel made a noncommittal sound, then changed the subject. "By the way, have you ever considered making hats to order?"

"I don't know." From the corner of her eye, she watched the trio make their way as far as Second Street, then they turned the corner and disappeared from view.

But Hazel was eyeing her with a knowing smirk so she quickly pulled her thoughts back to the conversation at hand. "Part of the fun for me in making hats is just going with whatever whimsy my imagination feeds me rather than trying to follow a set pattern or copy something from a picture. Why?"

"Eula Fay stopped by the shop yesterday to order a new dress to wear when she presides over the festival's opening ceremony. She asked if you'd consider making her a hat to match."

As Mayor Sanders's wife, Eula Fay always liked to look her best when she was attending some sort of official function. "I suppose, if the only parameter I had was that it should match a particular dress, I could do that."

Hazel nodded. "It would be a guaranteed sale for you. And it could generate some additional orders. You know how Eula Fay is—if she likes something she'll let everyone know."

"All right, you've convinced me." Verity hooked her arm through Hazel's and the two started down the sidewalk together. "I'll come by your shop tomorrow and take a look at the fabric and pattern you're using for the dress."

If she were to ever realize her dream of someday owning a millinery shop, she would definitely have to learn to create hats to order. Might as well start now.

But at the moment her thoughts were not entirely on hats. Part of her mind was focused on the fact that when she and Hazel turned on Second Street, neither

Mr. Cooper nor the Ortolon ladies were in sight. Had they separated at Mr. Cooper's shop?

Or had they continued on to the boardinghouse together?

Chapter Nine

Nate turned onto Schoolhouse Road, Beans trotting at his heels. He wasn't sure why he'd invited Mrs. Leggett and her daughter to join him, especially after he'd promised himself to minimize his contact with her. He was already pushing matters by working with the choir and now with her children's program.

He could tell himself he'd only intended to invite Joy, but that would be a lie. He knew good and well inviting Joy would also mean he was inviting Joy's mother.

Beans's sudden yip brought him back to the present. The dog bounded away from him toward the school-yard. Joy was already there, waiting on him. As was her mother.

Despite his resolve to remain merely polite, his pulse kicked up a notch. Okay, so he was attracted to her. But that didn't mean he had to do anything about it. If there was one thing the past nine years had taught him, it was to curb his impulsiveness. This was just a simple outing to give Joy an opportunity to play with Beans—nothing more.

Of course it was.

By the time he reached the schoolyard proper, Joy and Beans were already playing near the teeter-totter. Mrs. Leggett stood in front of the schoolhouse steps.

"Am I late?" he asked by way of greeting.

She shook her head. "I'm afraid Joy was getting impatient so we came out a bit early." She waved behind her toward the steps. "Shall we sit?"

He nodded and swept a hand, indicating she should precede him. She took her seat and fussily arranged her skirt, then looked up at him. "Aren't you going to sit, as well?"

Nate shook his head, thinking it best to maintain his distance. "I prefer to stand."

She frowned. "But your foot—"

"Is getting better every day. And don't worry, I'm not putting much weight on it." Ready to change the subject, he glanced toward the other members of their party. "It appears Joy and Beans are having a grand time."

She followed his gaze with her own. "Thank you so much for indulging Joy this way. I know you didn't have to include her in this outing."

He shrugged, uncomfortable as always with her gratitude. "It's just a walk I was planning to take, anyway."

"Still, it was a nice thing to do." She brushed at her skirt. "Did you enjoy your lunch with your friends?"

There was something odd about her tone, but he couldn't quite put his finger on what. Was she upset that he hadn't accepted her invitation? More to the point, how should he respond to her question? He hadn't lied to her earlier, but he'd done his best to mislead her so he could refuse her invitation without hurting her feelings. Truth was, he had eaten alone in his own apartment. He chose his words carefully. "It's always good to spend time with friends."

She looked at him as if she knew he hadn't really answered her question, but then nodded. "It is." Then she shifted and sat up straighter. "Perhaps now would be a good time to discuss the children's program in more detail."

Good, something neutral to discuss. "Of course. What size choir will you have?"

"I'm not certain yet—Janell, the schoolteacher, is going to cast her play tomorrow so she won't know for certain which children will participate in the choir until then. I'm meeting with her and the children at the end of the school day so I can meet them all. But Janell has already told me she anticipates there will be a dozen or so."

"That's a nice size. I assume they will be of various ages."

"Yes, including some children who are not yet school-age." She waved toward her daughter. "Joy for one. And at least two other children about her age—maybe three."

"Won't that be challenging?"

She grinned, not at all daunted. "Indeed it will." Then she raised her brow. "Does that make you want to back out?"

"Not at all." Truth be told, he was actually looking forward to it. "So how many songs will be on the program and how long do we have to put it all together?"

"I think three songs will make for a good program. And we have three weeks."

It seemed she wasn't afraid of a challenge. Of course, if anyone could pull this off, it was her. "So yesterday when we talked about this we decided the songs needed to be simple enough for four- and five-year-olds to learn, but interesting enough for the older children to not feel like it's beneath them. Did you come up with any songs that met those criteria?"

"I thought we'd start with something simple that most of them already know, 'Jesus Loves Me.' Do you know how to play that?"

"I haven't played it before, but I'm familiar with it. It shouldn't be a problem."

"Good." She cut a quick glance toward her daughter, then turned back to him. "Another song I thought of that might work with this group is 'Row, Row, Row Your Boat.' I know it's very simple, but if we have them perform it as a round, and add some hand motions with it, the older kids might find it challenging enough to be fun. What do you think?"

He nodded. "I think it will work. And since that one doesn't require a piano, I can help you with the rounds."

She nodded absently, her mind already seeming to move ahead. "I still need to figure out a third song. You don't have any suggestions by any chance?"

Nate hesitated. Then he decided that since she'd asked his opinion, that's what she'd get. "How about 'Down in the Valley to Pray'? It's easily divided into parts and simple enough for a children's choir. It can also be done a cappella."

A small frown line appeared between her eyes and he thought for a moment she was trying to find a polite way to tell him no. Then she lifted a hand, palm upward. "I'm afraid I don't know that one. Can you sing it for me?"

Sing it? On his own? That was definitely not something he was comfortable doing. "If you're not familiar with it, then perhaps we should go with something else."

"Oh, but you made it sound so intriguing. And I always love learning new songs." Then she tilted her head and gave him that challenging grin he found so irresistible. "You're not *afraid* to sing it, are you?"

"Afraid? No." He gave a self-deprecating smile. "I just know my own limitations and don't want to assault your ears with my braying."

She cast a watchful eye Joy's way again, then waved a hand dismissively. "Nonsense. I've heard you sing in church, remember? And I expect you to set a good example for the children. So you might as well get used to singing out with confidence."

He frowned and slid his fingers through his hair. Then, deciding he wasn't going to be able to get out of this, he gave in and sang the first verse and the chorus. When he was finished, he rubbed the back of his neck. He'd never done that before, sang solo for someone, not even Susanna. It made him feel more vulnerable, more exposed, than he liked.

But Mrs. Leggett was beaming at him approvingly. "What a lovely song!" She placed a hand on his arm. "Thank you so much for sharing it with me."

Everything inside him seemed to still for a heartbeat, as if wanting to soak in that unexpected touch. What was it about this woman that affected him so strongly? He fought to keep his expression in check and maintain an easy smile.

But either he failed or she felt something, too, because her expression shifted just the tiniest bit. Her eyes darkened and her breathing seemed to quicken. For a moment it felt as if something flowed between them at that point of contact. Then she abruptly withdrew her hand and the feeling was gone.

Averting her gaze, she called out to her daughter. "Joy, move away from the street."

"Yes, ma'am," the little girl responded with a wave. Mrs. Leggett kept her gaze on her daughter until the child had complied, which gave him time to collect himself.

When she turned back to him, her expression was once again serene. Had she felt what he felt?

"Where did you learn that song?" she asked.

In prison from a fellow inmate known only as Preacher. But he couldn't tell her that. "From an acquaintance. It was his favorite hymn." Hedging his answers like this felt as bad as lying.

"Well, I can certainly see why. You said it could be divided?"

He nodded. "You just repeat the whole thing four more times, replacing the word *father* in the chorus with *mother, brother, sister* and *sinner* respectively on each pass."

"The children are going to love it and so will their parents when they hear it. Thank you so much for singing it for me."

"Look." Joy's hail interrupted them. "I've taught Beans a trick."

Mrs. Leggett rose to go admire Joy and Beans's accomplishment and he slowly followed. Perhaps he should come clean, tell her the whole story of his past.

It would solve the problem of her sending those admiring glances his way.

But could he bear to see her look at him with loathing?

Verity held firmly on to Joy's hand as they made their way to Hazel's dress shop the next morning. She had to admit, knowing she would be passing Mr. Cooper's shop to reach Hazel's added a certain zest to the trip.

Mr. Cooper wasn't out on the sidewalk this morning, but the door to his shop was already open. He looked up from his workbench as they passed, giving them a smile.

Joy tugged on her hand. "Can I go visit Beans?"

"Maybe after we get finished at Miss Hazel's. In the meantime, you can visit with Buttons."

That seemed to mollify the child and she continued on without further resistance.

"There you are," Hazel said by way of greeting.

Verity nodded as Joy immediately sought out the feline. "We had a patient at the clinic first thing this morning so I was a little late heading out." She closed the shop door behind her, unwilling to trust her daughter to remain inside.

"Nothing serious I hope."

"Turned out to be just a bad case of indigestion." Verity set her drawstring purse on the counter. "Now, let's see this material you have picked out for Mrs. Sanders's dress."

Hazel drew out a bolt of a deep orange fabric shot through with delicate stripes of yellow. As she fingered the soft material, Verity felt her mind playing with several possibilities. "You said this is for the festival's opening ceremonies?"

"It is."

Studying the fabric and thinking of the woman herself, Verity nodded. "I believe I can come up with something that will look fetching and that she'll like. Can you reserve about a half yard of this that I can use for trim?"

"Of course."

"And if you have some netting in this shade of yellow, I'll need some of it, as well."

"Just let me know what else you'll be needing and I'll get it gathered up. And of course I'll bill Eula Fay for it."

"I'll stop by her place and discuss some ideas with her before I get started, but I already have a few thoughts as to what I'd like to do."

Another customer walked in and Verity stepped back to let Hazel conduct business. But rather than taking her leave, she found herself studying some of the bolts of fabric on display. There was one in particular that caught her eye. It was a muted blue, a hazy-sky kind of color, just the shade she loved. She fingered the fabric and liked the suppleness of it, as well.

"That would look lovely on you."

Verity dropped the fabric guiltily. Then had second thoughts. "I've been thinking about what you said the other day, and my black dress *is* getting a bit worn. Perhaps a new Sunday dress wouldn't be amiss."

Hazel's smile widened. "Well, it's about time." Before Verity could stop her, she grabbed up the bolt and carried it to her worktable. "And I have the perfect pattern in mind."

"Whoa." Verity held up a hand. "I said *perhaps*—I haven't made up my mind yet. And this fabric is much too fancy for me. I would need to choose something a bit more conservative."

"Nonsense. If you've gotten far enough in your thinking to say it out loud, then you're definitely ready. And this fabric is perfect. Now, I insist you let me make this for you."

"Oh, no, you don't. I can take care of this. Besides, I have another project for you."

"What's that?"

"The children's choir I'm forming for the Founders' Day Festival, I don't want them or their parents to worry about finding new clothing. I was thinking that if I could provide some smocks for each of them, sort of like short, simple choir robes, that might sort of even things out for everyone."

"Of course. I can get a bolt of simple, inexpensive fabric and whip something like that up in no time."

"Actually, I thought we might get some of the members of the Ladies Auxiliary to help with the stitching if you can do the cutting and oversee their work. I know Aunt Betty was asking how she might help, and I'm sure there are other ladies who feel the same way."

Hazel grinned. "Even better."

"Good. I'll ask Aunt Betty to round up some volunteers and report to you." She retrieved her purse. "I'll find out which children will be involved this afternoon so I can give you a head count and rough sizes after that. And of course I'll pay for the fabric."

Hazel waved that offer aside. "Don't worry about that. I can cover it, especially since I won't be doing all the sewing." She put a finger to her chin. "Now, about this new dress of yours?"

"Let me think about it."

"Don't think about it too long. I'm going to set this fabric behind the counter for you so it will be there whenever you get ready."

Verity tried to tell her friend not to bother but finally gave up. Whenever Hazel got something in her head, it was difficult to dissuade her. "Come along, Joy. Time to go. Tell Buttons and Miss Hazel goodbye."

Joy popped up and said her goodbyes. Then she took hold of Verity's hand. "Can we go see Beans now?"

"Beans?" Hazel raised a brow in question.

"It's Mr. Cooper's dog," Joy volunteered. "I taught him a new trick when Mama and me visited them in the schoolyard yesterday."

"You did?" She turned to Verity. "And why didn't you tell me about this little expedition? I want details."

Verity shrugged. "There's nothing to tell—Mr. Cooper just allowed Joy to play with his dog yesterday. Now, if you'll excuse us, it's time for us to go."

Verity breezed out the door with head held high, perfectly aware that Hazel was not at all satisfied with that explanation.

But thoughts of her friend faded quickly, replaced by a mood-lifting touch of anticipation at the thought of seeing Mr. Cooper again. However, when she and Joy stepped through the doorway of his shop, she came to an abrupt stop. Standing there, talking to Mr. Cooper with a bright smile and sparkling eyes, was Belva Ortolon.

Chapter Ten

Joy immediately rushed forward to greet Beans, drawing Mr. Cooper's and Belva's attention. Verity pasted her smile back on and stepped forward. There was no reason for her to give in to that stab of jealousy. She and Mr. Cooper were merely friends, nothing more. If he and Belva were forming some sort of attachment, well, she was happy for them. Of course.

With that not-quite-true thought firmly in mind, she waved a hand. "Hello. Don't let me interrupt you. We just stopped in for a minute so Joy could say a quick hello to Beans."

Belva shook her head, her cheerful demeanor never faltering. "Oh, you weren't interrupting anything—I was ordering a saddle from Mr. Cooper, but we were done."

Ordering a saddle? As far as Verity knew, Belva didn't own a horse. But again, that was none of her business.

"Besides," Belva continued, "you're just the person I need to see."

Verity took a heartbeat to absorb this unexpected statement. "Is there something I can do for you?"

"I was just congratulating Mr. Cooper here on his piano playing Sunday—wasn't it lovely?" She barely waited for Verity's bemused nod before continuing on. "Anyway, I mentioned that I had been thinking about joining the choir and he told me to stop thinking about it and just do it. So, since you're the choir director, I figure you would be the one to talk to."

Why the sudden interest in joining the choir? Belva had been in town for four months and this was the first time she'd mentioned it. Could it have anything to do with Mr. Cooper's involvement?

Not that that was either here or there. "Anyone with an interest is welcome to join," she answered with a smile she hoped was welcoming. "We practice every Saturday at four o'clock."

She hesitated a moment before issuing the second invitation, then chided herself for such churlishness. "And several us get together an hour earlier at the Blue Bottle for tea and conversation. You'd be most welcome to join us there as well, if you like. It's strictly optional." And since Constance had left this morning for her new adventure back east, there was an empty spot at the table.

"Oh, how lovely. Thank you."

"Hey," Mr. Cooper interjected. "How come no one invited me to this get-together? Aren't I a member of the choir now?"

Verity gave him a mock frown. "Technically you're the pianist, not a choir member."

Belva, who appeared confused by Verity's response, looked from her to Mr. Cooper and then back again.

"But surely, if he truly wants to join you, I mean, I can sit out—"

Verity laughed, though it wasn't lost on her how quickly Belva came to Mr. Cooper's defense. "I was just teasing. Of course, if he was serious about wanting to join our little tea party on Saturdays, Mr. Cooper is welcome to join us. I meant it when I said everyone was welcome."

"Oh." Belva gave a sheepish grin. "I should have known you were just having a bit of fun." Then she turned to Mr. Cooper. "What about it? Are you going to join us?"

He rubbed his chin, as if giving it serious consideration. "It's tempting, but it sounds as if this is a ladies-only affair." Then he raised a brow. "Then again, I do like a good cup of tea."

Did the look he shot her have a glint of challenge in it? Verity lifted her chin. "Eve's teas are special—she adds syrups and spices to give them unique flavors. She has something new just about every time we go in. Most of the menfolk around here, though, consider it too froufrou for their tastes."

He raised a brow at that. "I'm not most men and I'm not from around here." His lips twitched into a half smile before he schooled his expression again. "And I prefer to make up my mind for myself when it comes to what I like and don't like."

The look he gave her as he said that made her heart do a little flip-flop in her chest.

Then he turned to Belva. "How soon will you be needing that saddle?"

Was she dismissed? She stood there awkwardly fiddling with the collar of her dress, wondering if she should stay or go.

"Not for about three weeks," Belva answered. "Will that be a problem?"

"Not at all. It'll be ready when you need it."

"Well, if you'll excuse me, I have a few errands to run for Aunt Eunice." She turned to Verity. "It was nice running into you. And I'll see you on Saturday at the sweet shop."

When Belva had gone, Mr. Cooper leaned back and studied her curiously. "So, is there something I can do for you, or did you really come in so Joy could play with Beans?"

"It was mostly for Joy. But I did want to invite you to join me at the school this afternoon to meet the children who'll be part of our choir. If you'd like to, that is."

He seemed to ponder that for a moment. Then nodded. "Of course. What time should I be there?"

"I told Janell I'd be there at two-thirty."

"Then two-thirty it is."

"Well, then, I'll let you get back to your work." She turned toward her daughter, who was seated on the floor with Beans in her lap. "Time to go, pumpkin."

"But Mama, Beans and I aren't through playing."

"I'm sorry, but we need to go. I have a few more errands to run and I promised Aunt Betty I'd be back in time to help her hang out the laundry."

Mr. Cooper leaned forward. "It's all right, Joy. You're welcome to come back and visit anytime."

"You mean it?" Her precocious daughter's tone was quite solemn.

"Absolutely."

"Can I bring Mama, too?"

He glanced her way, his blue eyes seeming to darken slightly. "You may. In fact, I insist."

"Okay." Joy turned back to Beans. "Did you hear that? I can come back to play with you whenever I want."

Verity mentally sighed at her daughter's convenient misinterpretation of what had been said.

She foresaw a few battles between the two of them in the coming days.

Once Mrs. Leggett and her daughter had made their exit, Nate went back to work. He probably should have come up with an excuse to turn down her invitation. After all, she really didn't need him to go with her this afternoon. But for some reason, he hadn't been able to say no. His one consolation was that they would be in a room full of schoolchildren, not relatively alone in an empty schoolyard.

Nate forced his thoughts back to the order Belva had placed with him. A new saddle. It was his first major commission since he'd opened his shop and he was determined to do a good job.

Adam had loaned him the seed money he'd needed to set up and stock this place. And while he had no doubt his friend would extend the loan if he needed it, Nate was determined to make the payments on schedule. Because if he couldn't make a go of this place, then he might as well pack up and move on. He refused to be a drag on the man to whom he owed so much.

Then his thoughts circled back around to Mrs. Leggett. Was it wrong that he was so eagerly looking forward to seeing her again this afternoon?

* * *

When Nate stepped out of his shop just before two thirty that afternoon, he saw Mrs. Leggett approaching. Of course, she'd have to pass this way to get from her uncle's home to the schoolhouse. He shut the door behind him, then turned to wait for her.

As they exchanged greetings, they fell into step together.

"Where's Joy?" he asked. "Isn't she going to be part of this choir, too?"

"I left her with Aunt Betty. She'll get her introduction to the choir at the same time as the other young ones."

"How many?" he asked. Anything to keep the conversation light and impersonal.

"In addition to the children we meet at school today, there will be at least four others who are not yet school-age."

He sensed a quiet kind of anticipation about her, an eagerness, as if they were approaching a fun outing. She really *was* looking forward to this children's choir.

"So how well do you know the children who go to school here?"

"Most of them I at least know by sight. And I know some better than others, of course."

"So you're about to be assigned a group of children to teach that you have no idea whether they can carry a tune or not and how well they'll work together."

She tapped his arm lightly. "Don't be such a pessimist. They're children. And they're going to join the choir because they *want* to be in it."

"Or because they don't want to be in the play. There is a difference, you know."

"My, my, you *are* in a contrary mood today, aren't you?"

"I'd prefer to think I'm being realistic."

"Then you must think of this as a challenge. It will be up to us to make them love the choir, whether they are going into it for the right reasons or not. Do you think you are up to the job?"

He executed a half bow. "I will strive to follow your lead."

She laughed outright at that. It was a sound that brought a smile to his own lips.

They'd reached the schoolyard by then and he allowed her to precede him up the steps, suppressing thoughts of that simple but altogether electrifying touch yesterday.

When she reached the top, Mrs. Leggett opened the door herself rather than waiting for him, and stuck her head inside the building. "Are you ready for us?"

"Come on in" was the response from inside, and she opened the door wider and threw a smile over her shoulder as she entered.

When Nate followed her inside he saw Miss Whitman along with about a dozen students of various ages.

"Welcome, Verity." The schoolteacher waved them in. "And Mr. Cooper, it's an unexpected pleasure to have you join us, as well."

He set his hat on a nearby school desk. "I've volunteered to help Mrs. Leggett with the music, at least until your regular pianist returns."

"And we are all most grateful to have someone as talented as you fill in for Mrs. Ford."

He was grateful that she didn't wait for a response but instead she swept a hand toward the students.

"These are the talented group you two will be working with on the musical performance. The rest of the students are in Mr. Parker's classroom reading over the play."

"And a fine-looking group it is," Mrs. Leggett said enthusiastically. "I already know many of you and I'm sure I'll get to know the rest of you quickly. But for Mr. Cooper's benefit, why don't you each step forward, one at a time, and give us your name and age?"

There was something about her tone and demeanor that made one want to please her. Did the children feel it, too?

One by one they stepped forward and introduced themselves, just as she'd asked. He hoped no one actually expected him to remember all these names. He did spot one familiar face in the group—Jack Barr, Adam's son. The boy gave him a toothy grin as he introduced himself, indicating he recognized him, as well.

Mrs. Leggett had a kind word for each of them. When the last child had given her information, Mrs. Leggett took the floor again. "Very good. Now, we're not going to have any sort of practice session today—I just wanted to get to meet you and let you meet me and Mr. Cooper. But we *are* going to discuss expectations."

One of the younger children raised her hand.

"Yes, Cora Ann?"

"What's expectations?"

"Expectations means I'm going to let you know what I expect you to do if you want to be part of this choir." Then she smiled. "I promise none of this is very difficult. First, practice sessions will be for one hour every Tuesday and Thursday right after school, over at the church. We expect you to attend every practice unless you are ill. Second, you must promise to do your very best."

Nate watched as she went down her list of far-from-onerous expectations. She had the children's full attention—they seemed to be listening closely and were nodding in the appropriate places. Would she be able to command their attention as easily when they got down to the practice sessions themselves?

When she was done, she turned to him. "Was there anything you wanted to add?"

He was caught off guard by the question, but rallied quickly. "Only that everyone be respectful of their fellow choir members. Remember, everyone learns things at a different pace."

She gave him an approving nod, then turned back to the children. "Do you all agree to try to meet these expectations?"

Almost as one they said, "Yes, ma'am."

"Very good." She beamed approvingly at the group. "And I hope you'll be pleased to know that there are four children who aren't quite school-age yet who will be joining us. They are Joey and Molly Tucker, Jeffery Unger and my little girl, Joy."

"But they're practically babies," one of the older boys protested. "Will they even be able to keep up with us?"

Nate frowned. "They will if we help them."

She shot him a surprised look that quickly changed to one of approval. Had she thought he had no opinion on such things?

Then she turned back to the children. "Mr. Cooper is right. The younger ones may require a little extra patience, but with some practice they should be fine, especially with the songs we've selected."

"What songs are we gonna be singing?"

"We've selected three songs for the program, but I think we'll wait until tomorrow, when the rest of our choir will join us, to announce what they are." She looked around the group. "Now, does anyone have any other questions for me or Mr. Cooper?"

When no one spoke up, Mrs. Leggett leaned back against the teacher's desk.

"Very well, then. I'm really looking forward to getting to know all of you better and to listen to the beautiful music we'll make together. Remember, our first practice is right after school tomorrow. Let your parents know and don't be late."

The schoolteacher stepped forward. "All right, children, you are dismissed for the day." As the children quickly filed out, Miss Whitman turned to the two of them. "Thank you both so much for taking this on. I know the children will do their best for you." She scooped up a stack of papers from her desk. "Now, if you'll excuse me, I saw Abigail arrive a few minutes ago so I need to go next door and help her get the children's play organized."

"Of course." Mrs. Leggett stepped aside to let the teacher pass and then, with a "shall we?" glance for him, headed toward the door.

Taking his cue, he followed her out. By the time they stepped out on the small porch, there were no children in sight.

"Well, what do you think of our choir members?" she asked.

"I think, as a whole, they're a much younger group

than I'd expected." He hadn't seen more than two or three who looked like they'd hit their teen years yet. "Especially when you consider the four who weren't here today aren't yet old enough to be in school."

"The majority of them *do* seem to fall in the eight-to ten-year-old range." She didn't seem the least bit concerned by that. "It's a blessing for us, really."

"How so?"

"I find younger children much more teachable than the older ones."

He hadn't thought of it that way. Not that he was entirely convinced.

But she was moving on to another subject. "For our practice sessions, I was thinking it would be best to start with one song and practice it until they get it down right before moving on to the next. But do you think we should introduce them to all three songs when we get together tomorrow before we settle down to practice the first one? Or would that overwhelm them?"

How would he know? But she was waiting for his answer. "It seems to me that introducing them to all three songs first would give them something to look forward to. And if we sing each of them at the beginning of each session, it would get them used to that last song that they are probably not already familiar with."

"Good point. So you and I will sing them for the group first, and then we'll settle in to practice 'Jesus Loves Me.'"

"You're assuming these children actually can sing. Not everyone has an ear for music, you know."

"True. But if nothing else they can make a joyful noise. And, as you told Robbie, they'll manage okay if we help them." She met his gaze, her expression earnest. "I don't want any of these children to feel they are any less important to the choir than any of the other members."

He gave a short nod. "Of course. A joyful noise it is."

"I was wondering…" She paused, her fingers plucking at her collar.

"What is it?"

"Well, that song you sang for me yesterday—'Down to the Valley.'"

Had she changed her mind about using it? "If you prefer to substitute something else—"

"No, no, I love the song. It's just that, if I'm going to teach the children, then someone really needs to teach it to me first."

Teach her? Watch her learn the words and melody, make them her own? It was very tempting.

But he wasn't sure he was much of a teacher.

Chapter Eleven

Verity saw his hesitation and wished she could take the question back. Had her request been out of line? Her cheeks warmed as she realized the spot she'd put him in. He had shut his shop to accompany her this afternoon, and now she'd asked for more of his time. He was undoubtedly trying to find a polite way to say no.

Before she could withdraw her request, however, he nodded.

"All right. Where would you like to do this? It's performed a cappella so we don't need a piano, but I'd prefer not to break into song right here on the sidewalk."

She appreciated his self-deprecating humor. And also his generosity. "Thank you, but I just realized you probably need to get back to your shop. Why don't we plan to meet a little early before practice starts tomorrow instead?"

But he shook his head. "Today is fine." By now they'd reached the corner of Schoolhouse Road and Second Street. He waved toward his shop. "As you can see, there's no line of customers waiting for me to open my doors. And the work I already have scheduled can wait a little longer without endangering any schedules."

Was his business slow, then? "I'm sure you'll get more customers as more people become aware of your work."

He merely nodded and changed the subject. "So, where shall we go?"

"We could go down by the church. It should be fairly quiet there today."

They turned their steps toward the church but hadn't gone far before they encountered Eunice Ortolon, Belva's aunt.

Verity intended to just exchange greetings and keep moving, but Eunice apparently wanted to have a conversation.

"Well, hello, Verity, Mr. Cooper. It's a fine afternoon for a walk, isn't it?"

Mr. Cooper nodded. "That it is, ma'am."

Verity could see the woman's mind working as she studied the two of them. Surely she didn't see this as anything other than what it was. But the woman was a notorious busybody—she loved speculating about anyone and anything she knew, or even thought she knew. And she didn't mind sharing those speculations with anyone who would listen.

Eunice gave Mr. Cooper an arch smile. "I hope your injuries are healing well. We've been missing you around the boardinghouse."

Mr. Cooper smiled politely. "I thank you for your concern, ma'am. And I certainly hope my absence hasn't caused you any inconvenience."

"We're getting by." She glanced at Verity and then back to him. "I understand you'll be helping Verity here with the children's choir. That's very kind of you. There's not many a gentleman who'd agree to step in for the church piano player, much less teach songs to a group of youngsters."

Verity's spine stiffened. Did Eunice think that such actions were beneath him?

"If that's true, then it's their loss," Mr. Cooper said easily. "I enjoyed playing for the church service. And I just met some of the children who'll be in the new choir and I'm certain I'll enjoy working with them, as well."

"It sounds like Verity here is lucky to have someone as enthusiastic as you are to help her." Eunice's tone still carried an edge of patronization

Verity lifted her chin, but kept her smile relaxed. "It's Turnabout that's lucky Mr. Cooper moved here, don't you think?"

Eunice's smile slipped momentarily, then came back in full force. "Of course. Well, I won't keep you from, well, from wherever you were headed."

Verity ignored Eunice's not-so-subtly buried question and moved on.

For a moment neither she nor Mr. Cooper said anything. What was he thinking? Had he been put off by Eunice's clumsy comments?

"It strikes me that Mrs. Ortolon is nothing like her niece."

Verity swung her gaze around to meet his. The words had been uttered in an idle tone, as if he'd been remarking on the weather, but there was a definite glint of amusement in his eyes.

She matched his impassive expression. "You mean she's shorter and has a brassier voice?"

"Exactly."

They shared a grin, and for a moment Verity felt an unfamiliar emotion tugging at her, an emotion she decided not to examine too closely.

When they reached the churchyard, Verity swept a hand out. "Will this do?"

"It seems quiet enough."

By which she knew he meant there was no one around to hear him sing. This little touch of insecurity, and the vulnerability that it lent to such an otherwise strong man, actually seemed quite endearing.

"Would you like to sit on the steps?" he asked.

His question brought her thoughts back to the here and now. "Actually, this may sound strange, but what if we stroll through the cemetery?" She could see she'd startled him. "I promise I'm not being morbid. I've just always thought it was such a peaceful, beautiful place, especially on a bright spring day like today. But if it makes you uncomfortable—"

"Not at all. Lead the way."

Nate strolled beside her, wondering again at her unexpectedness, at how she could so enchant him without any obvious effort. The man who'd been her husband had been a lucky fellow.

She led him through the gate and then around the perimeter until they came to a large oak. There were two simple wooden benches, one on each side of the tree. She turned to him with a smile. "How's this?"

"It'll do." Actually, with her smiling at him like that, he would have agreed to sing in the middle of Main Street.

She took a seat on one of the benches, then looked up at him expectantly. "Well, then, teach me."

He cleared his throat and launched into the song, singing the first verse and chorus at a respectable volume. His reward when he was done was an absent, inwardly focused glance from his pupil.

"I think I have it," she said. "If you'll go over it again, I'll try to sing along."

With a nod he started again. She immediately added her voice to his. The sound of their voices together both startled and pleased him.

When they were done, she grimaced. "I mangled a few notes. Let's try it one more time."

He hadn't noticed her mangling anything, but he decided he could do this all day. He started again and this time when she joined in her voice was stronger, surer. And to his surprise, rather than copying him this time, she sang harmony, playing with some of the notes, making it up right there on the spot. And it sounded amazing. The beauty of their joined voices was something he could listen to forever.

When they were finished this time, she clapped her hands in pure joy. "Oh, that was fun. The kids are going to love this song."

Right now, it was his favorite, as well.

"I'll definitely need your help teaching it to the children, but at least now I feel like I can hold my own with it." She straightened. "Now, I'm sure you're eager to get back to your shop."

Not particularly, but he knew a dismissal when he heard one.

She led him out a different way than the one they'd taken earlier. Rather than following the perimeter, she silently led him on a winding path between the headstones.

Then she paused and placed her hands lightly on a pair of side-by-side headstones. "These are my parents," she said softly. "I like to stop by and say hello whenever I'm here."

He studied her bittersweet expression. "Have they been gone long?"

"They passed when I was five. Uncle Grover and Aunt Betty raised me."

"It was good that you had someone to take you in."

She removed her hands from the headstones and smiled up at him. "They were great substitute parents—I never doubted I was loved."

But she was still studying her parents' graves pensively.

"Do you remember them?" he asked.

She nodded. "Not a lot, of course, but images, emotions. I loved my mother, but I adored my father."

He could tell be the faraway look in her eyes that she was remembering another time and place.

"He was bigger than life, always full of energy, and he seemed to live to make me and Mother happy."

"Sounds like quite a man."

"He was. He had a way of making everything we did seem like fun. And he liked to take Mother on what he called adventuring—take hikes, camp out in the woods, canoe on water rapids, climb peaks—anything that seemed new or exciting. I have great memories of the two of them laughingly setting off on what looked, to my five-year-old self, like really fun excursions."

Her smile had a faraway quality to it. "They included me occasionally, in what I now know were the tamer of these outings." She touched the little scar near her lip. "I got this on one of the camping trips. Father said it was my badge of honor, the proof that I was an adventurer like him and mother."

"Did their death occur on one of these adventures?"

She nodded. "It was a hot air balloon."

Realizing what must have happened, Nate immediately held up his hand. "There's no need to tell me the details."

She seemed not to hear him. "I stood on the ground with a family friend and watched the balloon go up with them in the basket below. They both blew me kisses and then turned and kissed each other. They looked so happy and my only thought was that I wanted very badly to be with them." She paused a moment. "Then, when they were so far up that I could no longer distinguish them, the balloon caught fire in a big whoosh. It was over almost before the woman who was holding my hand fainted and hit the ground."

He quickly reached for her hand, wanting to offer her what comfort he could. "Verity, I'm so, so sorry that happened to you. That must have been horrific to see."

Her gaze slowly lost its unfocused quality and she smiled at him. "As you yourself said, Uncle Grover and Aunt Betty were really wonderful. Uncle Grover blamed my father's reckless, impulsive nature for getting my mother—his sister—killed, but he never held that against me. And anyway, I'm nothing like my father. I lack his thirst for adventure."

And then she seemed to suddenly realize he was holding her hand. Her cheeks pinkened and gaze dropped.

He gave her hand a quick squeeze and then released

it. But he didn't apologize. Mainly because he wasn't sorry.

Did she also realize he'd called her by her first name? Because she certainly hadn't objected.

Then he struck an idle tone as he prepared to do a little more probing. "Is your former husband buried here, as well?"

She didn't seem put out by the question. She merely shook her head. "Arthur is buried in Kansas, beside his first wife."

So she had been the man's second wife. "Do you mind if I ask you what sort of man he was?"

She started walking again, and for a moment he thought she wasn't going to answer. He didn't blame her—it was something he had no right to ask.

Then she spoke up. "I don't mind. In fact, Arthur deserves to be remembered and spoken of from time to time."

There was a fondness in her voice, and some sense of reflection, as well.

"Arthur was a fine, decent man," she continued. "He was a good doctor, and a respected member of the community where we lived. And he absolutely adored Joy."

"Did he have an adventurous streak like your father?"

She smiled at that. "I'm afraid not. For one thing Arthur was somewhat older, nearly fifteen years my senior. And he had a more analytical approach to life, a trait that served him well in his work as a doctor."

But how had it served him in his role as a husband? Had he been dispassionate and analytical there, as well?

Nate didn't press her any further. But he did find it odd that she never once spoke of loving him.

Verity lay in bed that night staring at the ceiling, going over the events of the day. Singing a duet with him had been such an amazing, exhilarating experience. It had felt…exciting. And fun. And, oh, so right. Almost as if their voices had been created specifically to complement each other.

Which was a totally ridiculous, fanciful thought.

Was that why she'd told him about her parents? A lot of people around here knew the story, of course, but she'd never spoken of it to anyone before.

The way he'd taken her hand, and looked at her with that sincere sympathy in his compelling blue eyes had been both comforting and affirming. His hands holding hers—strong, callused hands, hands that belonged to both a craftsman and a pianist—had made her feel both safe and empowered.

Which she supposed was why she had spoken so freely about Arthur today. Strange, but, except for the conversations she sometimes had with Joy, she'd spoken of her former husband more in that short discussion with Mr. Cooper than she had since she'd returned to Turnabout.

But even without Mr. Cooper's questions, she'd found herself ruminating on her marriage. Because telling him about her memories of her parents had had her making some comparisons with her own life.

Arthur had been a good husband to her and she'd been quite fond of him. She'd admired him, too. He'd been predictable, responsible and even-tempered. He was everything she'd told herself she wanted in a husband.

But thinking today of the all-encompassing, zestful love she'd witnessed between her own parents, she realized that she and Arthur had never shared anything like what her parents had. And she wondered now what it would be like to experience such a love.

She rolled over on her side and hugged her pillow. Arthur had never shared her love of music, either. Singing together with Mr. Cooper today, however, had been a surprisingly emotional experience. The way their voices had blended and intertwined, the look in his eyes as their gazes locked together—she'd never experienced that kind of connection before. It had been altogether addictively exhilarating.

Had Mr. Cooper felt the same thing?

And he'd called her by her first name. That had to mean something.

Didn't it?

Chapter Twelve

Verity nodded her thanks to Nate—that's how she thought of him now, even if she still used the more formal Mr. Cooper when she said his name aloud.

The two of them had just finished singing all three selected songs for the children. She had enjoyed singing with him today every bit as much as she had yesterday. Once Zella returned, would he consider joining the choir? It would be nice to sing alongside him every Sunday. Would the experience be the same as part of a larger group?

But right now it was time to focus on the gathered group of sixteen children. "So what do you all think? Doesn't that sound like a great program?"

Her question was met with mostly smiles and nods, but she also made note of the few who looked doubtful.

"Today we're going to focus on practicing 'Jesus Loves Me.'" That was the easiest and the one most familiar to the children. Hopefully it would help build the confidence of those who were feeling a bit overwhelmed.

"But we all already know that one, Mrs. Leggett," Derbin said.

"But do you know all four verses?"

"There's *four* verses?"

"There are." She looked around to include all the children in her remarks. "And I have an idea about how to perform this so that every one of you has an opportunity to really be heard."

The children leaned forward slightly. She noticed that even Nate raised a brow at that.

"Since there are sixteen of you, and the song has four verses, I'm going to divide you up into four groups of four singers each, and each group will be responsible for one of the verses."

"Do we get to pick which team we're on?"

Verity grinned at Jack's question. "No, Mr. Cooper and I will be figuring out the teams." She held up a finger. "But first, let's sing the first verse, the one all of you know, all together so I can get a feel for each of your voices."

She glanced toward Nate and without her saying a word he took his place at the piano. She turned back to the children. "Form a line here in front of me, oldest to youngest."

The kids scrambled to do as she asked. There was a little bit of giggling and rearranging as they figured out relative ages. Finally they were settled.

"Okay, now, stand up straight." She nodded to Nate. He played a short intro and then went right into the melody. She sang with them the first time, walking back and forth in front of them. When they got to the end, she nodded. "Sing it again, please."

This time she didn't sing along, but rather listened

to each of the children in turn, assessing the strength of their voices and their ability to carry a tune.

When they were done for the second time, she smiled and nodded. "Well done. Let me discuss this with Mr. Cooper for a few minutes and then we'll form your groups." She moved to stand next to him at the piano bench.

"I want to put the four youngest together," she said. "They know the first verse really well and this will give them an opportunity to be heard rather than hidden behind the older ones. And I'm sure their parents will appreciate giving them a bit of the limelight, as well."

"That sounds like a good plan."

"As for the others, I think grouping them by voice range would be best, don't you?"

He nodded. "But you also want to be sure you don't group all the weakest singers together, regardless of range."

"Agreed." She made a few mental adjustments to her thoughts on the groupings, then signaled him to follow her as she turned back to the children.

"Okay, here we go. When I call your name, stand together with your group. Group one—Molly, Joey, Robbie and Joy. Group two—Mina, Jack, Peter and Alice. Group three—Harriet, Cora Ann, Susie and Derbin. And that leaves Becky, Mary Ellen, Fern and Kevin for group four."

She waited until all the children had arranged themselves into their groups, then spoke again. "As I said, each group will learn one of the verses to sing. But all of you will sing the chorus together. Now, I've written down the words for each verse." She began passing the pages around, one sheet per group. "I want each group to pick a corner of the church and go there to practice your part. In about thirty minutes we'll get back together and try to run through the whole thing."

Responding to her glance, Nate stepped forward. It was really nice to work with someone who seemed to be so in tune with her thoughts.

"If you'll work with group one—" she pointed to the youngest children "—I'll work with group two." She figured the older children could probably handle this one on their own. Fern Tucker was in group four and Derbin Greene was in group three. Both were good singers and good kids—they'd be able to lead the others.

She'd given Nate the youngest group to work with mainly because Joy was in it. She figured it would be better for everyone if she didn't work with her own daughter. And since the children were already familiar with the words and melody to this one, his biggest challenge would be making sure they all started and ended the song at the same time.

She forced her focus away from him and his group and onto her group. Since they were not as familiar with the second verse as they were with the first, they had to go through it a couple of times before the children were comfortable singing it through by memory. Once they had that down, she focused on their timing and harmonizing.

Finally, it was time to pull them all back together. "Okay, everyone, let's gather back in the front here. And this time when you line up, do it by groups. Group one stand here, then group two next to them and so forth. Mr. Cooper, if you'd return to the piano."

Once they were all in place, she gave them a big smile. "From what I heard coming from your groups, it sounds like everyone is ready. So, let's try it together. Remember, each verse will be sung by only one group, but you will all sing the chorus together each time."

She waited for their nods before continuing. "One other thing before we start. I'm going to use a few hand signals to communicate with you during the performance. When I do this—" she held up a hand, palm out "—that means to stand up straight and focus on me. When Mr. Cooper plays the introduction, I will give you a countdown as so." She held up three fingers, one at a time. "And then when I do this—" she jabbed her index finger out in an aggressive pointing motion "—that means start singing. And when I do this—" she made a sweeping motion with her hand "—that means everyone join in. So keep your eye on me, okay?" She held up a hand and they all came to attention.

She nodded to Nate and he started the intro. She counted down with her fingers, then pointed to the youngest group. She had to smile as they sang. They weren't completely together, but what they lacked in technique, they made up for in enthusiasm. Even if they didn't improve before the actual performance, their parents would love watching them.

Though by no means perfect, they made it through the entire hymn without having to stop. They went through it a few more times, and once Verity thought they were comfortable with the song, she asked them to add some minor movement. As the time came for each verse, she had the group responsible step forward, then return to their places when they were done.

There were a few missteps, naturally, but all in all she was pleased with this first practice. When they came back together on Thursday they could polish this up and begin work on the next song.

Just as she was ready to dismiss the group, Hazel showed up with a measuring tape and notebook in hand. The dressmaker took quick measurements of each of the children for the smocks she planned to make.

When the final measurement had been taken and all of the children but Joy had gone, Hazel turned to Verity. "So how was the first practice?"

"I think it went quite well." Verity turned to Nate. "What did you think?"

"They're a good group of kids. Some of them already have excellent singing voices, some are going to need a little more work. But I think in the end we'll have a program the parents and friends will be able to appreciate."

Verity nodded. "I agree. And all of them seem willing to put in the work."

"Well, I have what I came for." Hazel gathered up her things. "If you two have additional work to do, I can take Joy back with me. You can stop in and get her on your way home."

Verity resisted the urge to roll her eyes at this not-so-subtle bit of matchmaking, but nodded, anyway. She knew Hazel would keep a close eye on her daughter, so she had no qualms on that account. "Well, there is something regarding our next practice I'd like to work out with Mr. Cooper." She turned to him. "If you don't mind staying a moment longer."

"Not at all."

Hazel held her hand out. "Come along, Joy. Buttons has a new bit of yarn he needs someone to dangle for him."

Joy went to her without hesitation. With one last grin over her shoulder toward Verity, Hazel led the little girl out the door.

A moment later, though, Joy raced back inside. What in the world was the matter?

"Joy, slow down before you fall and hurt yourself."

The girl immediately slowed her steps but continued forward. Verity saw Hazel step inside and pause.

She turned back to her daughter. "What's the matter? Did you change your mind about going with Miss Hazel?"

Joy shook her head. "I forgot Lulu." She reached into one of the pews near the front of the church and triumphantly picked up her doll. Squeezing her ever-present companion tightly, she turned back toward Hazel and made her exit for the second time.

Nate watched Joy leave, then turned to her mother. "That doll seems to be very dear to her." Susanna had had a special doll, also. Unlike Joy's wooden-headed cloth figure, though, Susanna's had been china and elegantly dressed in lace and silk. Still, it seemed both girls shared a similar love for their playthings.

Verity nodded. "It was given to her by her father." Her expression grew more solemn. "Just one week before he died."

Nate stilled at that reminder of her loss. And of the secret he was keeping from her.

But Verity didn't seem aware of him. Her gaze was unfocused, turned inward. "She was only four at the time and I think she's forgotten so much of him. He loved her very much—I'm glad she has that one thing of his she can cling to."

What about her? Was her memory of her deceased husband still fresh and raw? Or was he a beloved but fading memory that she thought fondly of from time to time?

And why did the answer to that very personal question matter so much to him?

"I'm sorry," she said, her cheeks pinkening. "I shouldn't have brought up such personal thoughts."

"No need to apologize. I'm honored that you would be comfortable sharing them with me."

Her smile immediately turned warmer.

Deciding his thoughts were now drifting toward dangerous territory again, he cleared his throat. "So what was this you needed to speak to me about?"

She took his cue and her expression took on a more businesslike cast. "I was thinking I'd like to change the second song to something else."

"And what brought this on?"

Her nose wrinkled slightly, as if she was trying to articulate a nebulous feeling. "It just doesn't seem to fit in with the other two."

He stilled at that. "And fitting in is important to you?"

Something in his tone must have caught her attention because she gave him a faintly puzzled look. "Well, of course. The program should be harmonious, don't you think?"

Fit in. Harmonious. Did she feel that way about the people she let into her life, as well?

Rather than answering her question, he asked one

of his own. "What did you have in mind to replace it with?"

"That's just it, I can't make up my mind."

He moved around the piano. "Do you mind if we walk while we discuss this? I need to head back to my shop. Miss Ortolon asked to talk to me about her saddle design again and I told her to come at four-thirty."

"Oh. Of course." She fell in step beside him as they headed down the aisle. "I apologize for holding you up. We can continue this conversation another time, if you like."

He heard something different in her voice, but he couldn't quite put his finger on what. "Not at all. There's time to figure this out before Miss Ortolon arrives." He opened the church door and allowed her to precede him. "So back to your question, what attributes would a song need to have in order to *fit in* with the other two songs? Are you looking for another hymn?"

"Not necessarily, though a hymn would definitely work better than a child's rhyme." She paused, as if gathering her thoughts. "I guess I'm looking for something with an uplifting message."

She waved a hand with an apologetic air. "I'm sorry I didn't think this through earlier. I hate changing things up now that we've set the children's expectations." She grimaced self-consciously. "Uncle Grover always says being wishy-washy shows a lack of character."

He felt strangely protective of her and was insulted on her behalf. "Not at all. And you're not being wishy-washy. You're merely being flexible enough to make an adjustment when you spot a weakness."

He was rewarded with a warm smile. "I guess I'd never thought of it that way. That does sound nicer, doesn't it?"

He forced himself not to bask in her smile but to get back to business. "So, a new song. Given our time frame, it would need to be either something the children are already familiar with or something very simple."

"Agreed."

He rubbed his chin. "How do you feel about adding a patriotic song? Something like 'America' or 'Columbia, the Gem of the Ocean'?"

"Why, that's a great idea." She smiled at him as if he'd said something brilliant. "I think 'America' will fit in perfectly. And you should be able to find the sheet music for it in the stack Zella left for you—she plays it every Independence Day. Which also means most of the children will at least have heard it before."

He nodded, a bit puffed up by her enthusiastic praise. "I'll come by tomorrow to look for it and maybe run through the song a couple of times just to make certain I can play it smoothly at Thursday's practice session."

"I'll be glad to help you with that if you like."

He definitely liked. But should he agree?

She spoke up again before he could decide. "It might be good for us to run through it together so we can decide whether to have the children sing it as a group or break it out by verses like we're doing the others."

How could he say no to that? "Of course." They'd reached his shop by then and he opened his door. "Would you like to continue our discussion inside?"

She started to say something then glanced down the

sidewalk and her expression changed. "I think we're done for now. I'll let you get back to work."

He followed her gaze and saw Belva approaching. He turned back to her and nodded. "I'll see you at the church tomorrow then. Shall we say four o'clock?"

With a nod and a wave, she retraced her steps as far as the dress shop. He watched as she stepped inside, then he turned to greet Belva.

Verity didn't tarry long at Hazel's. Joy, naturally, didn't want to part from Buttons but reluctantly followed her mother out. Verity determinedly kept her gaze on her daughter as they walked past Nate's shop, though she was quite tempted to look. Were he and Belva laughing the way they'd been the last time she saw them together?

Nate had said Belva was stopping by to discuss her saddle design. What was there about saddle design that needed further discussion once the order had been placed?

Verity didn't like the idea that she was giving jealousy a toehold in her heart, but there was no denying she had. If she couldn't control her heart, she at least had to control where she let her thoughts take her.

With that in mind, she turned to her daughter. "So, Joy, what did you think of choir practice today?"

"It was fun."

"And what was your favorite part?"

"It was when Mr. Cooper practiced with our group. He has a nice voice."

It seemed Nate had managed to steal her daughter's heart, as well.

She let Joy's happy chatter, which required very little response, carry them the rest of the way home.

Nate listened to Belva's suggestions and took the appropriate notes. Back when he had been working part-time at the boardinghouse, Belva had gotten into the habit of chatting with him while he chopped wood or performed some of the other maintenance chores her aunt had lined up for him.

He wasn't sure why she'd taken to him the way she had—perhaps it was because she was fairly new to town herself and hadn't made any close friends yet. Or perhaps it was because, as she'd told him recently, he reminded her of a schoolteacher she'd had when she was younger, a man she admired and trusted very much. Whatever the case, it seemed he'd become a confidant of sorts for her. She'd confided secrets that she hadn't shared with anyone else. He hadn't reciprocated, of course, which made him feel even more of a fraud. But he hadn't asked to be put into that role, and there was nothing he could do about it now.

All that being said, normally he enjoyed her chatter—she almost felt like a younger sister—but today his mind was on Verity.

The doctor's niece was beginning to look at him with a certain softness, a certain interest that he couldn't mistake. The thing was, he wasn't sure if she liked him for who he truly was, or if she still had some kind of misguided sense of gratitude that she was mistaking for something deeper. And the answer to that mattered a great deal to him.

Whatever the case, he wasn't sure how much longer he could maintain a "just friends" attitude, especially when she looked at him with those lovely eyes of hers and that sweet smile on her lips. And even worse was this gnawing guilt that he was lying to her by omission.

The time was drawing near when he'd have to summon the courage to tell her his past.

And once he did, he wouldn't have the problem of having her look at him with such admiration at all.

"Mr. Cooper."

Belva's voice pulled him back to the present. "Yes."

She had a fist planted on her hip. "I don't think you've heard anything I've said for the past few minutes."

He didn't bother denying the accusation. "I'm sorry. What were you saying?"

She relaxed and waved a hand dismissively. "Oh, nothing much. Just nattering on like always. But it looks like this time, it's you who needs to talk. Anything I can help with?"

"Oh, it's nothing. I'm just distracted today." He tapped his notebook with his pencil. "I think I have your new specifications down and I don't see any problems incorporating them in the final product. Was there anything else?"

She shook her head. "That's all for now. I can't wait to see the finished saddle."

"Have you told your aunt about your horse yet?"

"I'm going to wait until the very last minute. I'm afraid something will happen to spoil my plans if I tell too many people." Then she gave him a little wave. "Thank you again. And remember, if you need someone to talk to, I'm available."

Someone to talk to—that would be very welcome.

But the only person here he could safely confide in was Adam, and Adam was a big part of his dilemma.

Because his story wasn't his alone. If he ever reached the point where he was ready to talk about his time in prison and what he'd done to land him there, if the person he told was an intelligent person, she might begin to wonder just how he and Adam met. And Nate would *not* allow himself to be the cause of speculation about Adam's past.

No matter how uncomfortable keeping secrets from certain people made him.

Chapter Thirteen

The next few days passed in a pleasantly busy fashion for Verity. She met Nate at church Wednesday afternoon as they'd planned, and together they practiced the new song in what Verity thought of as perfect harmony. Singing with him had become a treasured experience for her. She loved the way their voices intertwined, the way his gaze held hers when they sang, the way they seemed to instinctively be able to anticipate one another. Perhaps, sometime soon, she could convince him to perform a duet with her during the Sunday service.

In the end they decided to go with the first three verses of "America" for the program and to let the children perform it as a group rather than assigning parts.

At Thursday's practice session, Verity had them start out by running through "Jesus Loves Me," the song they'd practiced during the prior session, a couple of times and then she introduced "America" as the replacement for "Row, Row, Row Your Boat." By the end of the hour-long session she was well pleased with their progress.

By the time Friday rolled around, Verity had Eula

Fay's hat completed. The mayor's wife seemed delighted with the result, lavishing effusive praise on Verity. It was enough to make her begin to think that perhaps she might just be ready to open her millinery business after all.

Despite his teasing comments earlier in the week, Nate didn't join them on Saturday for their weekly tea, but Verity hadn't really expected him to.

Belva, however, *did* join them. The other members of the group welcomed her and seemed genuinely delighted to learn she was joining the choir.

Despite the remaining pinprick of jealousy, Verity couldn't help but like the girl. She was perpetually optimistic, had a bit of coltish awkwardness about her and was always willing to pitch in and help where she could.

And later, at choir practice, she proved to have a tolerable enough voice to blend in with the rest of the group.

After choir practice, Hazel approached her. "Come with me and stop by the shop on your way home. There's something I want to show you."

Verity had hoped to walk with Nate but hid her disappointment. "Of course. Is it something to do with the choir smocks?"

"No questions—it's a surprise."

Verity rolled her eyes—Hazel and her love of the dramatic. But it was always easier to go along with her than try to argue.

"So, how are things going between you and Mr. Cooper?" her friend asked.

"He's been a big help to me with the children's choir. He has a way about him that they all respond to."

Hazel gave her a little nudge. "I didn't ask how he was getting along with the children. I asked how he was getting along with *you*."

Verity waved a hand airily. "We've become good friends, and of course I have no complaints about his performance as a musician."

Hazel gave her a severe frown. "You, my dear, can be a most frustrating friend. I want details, not boring platitudes."

Verity placed a hand over her heart in feigned shock. "Boring?"

"Don't play the innocent with me, Verity Magdalena Leggett. You know exactly what I mean."

Verity laughed. "Let's just say we get along very well." By this time they'd reached Hazel's shop. "Now, what is this surprise you wanted to show me?"

"Patience, my dear." Hazel opened the door and led the way inside.

Verity's gaze went immediately to a dress form in the center of the shop. Draped on it was a lovely dress fashioned from that same shadow-blue fabric she had so admired last week.

She moved closer to examine it. Hazel had done an amazing job of keeping it simple but at the same time giving it a special feel. The slightly flared skirt was trimmed on the bottom with two rows of a darker blue ribbon, as was the waistband. The sleeves were puffed from the shoulder and then gathered at the elbow and snug on the forearm. Again there was dark trim on the bodice, but here it was done in a vertical pattern that Verity could tell would be quite flattering to the wearer.

"So, what do you think?"

Verity turned to her friend. "It's really lovely. I knew this fabric would drape beautifully, but I think you outdid yourself here. You should have no trouble selling this one."

"Oh, it's not for sale." Her friend had a very smug look on her face. "I made it for you."

Verity was taken aback. She couldn't accept such a gift. And yet…

"And before you say anything," Hazel continued, "you should know that I won't take no for an answer. In fact, I will be highly insulted if you don't accept my gift since I went to a lot of trouble to tailor it just for you."

Verity fingered the dress, enjoying the suppleness of it. It had been a long time since she'd had a new dress, at least one that wasn't made from pieces of other dresses and a new bit of ribbon or trim. "If I do accept it," she said carefully, "then you must at least let me pay for it." She'd find the money somehow.

"If you insist on repaying me, you can make one of your fabulous hats just for me and I will consider us even."

Verity knew it wasn't an even trade but she nodded agreement. She'd find other ways to repay her friend.

"Good." Hazel stepped forward to remove the dress from the form. "Let me just package this for you and you can take it home with you. And I expect to see you wearing it at church tomorrow."

A few minutes later Verity was headed toward home, a package in her arms and the humming melody of a song on her lips.

Yes, all in all, it had been a good week. And she

had the glimmer of an idea how to make tomorrow even better.

Clothed in this new dress, she might just find the courage to translate her idea into action.

"There's something I'd like to talk to you about," Nate said as he followed Adam into the study.

Adam had invited him to join his family for supper Saturday evening and Nate had gladly taken him up on it. The meal was over now, and he and Adam had moved from the dining room to the study.

"Of course." Adam took a seat in one of a pair of large leather chairs that fronted the desk and signaled Nate to take the other.

Once seated, Nate rubbed the back of his neck, suddenly unsure how to start.

Adam steepled his fingers. "Would this, perchance, have anything to do with Mrs. Leggett?"

Nate noted the amused glint in his friend's eyes and nodded sheepishly. "Am I so obvious?"

"Let's just say I've noted the glances you've been giving each other." He propped his left leg on his right knee as he leaned back. "So, is it serious?"

Nate had no problem answering that question. "If you're asking if I'd like to pursue something more than a mere friendship with her, then the answer is yes."

"So why did you feel the need to speak to me about this rather than her? Do you want some information about her?"

"No, nothing like that. The thing is, I don't think I can take this any further without being honest with her about my past."

"I see."

He couldn't read anything one way or the other in Adam's demeanor. Did his friend understand what the implication was? "Of course I don't plan to mention anything about your connection to any of this. But Mrs. Leggett is an intelligent woman." It was one of the things he admired about her. "She might very well put some of the pieces together."

"Nate, I know I've told you that my history is not well-known around here. But that wasn't meant to keep you from telling your own story if you felt the need." He leaned forward, his expression earnest. "The people who matter the most to me know all about my history. As for the rest of my friends and neighbors here—" he shrugged "—I hope I've proven myself to them in the three years that I've lived here. But, if some choose to believe the worst, then I'd like to think I can survive that."

He gave Nate a pointed look. "If Mrs. Leggett is important to you, and you feel led to tell her your story, then don't let any concerns about my feelings hold you back."

Nate felt humbled by his friend's trust. "Thanks. Mind you, I don't plan to tell her tomorrow, and it may not be next week, or next month, or even at all. I just needed to know that, if the time does come, I won't be betraying any spoken or implied confidence between us."

Later, as Nate walked home, he thought over what Adam had said. His family and close friends knew the truth and still accepted him. Of course, in Adam's case, he had been innocent of the crime he'd been imprisoned for. Not that his innocence had ever been officially established. Still, that had to have played into how those who knew his story viewed him.

Would that same kind of trust be afforded to him?

He supposed that depended on whom he told his story to. And how he told it.

This wasn't something he could figure out on his own. Bowing his head, he offered up a prayer, asking for guidance.

After church on Sunday, Verity approached Nate with a lunch invitation. "Aunt Betty has cooked a lovely pot roast and there is plenty to go around."

"Thank you, I'd be quite pleased to accept your invitation." He quirked an eyebrow. "Should I bring Beans? For Joy to play with, I mean?"

One of the things that endeared him to her was the bond that had formed between him and her daughter. "Of course. She'd like that."

Then, emboldened by the pretty new dress she wore, she gathered up her courage to take her invitation one step further. "Aunt Betty's been after me to gather some dewberries so she can make a cobbler. I thought, after lunch, I might take care of that for her. You're welcome to come along with me if you like."

He hesitated, and she thought for a moment he would decline. Had she been too forward after all? But he finally smiled and nodded. "It's a fine day for an outing and I'd be happy to repay your aunt with such a pleasant chore."

Verity exhaled the breath she hadn't been aware until now that she held. Issuing such an invitation to a single gentleman had called for a forwardness she hadn't been sure she had in her. It had felt both scary and exhilarating. Hazel would be proud.

She smoothed the skirt of her new dress. Perhaps she should have followed Hazel's advice and added some color to her life a long time ago.

Chapter Fourteen

"I see you've put away your walking stick. How's your arm and ankle doing?"

Nate turned to pass the breadbasket to Verity as he answered her uncle's question.

"They're healing nicely, sir. In fact, I'm thinking about resuming my work at the boardinghouse in another day or so."

He saw Verity's fingers tighten on the basket so he held on to it a moment longer until he was certain she had a proper hold.

"Do you think that's wise?" she asked. "I mean, given the kind of work she'll have you doing."

Her uncle spoke up before he could. "That depends." He turned to Nate. "Just be careful to start slow—I wouldn't be chopping any firewood or carrying heavy loads." He pointed his index finger at Nate in the manner of a judge pointing to an accused. "And mind you, if those injuries protest in any way, you stop what you're doing immediately."

"Yes, sir."

The conversation turned to inconsequential matters after that. Nate enjoyed the meal, but even more, he enjoyed the company, the give-and-take that could only happen in a gathering of folk who were comfortable with each other. That was one of the things he'd missed most after he was thrown in prison.

He also couldn't help but notice the difference in Verity. He'd been pleasantly surprised by that new dress she was wearing today. Not only because the cut and color were flattering on her, but because of what it signified—she had put away her mourning clothes. Could it possibly be a signal of other, more subtle changes in her outlook?

And it wasn't just the dress. There was a new energy about her, a certain spark that hadn't been there before. It could just be her pleasure in wearing that new garment, but he didn't think so. Something internal seemed to have shifted and changed in her, as well.

Perhaps, when they went berry picking this afternoon, he'd be able to get some clues as to just what this all meant.

When at last the meal was over, Verity insisted on helping her aunt clean up before they went on their excursion.

As the women started clearing the table, Dr. Pratt turned to Nate. "What do you say we get out of the ladies' way? How do you feel about a game of chess? Verity tells me you're quite the strategic player."

So she talked about him to her uncle, did she? "It would be my pleasure, sir."

As he followed the older gentleman into the parlor, he couldn't help but remember what Verity had told him about how her uncle had such disdain for her father, but hadn't held her father's adventurous nature against her. It had been a rather peculiar statement to make and he wasn't above doing some subtle probing.

Nate waited until they were seated and the game was set up. "I understand Mrs. Leggett grew up here with you and your wife." That was a nice neutral opening.

"That's right." Dr. Pratt glanced up from the chessboard. "She's like a daughter to us."

Had that been a warning of some sort? "She told me what happened to her parents."

The doctor moved a pawn, then leaned back. "Did she, now? I'll admit to being surprised. She doesn't ever talk about the accident. Or about her parents at all."

"Not even with you?"

The older gentleman tugged on the corners of his vest. "When she was younger I used to tell her tales of her mother as a little girl. But it's been some years now since we spoke of it."

Nate made his opening move. "And her father?"

Dr. Pratt's face hardened. "We don't speak of her father. Sturgis was a foolish, reckless man who thought nothing of putting the lives of those around him in danger."

Nate couldn't let that statement stand. "But surely there was good in him, too? If your niece and her mother loved him as much as they obviously did, then they had to see something in him worthy of that love."

"I'll allow that he *did* have a way about him, a certain charm and wit that most ladies found hard to resist."

From Dr. Pratt's tone, Nate could tell he didn't consider those good qualities.

Then his host shook his head and straightened. "How did we get started on this topic? It's *your* history I intended to discuss this afternoon."

Nate shifted uncomfortably, returning his focus to the chessboard. That was one topic he didn't want to discuss. "There's not much to tell, sir." He moved his next piece. "I grew up in fairly comfortable circumstances in the town of Plattisburg, Pennsylvania. I had one sibling, a younger sister. Unfortunately, she and my parents have all passed away so I have no family left to speak of."

Dr. Pratt's expression turned sympathetic. "I'm sorry. A man's life is so much richer if he has family around him to share it with."

Nate couldn't agree more.

But Verity's uncle wasn't through interrogating him yet. "Why did you come to Turnabout? I know you're a friend of Adam Barr's, but I figure it would take more than that to cause a man to pick up and move halfway across the country with little more than the clothes on his back."

This was getting into very uncomfortable territory— he needed to redirect the discussion. "I suppose we all have a few things in our past that are painful to look back on or that we wish we could erase." He met the man's gaze without blinking. "I just reached a point in my life where there was nothing left for me in Plattisburg and getting a fresh start somewhere else felt like a good idea." He allowed a touch of cynicism to color his voice. "As for the dearth of possessions I arrived with, it was everything I owned."

Everything he'd said was true, as far as it went. But it was time to change the topic before the man boxed him into a corner he couldn't maneuver out of. "Has your niece always been interested in medicine?"

Dr. Pratt's expression softened. "Almost as soon as she moved in here, Verity wanted to help me in the clinic. She was always getting underfoot, asking for things to do. She would handle any household tasks my wife gave her but then would head right back to the clinic to see if I'd let her help me with anything. I finally gave in and decided to teach her a few simple tasks that would allow her to assist me."

It sounded as if Dr. Pratt loved his niece very much. It also sounded to him as if young Verity had been trying to replace her beloved father with her uncle.

"She was a fast learner," Dr. Pratt continued. "Never saw anyone take to it that quickly or at so young an age."

Nate had never doubted Verity was an intelligent woman—it was part of what appealed to him about her. But it seemed she had a natural talent, as well.

Verity appeared in the doorway just then, putting an end to their conversation. He noticed she'd changed out of her pretty new dress and into an everyday dress. But there was no touch of black to be found on this one either. He took that as a good sign.

"So who's winning?" she asked.

Nate sent a smile her way. "It appears your uncle currently has the upper hand." The doctor was a skilled player who was making him work to find any advantage he could. This game could potentially go on for quite some time.

Apparently Dr. Pratt thought the same thing. "I see my niece has some pails and a basket in hand. I believe that's her not-so-subtle hint that she's ready to go."

Verity gave him an affectionate smile. "Perhaps I *was* being a little too obvious."

Dr. Pratt leaned back and waved them on. "Why don't you two go on. We can finish this game another time."

Nate didn't have to be told twice. With a nod to his opponent, he stood and joined Verity.

She allowed him to take the pails from her, but held on to the basket. "Aunt Betty packed us some lemonade and a couple of pieces of gingerbread in case we feel the urge to snack while we are out."

"Your aunt Betty is a woman after my own heart."

Verity laughed. "Well, she's keeping an eye on Joy, and Joy is keeping an eye on Beans," she said. "So I think we can safely slip out now."

As they stepped outside, he lent her his arm to descend the porch steps. "So where do we find these dewberries your aunt is coveting?"

"There are some vines near the tree line out past the schoolyard. But they've likely been picked over already." She slid him a touchingly shy look. "There's another really great spot a little ways west of town, but it's too far to walk comfortably. However, Uncle Grover already agreed to loan us the use of his buggy, if you're of a mind to go for a ride that is."

A buggy ride with a pretty girl on a fine spring day—he couldn't think of anything he'd rather do. "So, where does he keep his buggy?"

Twenty minutes later Nate was maneuvering the buggy out of the livery's carriage house, Verity seated by his side.

Once they left the town behind them, Verity began pointing out landmarks of interest—the grove where she always harvested pecans in the fall, the meadow where she liked to take Joy for picnics, the pond where she and her uncle fished when she was a child.

He thoroughly enjoyed these glimpses into her life and wondered if there would come a day when he could share them with her.

"I see you brought two pails along," he said. "Do you really expect us to fill both of them?"

She raised a brow at that. "Well, I certainly expect to fill *my* pail. Whether you fill up yours is entirely up to you."

"Oh ho, are you issuing a challenge, Mrs. Leggett?"

Her eyes were sparkling in a most attractive manner. "And if I were—are you planning to take me up on it, Mr. Cooper?"

"I do believe I am. As for stakes, shall we say the first one to fill their pail forfeits their slice of gingerbread."

She raised a brow. "High stakes indeed. I'll have to rethink my plan to go easy on you."

"Then we are agreed—no mercy from either quarter!"

She grinned but rather than return his verbal salvo, she pointed to an open area just off the road. "We're here. You can turn the carriage in over there."

He complied, then tied off the reins and hopped down. He quickly moved around the carriage to help her down, forcing himself to just offer her a hand rather than take her by the waist like he really wanted to.

"There's no need to tether Banjo," she said as she stepped down. "He's docile and won't wander far."

Nate reached inside the buggy to fetch the pails.

By the time he turned back around, she was moving away from the buggy.

"Hold on there," he said. "Don't think I'm going to let you get a head start on me."

She laughed. "Don't worry, I can't start without my pail. I just wanted to sample a few before we get started." She put her hand to her chest in an exaggeratedly virtuous pose. "Just to make certain they're good enough for Aunt Betty's cobbler, of course."

"Of course." He quickly caught up with her and tucked her hand on his arm. "This ground is rough," he said by way of explanation. "One of us with a bad ankle is enough."

Nate was thoroughly enjoying this newly revealed playful side of her. If a new dress was what it took to bring it out, he hoped she had plans to purchase quite a few more.

He allowed her to "teach" him how to pick the berries—how to tell which berries were ripe and which were not and how to pluck them from the vine to do the least damage to the fruit. It was endearing to see her earnestness and her concern that he had a clear understanding.

"One of the things you need to be careful about," she said as they got started, "is to check the area around the vines for snakes, yellow jackets and other pests, like spiders." She gave a delicate little shiver on the last.

"Spiders?"

She turned to her berry picking. "Yes. I absolutely hate the things." Then she colored and glanced at him from the corner of her eye. "The truth is they absolutely terrify me—especially those daddy-longlegs type. I can tolerate them from a distance but if one gets near me—" She shuddered. "I suppose you think I'm a cowardly ninny."

"What I think is that you don't care much for spiders," he said drily.

She gave a little gurgling laugh at that. "You certainly believe in understatements, don't you?"

"Actually, it reassures me to know that you're not perfect."

She did finally meet his gaze. "Perfect? Now you're just being sarcastic."

"Not at all. You, Mrs. Leggett, are dauntingly accomplished. You are a good mother, you ably assist your uncle in his medical practice, you lead the Sunday choir, you agree to form a children's choir at the drop of a hat, and speaking of hats, on top of all the rest, you're a talented milliner. You have to admit, that is quite an impressive list."

She shook her head. "Thank you, but there are a lot of folks whose list would be much more impressive." She waved a hand in his direction. "Look at you. You can play the piano better than anyone I ever heard before, you've agreed to help with the children's choir, you can craft beautiful leather goods, and, most impressive of all, you had the courage to pick up and move halfway across the country to start a new life."

He'd been enjoying her praise—up until that last. Was that how she saw his transplanting himself to Turnabout? It made him feel more of a fraud than ever.

He turned back to the berries and for a while they worked in silence. Then he became aware that she was surreptitiously watching him with a touch of concern in her expression. So he plucked a berry and rather than tossing it in his pail turned to her. "I'm not sure of the etiquette surrounding picking dewberries. Are we allowed to eat as we go?"

She nodded solemnly. "Not only is it allowed, it is considered mandatory. One must taste the berries every so often, just to make certain they are worth harvesting." Then she grinned. "I've already partaken, and at the pace you're going, I can eat quite a few more and still fill my pail before you."

"Is that so? Well, my dear Mrs. Leggett, we'll just see about that." And he popped the berry in his mouth.

She laughed, then her expression took on a shy cast as she nervously tucked a tendril of hair behind her ear. "Actually, I was thinking it would be nice if you'd call me by my given name."

He was deeply touched, especially knowing that had probably been difficult for her to say. He gave a slight bow. "I'm honored. And would be even more honored if you would return the favor." Then, to lighten the mood, he gave her his best scowl. "But if you think that will make me go easy on you, *Verity*, you're mistaken. I still plan to win this competition."

She laughed and tossed a berry at him. With that, the mood lightened again. The friendly banter passed between them with the ease of longtime friends. He was called on a few times to slay spiders for her, though he noticed she had no trouble with the lizards, bees and various insects they encountered.

And if their hands and arms seemed to "accidentally" brush against each other with a remarkable frequency, well, she didn't seem any more interested in complaining than he did.

It was the most perfect afternoon he'd experienced since well before he'd gone into prison.

It took a while to fill their pails, partly because they ate liberally as they picked. But finally, all too soon, she held up her pail triumphantly. "Mine is full. I do believe I win."

He stroked his chin, keeping his expression solemn as he studied the contents of her pail. "Hmm, I suppose I shall have to concede." He gave an exaggerated bow. "My slice of gingerbread is hereby awarded to you."

She laughed. "Don't feel too bad. I had experience on my side." She peered at his pail. "And it looks like you were close. Perhaps if you'd eaten a few less…"

He grinned. "Guilty. But I didn't notice you being particularly restrained in that area yourself."

She raised a brow. "Remind me—who won this little contest?"

He laughed, then took her elbow again as they turned toward the buggy. This time it felt more natural and at the same time more special. Did she feel any of this? Or was it just him?

Suddenly she stopped beside a moss-covered log. "I think I have something lodged in my shoe. If you'll carry my pail back to the buggy and fetch the basket, I think I'll sit here and empty it." She grinned up at him. "And I might just let you have a bite or two of *my* gingerbread."

"With incentive like that, how can I refuse?" He took her pail and helped her sit, then straightened. "I'll be right back."

She waved him away. "No need to rush. This may take me a few minutes."

He'd just stowed the berry-filled pails and grabbed the basket when he heard her yelp. Startled, he whirled around and saw her pop up and begin shaking one arm frantically. Nate dropped the basket back into the buggy and sprinted toward her. He'd seen some wasps earlier and was certain she'd been stung. "What is it? Hold still and let me see."

But she wouldn't stop her frantic movements and he had to forcibly take her arm to still her. She was trembling so much that his concern doubled. What in the world had turned her into this shaky, hysterical person? "Tell me what's wrong."

Her only response was a near-hysterical "Get it off of me. Please, get it off of me."

Finally, understanding dawned. It took him a moment longer before he saw not one but two of the long-legged but perfectly harmless spiders clinging to her sleeve. He quickly brushed them away. "There, they're gone now." Apparently he'd been wrong to assume she'd exaggerated her fear of the things.

She finally stilled her frantic movements and buried her face in his chest, wrapping her arms tightly around him. Startled, he instinctively wrapped his arms around her. He could feel the frantic beating of her heart and he gently rubbed her back, whispering soothing nothings until her heartbeat slowed to something close to normal and her hold on him relaxed. She didn't pull away, though, just stood there in the circle of his arms, which was fine by him.

"I'm sorry." Her voice was low and embarrassed.

"I'm not." The words were out of his mouth before he could stop them, but he couldn't regret them.

She pulled slightly back, just enough to look into his eyes. And what he saw there took his breath away. Vulnerability. Need. Longing.

With a shaky hand, he stroked the soft curve of

her cheek. "Sweet Verity." Her name felt so right on his lips.

She closed her eyes for just a moment and leaned into his palm. When she opened her eyes again there was a soft, shy invitation. Slowly he lowered his face to hers, holding her gaze, trying to attune himself to the least nuance of doubt or withdrawal.

Then their lips met and he was lost.

Chapter Fifteen

Verity was lost in a sea of emotions. Nate's kiss made her feel such warring sensations—both safe and wild, vulnerable and empowered, cherished and cherishing. Never, not even during her five-year marriage, had she felt this way.

She could lose herself in this kiss, this embrace, forever.

Then, abruptly, he ended it and pulled back.

She blinked, momentarily disoriented by the brusqueness of his action. She searched his face for some clue as to what he was feeling right now, why he had suddenly turned cold. His guard was up again, his expression suddenly distant, unreadable. The only sign that he had been affected by that kiss was a slight change in the rhythm of his breathing.

The smile he gave her was almost perfunctory. "I think it's probably time we head back to town."

That was it? No acknowledgment of that kiss they'd just shared? What was wrong? It felt like a very clear and very definite rejection.

Trying to disguise the sick feeling in her stomach

and hoping the warmth in her cheeks didn't translate to heightened color, Verity nodded. Without waiting for him to take her arm, she turned toward the buggy. She didn't want him to see her face right now. Because she knew it would show how very flustered and confused and utterly miserable she felt.

She hadn't taken more than a couple of steps, however, before she stumbled. He had a hand on her arm before she could truly fall, and he kept it there as they walked in silence the rest of the way to the buggy. He helped her up with all the care he'd show a stranger, then moved around to the other side. In a matter of minutes they were on the road and headed toward town, all without another word.

Verity tried to figure out what had gone so terribly wrong on this afternoon that had seemed to be going so well.

The teasing banter they'd exchanged during the berry picking had been exhilarating and he'd appeared to enjoy it, as well. And even when she'd made a fool of herself over the spiders, he had reacted with genuine concern for her, never once making her feel silly or annoying. In fact, the way he'd held her, had done his best to calm and soothe her, had seemed to convey something more than mere friendship. And she was almost certain she hadn't imagined that tenderness she'd seen in his eyes when he'd caressed her cheek.

And, oh, how that caress had made her feel.

With her former husband, a man fifteen years her senior, she'd felt safe and comfortable. But there was nothing comfortable about the way Nate made her feel.

The sweet wonder in his gaze, the gentleness that came through the touch of those rough, work-callused fingers, had combined to make her feel as if she was safe, yes, but also cherished and desired, as if she was someone special, in his eyes at least. It had emboldened her to try to show him how she felt, as well.

But she'd obviously done something wrong. Had she misread his feelings? Or had her own unseemly boldness made him reconsider any affection he might have felt?

The ride back to town seemed to take forever. And for most of it she mentally berated herself. Why hadn't she held herself in check, squelched this impulsive display the way she had so many others?

Had she irreparably ruined her friendship with Nate?

Finally she could stand it no longer. She had to do something, had to try to do what she could to cut through this stiff silence between them.

"Nate, I'm so sorry. I shouldn't have—"

"Don't."

His sharp command, more growled than spoken, startled her into silence. Why was he so angry with her?

He clenched his jaw and raked his fingers through his hair with an angry, jerky thrust. "Don't apologize. You didn't do anything wrong."

Was he just being polite, trying to spare her feelings? "I don't understand."

He took a deep, defeated-sounding breath. "You think I'm a hero. But I'm not."

That again. "You're being too modest. You—"

But he wouldn't let her finish. "Verity, I *don't* deserve hero worship. Not from you, not from anyone. You don't know—"

It was her turn to interrupt. "Stop right there." Relief flooded through her. *That's* what was bothering him.

"First, you're not the best judge of what you *do* and *do not* deserve in the area of hero worship. The fact that you won't acknowledge what a courageous thing you did for Joy only proves that you are a genuine hero." She held up a hand to halt the argument she saw forming on his lips. "And second, what I was very clumsily attempting to convey back there had nothing at all to do with hero worship." If she'd left him with any doubts as to her feelings, surely she'd just settled the matter. Had she made the situation better or worse?

The muscles in his jaw worked for several heartbeats before he finally seemed to come to a decision. A decision he did not seem to be happy with. "That only makes it worse."

There was her answer. "I see." Everything inside her seemed to shrivel. "I'm sorry. I didn't intend to make you uncomfortable. Let's speak no more of it." Please let this ride be over soon. All she wanted was to lock herself in her bedroom and fall apart in private.

Abruptly, Nate steered the horses to the side of the road and pulled the wagon to a stop. The town was in sight but they still had a fair amount of privacy from here.

"What are you doing?"

He set the brake with a sharp, angry motion, then turned to face her. "I will not let you feel any guilt, or shame—" he waved a hand "—or whatever other negative feeling is rattling around in that mind of yours." His expression was fierce. "And don't try to deny it. I can see from the look on your face that you're second-guessing every word you uttered or gesture you made since we set out this afternoon."

She hadn't even been aware that he was watching her, much less that he was able to read all of that.

"I'll say again—you did *nothing* wrong. I treasure every moment of our time together this afternoon, more than you will ever know. But I realize now that you won't believe that, not without an explanation. So now I'm going to give you that explanation."

Seeing the dread in his expression, she wasn't really sure she wanted to hear what he had to say. "If it's something you'd rather not talk about, don't feel you need to tell me."

His smile had more grimace than humor to it. "Too late. I need to tell you this for myself as well as for you. There's something you don't know about me, about what I've done, where I've been."

She saw the guilt and something darker cloud his eyes, turning that beautiful blue to a murky, storm-cloud gray. "Whatever all of that is, it can't possibly be as bad as you're making out."

"Can't it?" The words were so softly uttered that she barely heard them.

His expression had such a poignant, bittersweet edge to it that she touched his arm, hoping he would feel something of her support, her faith in him. "Then tell me so we can put it behind us."

He reached up to cover her hand with his own and just stared at them for a moment. Then he gently disengaged and straightened. He turned so that he was facing her fully and met her gaze almost dispassionately. "Nine and a half years ago I robbed a bank. I've spent the majority of the time since then in federal prison."

Verity froze. She wasn't sure what she'd expected, but it wasn't this.

He was a bank robber.

Just like the man who'd shot and killed Arthur.

Just like the man who'd taken her little girl's daddy from her.

Nate watched Verity's instinctive recoil, the hand that shot to her mouth, the horror in her eyes. It was every bit as nightmarish as he'd imagined it would be.

Because back there, when he'd shared that kiss with her, he'd realized he loved her—deeply and completely. And that scared him as nothing had before.

Before he realized what he was doing, he reached a hand out. "Verity—"

She crossed her arms tightly over her chest. "Perhaps we should go." Her voice had a cold, lifeless quality to it.

Nate dropped his hand and gave a short nod. "Of course." He faced forward and set the buggy in motion again. Verity had moved as far from him as she could on the seat of the buggy, and she was so stiff she looked to be in danger of snapping in two.

This is what he'd done to the woman he loved. Why had he thought he could play with fire and not get burned? Or worse, get someone else burned.

Rather than going directly to the livery, Nate stopped the buggy in front of her uncle's home. "I'll let you out here so we don't have to walk from the livery with those full pails." He planned to climb down to lend her a hand, but she had scrambled down before he could so much as set the brake. As she reached in the buggy to retrieve the pails, he cleared his throat. "I'll be back to get Beans after I've tended to the buggy."

She froze a moment, then shook her head. "That won't be necessary. Wait here and I'll get him for you now."

That stung. She obviously wanted him entirely gone from her life as soon as possible.

Without waiting for his answer, she turned and marched quickly up her front walk. A moment later she was back with Beans in her arms. She set the dog on the buggy floor then straightened. "I'll give Uncle Grover and Aunt Betty your regards."

What else could he say? He nodded, but she had already turned and headed back toward the house. He watched her until she disappeared inside, but she never once turned back around.

He set the buggy in motion again. Had he made a mistake telling her? Would she keep his secret? What did this mean for his work with the church choir and children's choir?

And would she put the pieces together and figure out Adam's secret, as well?

He raked his fingers through his hair. He'd made a grand mess of things.

Beans, as if aware of his mood, whined at his feet. He scooped the dog up with one hand and set him on the seat beside him. He gave the animal a scratch behind the ears, not sure which one of them drew more comfort from the contact.

"I hate to tell you this, boy, but that may be the last time you get to play with Joy. I'm afraid I've made a royal mess of everything."

Because, if he wasn't mistaken, he'd lost any chance at all he had with Verity.

* * *

Verity tried to go through the rest of the afternoon and evening as if nothing untoward had happened. And for the most part she just felt numb.

She helped her aunt wash and store the berries.

She read a book to Joy, though later she couldn't remember what story she'd read.

She even organized the supplies in her tiny workroom.

When supper time finally rolled around, Verity did her best to keep up her end of the conversation, deflecting talk of the berry-picking expedition as much as possible.

At last the meal was at an end and the kitchen was cleaned. She took Joy upstairs and got her ready for bed, going through their nightly rituals of prayers and a lullaby.

When she tucked the covers up under Joy's chin, the little girl looked up at her with concern in her gaze. "Did you see a spider while you and Mr. Cooper were out picking dewberries?"

Verity gently brushed the wisps of hair from her daughter's forehead and attempted a smile. "Yes, pumpkin, I did. In fact, two of them got on the sleeve of my dress." She still remembered the sweet way Nate had held her after his "rescue" of her, the way he'd tried to comfort her and make her feel safe and not at all foolish. How could this be the same man who'd done something so awful, so disregarding of the hurt he was doing to others?

"I thought so." Joy's self-congratulatory words brought her back to the present. "Because you looked all dis-bob-u-lated when you got home."

Verity smiled at her daughter's mispronunciation of *discombobulated*, one of her aunt's favorite words. But the smile faded quickly. "You're a very smart little girl to figure that out, but I'm all better now."

"You don't look all better." Joy dragged her hand out from under the covers and patted Verity's cheek. "Don't worry, Mama, I don't think those bad spiders followed you home."

Touched beyond words by her daughter's love and concern, Verity gathered her in a tight hug. "Thank you, pumpkin, I'm sure you're right." Then she let her go and tucked her back in. "Now, you get a good night's sleep and don't worry about me and the spiders anymore. Okay?"

"Okay." And the girl rolled over on her side and shut her eyes.

Verity knew from past experience that Joy would be sound asleep in a matter of minutes.

Pleading a headache, she bid good-night to her aunt and uncle then escaped to her own room to turn in early.

But not to sleep. Because the numbness she'd felt since Nate—no, Mr. Cooper—had driven away was wearing off. In its place was an aching sense of loss.

She sat on the edge of her bed and grabbed a pillow, hugging it to her chest and rocking back and forth.

She kept trying to reconcile the man she'd come to admire so deeply with the man who'd done that terrible thing he'd admitted to this afternoon.

He was a bank robber. A man who'd carried a gun into a place of business, a place where innocent people, people with families who loved them, would be present. And he'd tried to forcibly, maybe even violently, take what didn't belong to him.

There was nothing heroic about such an act. About such a man.

No wonder he'd felt so guilty whenever she used that word. Why hadn't she believed his protests?

When she thought about how she'd acted around him today—teasing him, *flirting* with him, throwing herself into his arms. And then letting him kiss her. No, more than that, she'd practically invited that kiss. What a besotted fool she'd been. She'd let herself be led by her emotions rather than reason. There'd been nothing reasonable about this afternoon, no thought about the consequences of her actions.

And look where it had gotten her.

She touched her lips. But for that moment—that moment just before he'd abruptly ended that kiss—it had been so sweet, so wonderful, so exhilarating.

No! She wouldn't think of that.

It had all been a lie.

But it hadn't felt that way.

Verity got very little sleep that night. At some point she began worrying about how she would act toward him next time they encountered each other. And given his involvement with the choirs, there would be no way to avoid him completely, not until Zella got back at any rate.

She supposed she could deal with his playing on Sunday mornings.

But to have him working with the children? That seemed wrong on a number of levels. It wasn't that she thought he would do anything to harm them—that thought was too ludicrous to even contemplate—but his influence over them would be questionable, and if his story ever came out, it would confuse the children.

Not that she would reveal his secrets. Even knowing what she now knew, she couldn't bring herself to expose him to such critical scrutiny. But for her peace of mind she'd have to replace him as her partner on the children's choir project, and she needed to do it before the next practice session on Tuesday.

First thing in the morning she'd have a talk with Mrs. Peavy. After all, she usually served as Zella's stand-in.

Just how had it happened that Mr. Cooper had ended up in that position this time, anyway?

Verity didn't get quite as early a start the next morning as she'd planned. She'd barely made it downstairs when Meechum Smith was brought into the clinic with a broken arm. It was a bad break and she'd worked beside her uncle for several hours to help him get the limb cleaned, set and splinted properly. By the time they'd completed the procedure, Mr. Smith was unconscious. So Verity had prepared a bed in the infirmary for him. She tried very hard not to remember the last patient who'd spent time there. Luckily his wife, Ellen, had accompanied him and she planned to spend the day with him, so Verity could make her escape as soon as he was properly installed there.

After cleaning up she was finally able to slip away. She trudged down the sidewalk toward the Barr home with a heavy heart. During the time she'd worked beside her uncle this morning, she'd been able to forget her world had been turned upside down yesterday. But as soon as she'd been dismissed it had all come flooding back.

She should never have let her emotions have sway over her. Much better to let reason be her guide. Her marriage to Arthur may not have been the fairy-tale rómantic relationship she sometimes found herself dreaming of, but it had been comfortable and safe. If Arthur hadn't made her feel the same fluttery anticipation she'd felt with Mr. Cooper, neither had he made her feel this dark, aching sadness.

She would ask Mrs. Peavy to help her with the children's program and would use the time this was taking away from Mr. Cooper's business as the reason. And in few weeks or so, when Zella returned, he would step down from the Sunday choir music, as well. There would be no need for her to have any further interaction with him.

Which should have made her feel a whole lot happier than it did.

When she arrived at the Barr residence, Verity bypassed the front entrance and went around to the back. Buck, the Barrs' big, fierce-looking dog, raced up to greet her. But his wagging tail let her know it was friendly curiosity rather than aggression.

She gave the animal a pat on the head and then climbed the back porch steps. The kitchen door was open, leaving only a screen door as a barrier against insects and other unwanted intruders. She could see Mrs. Peavy inside, already busy at the stove.

Verity tapped on the door frame and called out a hello.

Mrs. Peavy glanced up and smiled when she recognized Verity. "The door's unlatched, come on in."

She wiped her hands on her apron as Verity complied. "Can I get you a cup of coffee?"

Verity shook her head. "No, thank you, I'm fine."

"If you're looking for Reggie, she's out taking a walk with Patricia. But she'll be back shortly, if you want to sit and visit for a spell."

Verity shook her head. "Actually, it was you I came to see." She looked at the pots simmering on the stove and the pie ready to go into the oven. "But if you're busy, I don't want to interrupt your work."

Mrs. Peavy smiled. "Actually, I'm ready to take a little break." She waved toward the table. "Have a seat and I'll join you in just a minute."

Verity pulled a chair out at the table as Mrs. Peavy slipped the pie into the oven. The older woman then moved to the counter, where she retrieved a small jar before taking a seat across from Verity.

"Well, now," she said as she opened the jar, "I hope you won't mind if I apply this liniment while we chat. I was just waiting until I got the pie in the oven."

"Not at all." Verity caught the familiar scent and it brought her up short. "Are you having problems with your hands?"

Mrs. Peavy nodded. "These old hands are beginning to show their age, I'm afraid. Some days are worse than others, but this liniment helps." She sighed as she worked the medication into her hands. "I was so glad to learn Mr. Cooper could play the piano and was willing to take over while Zella was away. I'm afraid my days of being her substitute have just about come to an end."

"I'm so sorry to hear that." For a number of reasons. Was this why Mr. Cooper had been asked to sit in for Zella rather than Mrs. Peavy?

"There now." Mrs. Peavy screwed the lid back on the jar and leaned back. "Much better," she said with a smile. "Now, what did you want to talk to me about?"

What could she say? Asking her to take Mr. Cooper's place was out of the question now. But there was something else she could ask. "Who will take your place as Zella's substitute now?"

Mrs. Peavy frowned slightly. "I haven't really given that much thought yet. But there are a couple of ladies here in Turnabout who could serve very capably."

"Like who?"

"Well, Maude Wick for one. And Viella Higgs. And of course, now we have Mr. Cooper." She gave Verity a probing look. "Why are you asking?"

Verity chose her words very carefully. "I was thinking I might ask someone to take over playing the piano for the children's program. Mr. Cooper's business is so new, it doesn't seem fair to ask him to close up two afternoons a week to help us out."

"I see." Mrs. Peavy tilted her head slightly, giving Verity a probing look. "Has he asked you to find him a substitute?"

"Oh, no. This was my idea." Though after yesterday she had no doubt Mr. Cooper would be relieved not to have to work with her any more than necessary. "It seems wrong to impose on him so heavily when he's barely settled into town."

"Well, you're a good friend."

Verity mentally winced at that far-from-accurate statement. But she was trapped, unable to reveal the true state of affairs without giving away the whole story. And she wasn't ready to expose him that way.

But Mrs. Peavy spoke up again, rescuing Verity from having to examine her motives for that last thought too closely.

"I'm afraid you're not going to have much luck with Maude and Viella, though. Maude's new baby is due in just a few weeks. And Viella's just moved her ailing grandmother in with her. That's why it was such a godsend to learn that Mr. Cooper was talented and available."

"I see." What did she do now?

"If you really think it would be best to let Mr. Cooper off the hook, perhaps I could—"

Verity quickly reached across the table and gently clasped the woman's knurled hands. "That's very generous of you, but please don't give it another thought. As I said, Mr. Cooper hasn't uttered one word of complaint. I'm likely making mountains out of molehills again."

She stood. "Now, I've taken up enough of your time. Please give Mr. Peavy and the Barrs my regards."

As Verity shut the screen door behind her, her mind was scrambling to figure out what to do now. The next practice with the children's choir was tomorrow, and she wanted to get this matter settled before then. She wasn't certain she could work so closely with him again, at least not without giving away her feelings to those around them.

Perhaps the solution was to not worry about getting another piano player. Perhaps they could do the entire program a cappella. She would need some help, but she could ask one or two members of the church choir to assist her. Of course that would mean going into explanations of why she wanted to make the change. She supposed she could always use the same excuse she'd given Mrs. Peavy.

* * *

The bell jangled as his shop door opened and Nate looked up hopefully. But it was Belva who had entered, not Verity.

He wasn't sure why he kept expecting to see her walk in. She'd made her feelings about him quite clear when he dropped her off yesterday.

Why in the world had he kissed her? If he hadn't given in to his own longings, they might still be friends at least.

Not that he could find it in him to truly regret that kiss. Everything in him had responded to her—he'd wanted to cherish her and protect her and claim her as his own. For those few moments she'd made him feel as if he could scale mountains and explore oceans and slay dragons.

And now, not only did he no longer have the right to hold her, but he'd lost her friendship, as well.

"Well, now, don't you look like someone just mowed down your prized flower patch. What's ailing you?"

He summoned up a smile. "I've just got a lot on my mind today. What can I do for you? You're not planning to change the design on your saddle again, are you?"

She laughed good-naturedly. "No, I think we're all done with that. I just came by to ask you something."

"And what's that?"

"I turn twenty in two weeks, and that's when I get the inheritance Aunt Imogene left for me."

He already knew all of that from their earlier discussions. Hard as it was to believe, this young lady was about to become a wealthy heiress.

He figured she'd get to her question in her own time, so he followed her conversational lead. "So, are you planning all the things you're going to do with the money?"

She nodded, her face split in a wide grin. "Well, getting my horse is the first thing. And then I figure I'll do some traveling. But before I can do any of that, I need to get my house in order, literally."

"What do you mean?"

"Part of my inheritance is Aunt Imogene's home over in Tyler. I haven't seen it yet, but I understand it's big and it's in need of some work. There's a caretaker, but the solicitor is telling me he's elderly and ready to retire." She traced a circle on his worktable with a finger. "Since I don't know very many people whom I would trust with that responsibility, I was wondering if you'd be interested in the position."

Nate leaned back and stared at her for a long minute. Was this the answer he was looking for? A chance to start over somewhere else.

But that felt an awful lot like running away. Was he ready to give up already? "Belva, I'm flattered that you'd ask me, but—"

"That was quick." She leaned back on her heels, disappointment coloring her all-too-readable face. "Is it because I'm a woman? Or because I'm younger than you? Or both?"

"Neither." He leaned forward and tried to explain things in a way she'd accept at face value. "I just moved here, just opened my shop. I want to see if I have what it takes to make a go of things. I'm sure you'll find someone else—"

"Please don't say no just yet, at least not until you've heard everything."

There was more? Ah, well, what could it hurt to

hear her out? He folded his arms across his chest and leaned back again. "All right, I'm listening."

"Okay." She took a deep breath, then launched into her pitch. "The solicitor tells me it's a fair-sized place with a large house and a stable in the back. There's staff to handle the day-to-day things. It's the caretaker's job to manage them and to keep an eye on the overall well-being of the entire place. You'd have lots of say in how the place is run, a small cabin of your own on the property to live in, and I'm sure we could even find a place to set you up a workroom if you wanted to continue with your saddle making."

She paused for a breath and he took the opportunity to ask a question. "Why me?"

Her brow furrowed. "What do you mean?"

"Why ask me to take the job? You barely know me, after all. And I have no experience with the sort of work you're describing."

"You're my friend. And it would be good to have a friend with me when I start my new life."

Nate saw her vulnerability then, the lonely girl who was heading into a new adventure she wasn't sure she was quite ready to face alone. His resolve wavered. A young woman in need was definitely his Achilles' heel.

Belva apparently felt his indecisiveness. "You don't have to give me an answer today," she said quickly. "Why don't you take a few days to think it over?"

"All right. But Belva—" he leaned forward, shooting her a very pointed gaze "—I would be thinking of a backup plan if I were you."

She nodded, but from her optimistic expression he wasn't certain if she really took his words to heart.

After she had gone, Nate bent over his work again.

Belva's visit had been a welcome, if temporary, distraction.

But it had also driven home one very disquieting fact.

That he seemed to be destined to always disappoint the women in his life.

Verity had returned from her visit with Mrs. Peavy to find their resident patient asleep, her uncle resting, and Aunt Betty teaching Joy how to prepare the dough for a dewberry cobbler. Needing something to occupy herself, she'd gone to her workroom. A half-finished hat sat perched on a wire form, waiting for her to complete it. But she decided she was in the mood to start from scratch. She grabbed netting and lengths of ribbon and silk flowers and went to work with almost manic focus.

But it was no use. She didn't find the sense of satisfaction and accomplishment she normally found when she worked on a hat. Instead, her thoughts turned to her own reprehensible lack of control. Ever since Mr. Cooper had appeared on the scene she hadn't been herself. She'd been acting impulsively and emotionally and without proper regard for consequences.

And look what it had gotten her.

She supposed she could understand why Mr. Cooper hadn't told her his history sooner—his idea of getting a fresh start probably included suppressing all traces of his past. Whether that was the ethical thing to do, however, seemed questionable.

If they hadn't kissed, would he have told her at all? Would she have been better off not knowing?

Because now he had turned her into a coconspirator in keeping his secret from everyone here, as well. Being the only one in town who knew his secret was…

She stilled.

No, that wasn't entirely true. Though Mr. Cooper hadn't said so, she knew there was one other person in Turnabout who had to already know of his past. The same man who had practically vouched for the newcomer to the rest of the townsfolk, who had, in fact, recruited Mr. Cooper for the church pianist job.

She set down her materials and began to forcefully roll down her sleeves.

Oh, yes, Adam Barr definitely had some explaining to do.

Chapter Sixteen

Verity entered the bank and went directly to the manager's office. She'd taken a circuitous route so she could avoid passing in front of either Mr. Cooper's or Hazel's shop. Cowardly and perhaps a bit foolish of her, but there it was.

To her satisfaction, Mr. Barr was alone in his office.

He looked up when she tapped on his door frame and greeted her with a smile as he stood. "Mrs. Leggett, hello."

She gave a stiff nod. "Mr. Barr."

"Please have a seat and tell me what I can do for you today."

She remained in the doorway. "Do you mind if I close the door first?"

There was a subtle shift in his expression from friend to businessman. "Not at all."

He waited until she was seated, and then took his own seat behind his desk again. "Now, what's on your mind?"

"Mr. Cooper."

His expression took on a wary aspect, as well it should.

"What about him?" he asked.

"He told me some troubling things about his past yesterday afternoon. I assume you are aware of where he's been for the past nine years and why."

There was the barest flicker of surprise before he schooled his expression again. "I am."

"And yet you said nothing." She didn't bother to mask her disapproval.

He spread his hands. "It wasn't my story to tell."

"Perhaps not." Verity could feel all of her pent-up emotions starting to spill out, but felt helpless to stop it. "But, if I understand the sequence of events properly, it was you who encouraged him to move here, you who helped him get established, and you who convinced him to take Zella's place while she is out of town, even though you knew that it meant working with the children's program."

"All of that is true. And I stand by all of it." He gave her a steady, unapologetic look. "And I also stand by him."

How could he say that?

He studied her for a heartbeat, then leaned forward. "Mrs. Leggett, I know what happened to your husband, so I know Nate's story was difficult for you to hear. But do you honestly believe he poses any kind of danger whatsoever to the children, or to anyone in Turnabout for that matter?"

She shifted in her seat. "Not directly. Not deliberately."

He spread his hands. "Then?"

"These are *children*, children I have some responsibility for. What if they learn to trust him, to…to care for him? And then later they learn the truth about who he is." To feel betrayal, as she had.

He raised a brow at that. "Who he is?"

She waved a hand impatiently. "A bank robber, of course."

"That's what he *did*. It's not who he *is*."

His matter-of-fact tone and steady gaze were making her feel defensive. "You're splitting hairs."

"I disagree. Those are two very different things." He leaned back in his chair. "But, be that as it may, if it's the children's sensibilities you're worried about, it's been my experience that children might give the adults they encounter a token respect, but they only give their trust—and their hearts—to those who deserve it."

He held her gaze. "And for that matter, how would anyone else ever find out the truth, unless Nate himself chooses to tell them?"

She heard the underlying question in his tone and stiffened. "They won't hear it from me."

"Nor will they hear it from me. As I said, it's his story to tell, when and if he chooses to do so." Then his expression softened slightly. "You say Nate told you what he did. Did he tell you *why* he did it?"

The question caught her by surprise. "No, but surely you don't believe the end justifies the means? You, of all people, should have a stronger sense of justice than that." In addition to managing the bank, Mr. Barr was a lawyer.

"No, but the kind of man that you know in your heart that Nate is, the kind of man who would set aside his own safety to rescue a child in danger, must have had a powerful motive to take such a step, don't you think?"

She winced at this not-so-subtle reminder of what she owed Nate.

But he had one more question for her. "Don't you believe in second chances, Mrs. Leggett? In leaving ultimate justice in God's hands, and in obeying His directive to forgive one another?"

"Of course. I just…" Verity let her words trail off, not sure how to finish the statement.

Then she stood. "Thank you, Mr. Barr. You've given me a lot to think about."

He stood, as well. "You're welcome." His gaze held a note of sympathy. "Despite what he did, Nate's a good man. I think if you'd just talk to him and give him a chance to explain, you'd agree with that, as well."

Verity nodded noncommittally, then made her way home at a slower, more deliberate pace than she'd used on her earlier march to Mr. Barr's office. She mulled over everything he'd said to her. Was he right? Would Nate's explanation of *why* he'd robbed that bank change her mind about him? She certainly wanted to believe she hadn't been *entirely* wrong about the sort of man he was.

Perhaps knowing the full story would bring her some peace with all that had happened. And she did owe him that chance.

But in her heart she knew that understanding his motives might help her look more kindly on him, might even heal their friendship, but it would never be enough to bring them back to that sweet, we-belong-together bond they'd shared ever so briefly.

That part of their relationship was dead before it

had really had an opportunity to set down roots in their hearts.

And that made her ache deep inside for what might have been.

Later that afternoon, Verity took a deep, bracing breath and walked into Nate's saddle shop. When he looked up she saw the surprise in his eyes, quickly followed by a strange mix of hope and wariness.

It seemed a reflection of how she herself was feeling.

Nate set down his tools but didn't rise. "Can I help you?" His tone was guardedly polite. Not unexpected.

Beans had popped up from his nap beneath the worktable and was now staring up at her with a tail-wagging welcome.

She bent down to pat the dog and tried to keep her tone equally businesslike. "Aunt Betty made a cobbler with some of the dewberries we picked yesterday."

"I'm glad they served her purpose."

"Since you didn't take any of the berries for yourself, she wanted to make certain you got some of the cobbler." She straightened and lifted the basket she was carrying. "I have it right here."

"That was very generous of your aunt. Please tell her thank you for me."

"Of course." He was certainly not making this easy for her. "Where would you like me to set this?"

He waved to the counter. "Right there, if you don't mind."

She crossed the room and carefully placed it just so on the counter. She could feel his gaze on her the entire time. Did she have the courage to go through with this?

She turned and met his gaze.

"Did you come here just to deliver the cobbler?" he asked softly.

"No."

"Then what?"

She tightened her lips a moment, then leaned back against the counter. "It's a nice day. I thought, if you were ready to take a break, we could go for a walk."

This time there was no mistaking the flicker of hope in his expression.

Before he could say anything, she clarified, "It would give us an opportunity to talk without interruption."

For a moment Nate just sat there, studying her face, as if trying to read something there. Then he nodded. "Very well." He stood and reached behind him to untie the leather apron he wore. His movements were calm and deliberate, but she once more had that sense of tension simmering below the surface.

Nate hung the apron on a peg, then moved around the table to open the door for her. She was very careful not to brush against him as she passed.

He started to follow her out and then paused. "Do you mind if Beans joins us?"

"Not at all."

The silence between them held as they left the shop. He let her take the lead and she headed for the churchyard. As before, she led him through the entrance to the cemetery and around to the bench beside the oak.

Nate remained standing. Beans took the opportunity to sniff around what was obviously new territory to him.

While she was still trying to figure out how to

start, Nate spoke up. "If this is about my continuing to work with the choir or the children, then I will make it easy—"

"That's not what I want to talk about." Was that a flicker of relief she saw in his face?

"Then what?"

She sat up straighter, determined to see this through no matter what. "I have two questions for you."

He seemed to brace himself. "All right. Ask."

"First—did you bring a gun with you when you robbed that bank?"

He clenched his jaw, but he nodded. "I did."

Her spirits dropped. How could he? Whether he intended to harm anyone or not, just by bringing a weapon to—

"But it wasn't loaded."

"Oh." Did that make it better? She wasn't sure.

"What's your second question?"

His tone was brusque. Was he in a hurry to get this over with, too?

She tilted her chin up. "I want to know why."

His guarded expression wavered for a moment, then returned. "Why?"

"Why did you rob that bank?"

A bitter smile twisted his lips. "Does it matter? You're not someone who believes that the ends justify the means, are you?"

Almost the exact same question she'd asked Mr. Barr. "No. But I want to understand. And the only way I can do that is to hear the whole story, complete with your reasons why."

Would he open up to her? And if he did, would it truly change anything?

* * *

She wanted to understand.

Nate thought about that for a moment. Would it do him any good to go through that whole sordid tale again, or would it only stir up those old wounds and still leave her unmoved?

It hadn't been lost on him that she was wearing mourning attire again—that solid black skirt and a drab gray shirtwaist. That was undoubtedly his doing.

He supposed he owed her that small satisfaction she'd asked for, regardless of the cost. But where to start? He raked a hand through his hair, trying to decide how much to tell her, or more to the point, how much of himself to reveal to her.

"That question is going to take me a little longer to answer than the first."

She shifted, as if settling more comfortably in her seat. "I have the time."

Nate glanced toward the graves that held the remains of her parents. "The other day you told me how your parents died." He had treasured the way she shared that part of herself with him. Would she feel even the tiniest bit of the same?

He turned back to meet her gaze. "Now I'll tell you about mine."

Her eyes widened a bit at that, but she merely nodded.

"My family was well-to-do. Not wealthy, mind you, but we didn't lack for anything and were able to enjoy some of the finer things of life." He hadn't realized just how good a life he'd had growing up, until he lost it.

"In addition to my parents, I had a sister, Susanna,

who was two years younger than me. We were a relatively happy family, with a wide circle of friends.

"Then, when I was seventeen, my father made some disastrous financial investments and lost nearly everything we had. We were forced to sell our home and move to more modest quarters just to get by. We also let go all the servants except Leena, our housekeeper, who was elderly and almost part of the family. My mother, who always had a somewhat delicate disposition, not only had to take on more of the household work herself, but she cut herself off from many of the friends in her social circle."

Verity folded her hands in her lap. "That must have been hard on all of you. But surely you don't mean you robbed a bank just to—"

"No, of course not." He waved a hand impatiently. "We were getting by well enough, even if it was without the luxuries we'd grown so used to. But my father felt a great deal of shame over what had happened and, two months after we moved, he hung himself."

He heard a small gasp and saw Verity's hand go to her throat. "Oh, Nate, I'm so sorry."

He took some comfort in her soft tone and use of his given name. At least, for the moment, she wasn't looking at him with loathing.

But she was waiting for him to continue. He skipped over the part of the story where it had been he who found his father's body, he who had had to shield his mother and sister from the gruesome sight, he who had had to deal with all the nightmare of official inquiries and paperwork. "Afterward, my mother took to her bed, leaving me and Susanna to deal with the day-to-day household things as best we could. Six months later she passed away in her sleep." It was Susanna who had found the body this time. He wished he could have spared her that at least.

"At the age of eighteen, I had sole responsibility for my sixteen-year-old sister, for Leena, who was staying to help even though we couldn't pay her, and for the upkeep of our home. All of that with no income and my only skill that of playing the piano."

"Is that when—"

He shook his head. He'd still had his pride, even then. "I got a job playing piano at a music hall. It wasn't much, and it wasn't socially acceptable, but it was enough to keep us going."

"That was resourceful of you."

"I thought, if I could just keep us together and make do for a few years, perhaps I could find a good, decent husband for Susanna and a viable position for Leena, and then I could strike out on my own."

"So what happened?" Sometime during the discussion she'd picked up Beans and now held him in her lap, stroking his back with gentle, even movements.

"Susanna got sick. And it was bad. Tuberculosis. She needed medical treatment that I couldn't afford to pay for. I tried every avenue I could, selling everything we owned that had any value, borrowing money until I was so far in debt it seemed I would never get out. And still it wasn't enough. I saw my little sister wasting away in front of my eyes. I thought, if I could just get her into a good sanatorium, one of those places that specialized in care for patients like her, then it would give her a fighting chance to get better."

"So that's when you robbed the bank." There was no question in her tone this time.

"I planned it all out, thought I had everything covered. Except I didn't plan for an off-duty policeman to walk into the bank just as I was making my getaway."

"What happened to your sister?" she asked softly.

This was the most difficult part, the part that had haunted him every day of his incarceration. "Leena, bless her heart, did her best to look after Susanna. At least my sister wasn't completely alone. But her illness got progressively worse. And because of her connection to me, a convicted felon, most of the so-called friends we had left shunned her. About a year after I went to prison I received word that she passed away. And I wasn't even able to go to her funeral." He clenched his jaw at the memory. "I know I got what I deserved, but Susanna deserved so much better."

He realized he'd balled his hands into tight fists at some point during the story. He forced them open, allowing his hands to hang loosely at his sides. "So there you have it, the whole sordid story." Had it made a difference? He couldn't tell.

"Thank you for sharing it with me." Her voice was subdued, but not unkind. "It makes things a whole lot clearer."

Regardless of how she now felt, there was one thing he had to ask of her. "I know I don't have the right to ask you this, but I'd appreciate it if you didn't tell anyone my story." He still had an obligation to protect Adam's reputation as best he could.

"I understand. And I assure you, I have many faults, but I don't gossip." Then she brought her hand up to fiddle with her collar. "Just so you know, however, I have already spoken to Mr. Barr."

He was hoping her mind wouldn't start down that path. "Adam? Whatever for?"

"I realized he had to already know your story since you and he were acquainted before you came here, and I wanted to confront him about it. He didn't give away any of your secrets, though. He merely told me to speak to you."

So maybe she hadn't already guessed Adam's secret. He needed to get the focus off his friend and back onto him. "So now that you've heard my story, where does that leave us? I mean, if you prefer to have someone else play the piano for the church service and the children's practice sessions, I'll understand. I can quietly step down without there being any awkwardness."

She'd started shaking her head before he'd even finished speaking. "I see no need for you to step down. You said you're here to start over, and I think you deserve that chance. Unless you do something to show me I'm wrong, I have no problem with proceeding as we'd planned." She paused, seeming to choose her words carefully. "As for where that leaves us personally, I'd like to think we can remain friends."

The slight emphasis she'd put on the word *friends* let him know there would be no repeat of that amazing kiss. But friendship was a start. He could be patient. Perhaps over time she would learn to trust him again.

She set Beans on the ground and stood, brushing her skirt. Then she glanced his way, a little frown wrinkle above her nose. "I have one more question for you, but don't feel like you have to answer it if you don't want to."

He braced himself, not sure what to expect. "Ask away."

"How did you end up as a saddler?"

That's what she wanted to know? Relieved that she was showing an interest in him beyond his crime, he felt a little more of his tension ease. "In prison, they like to keep the inmates busy. And they also make money hiring out the prisoners to the locals in the area, money that supposedly goes into the upkeep of the place." He gave a self-mocking smile. "Piano playing was not a very marketable skill, and I didn't know how to do much else of any real value. So I offered to work with a fellow prisoner who was a skilled leather worker. Mack taught me just about everything he knew about working with leather. And I found I enjoyed the work. Like with playing the piano, there is a real artistic component to the craft."

It was a bit anticlimactic to be talking about such everyday things after the charged conversation they'd just had. Of more concern was the question of whether she was really comfortable with putting his less than stellar past behind them now.

It seemed, for now at least, that she was.

But could he live with that? He longed to take her hand again, to have her look at him with the soft admiration and warm feelings he'd seen in her gaze yesterday afternoon, to have her feel comfortable teasing and being teased by him.

To be able to wrap his arms around her to offer her comfort when she needed it, or something more.

He should be glad that their friendship was restored.

But he was greedy and wanted more.

A lot more.

Verity, not wanting to talk to anyone, went outside to work in the garden when she returned home. Nate's story had broken her heart. He'd been through so much tragedy, so much heartache, and at such a young age. By her reckoning he'd spent nearly a third of his life behind bars. How had he managed to come out of that with his spirit intact?

No, the ends didn't justify the means, but he'd been desperate, and he did what he did not to save himself but his sister. She could understand such feelings. If it had been her and Joy in such a situation, there was very little she wouldn't do to somehow provide what her daughter needed to survive.

And, as Mr. Barr had pointed out, Nate had paid the price for what he'd done. Knowing what she knew now, she was certain they could return to their friendship and work together without any tension between them.

And perhaps, in time, they could be more than friends.

But she wouldn't rush it this time. She'd learned her lesson there, as well. Acting impulsively only led to disaster. Better to take slow, measured steps, to tamp down any temptation to be impulsive, just as she'd always done before Nate came along.

Because, yes, she was still very much attracted to him, but she also knew that simple attraction was not enough. There were certain qualities that she required of a husband for herself and father for Joy—qualities such as stability, reliability, caution.

Other things, such as how special he made her feel and how her pulse always quickened when he was near, were merely frivolous emotional trappings that were fleeting at best and that muddied the waters of how to build true, lasting relationships.

Relationships like the comfortable one she'd had with Arthur.

And if there was a piece of her heart that disagreed, that yearned for those frivolous emotional trappings, well, she'd just have to work harder to tamp that down, as well.

Chapter Seventeen

The Tuesday afternoon practice session with the children went well. She and Nate were able to work together without any awkwardness. If there was none of the shared glances and exchanges of banter that had crept into their conversations of the past few weeks, that didn't really affect the way they worked with the children.

And at the end of the session, she and Joy walked with Nate as far as his shop, just as they usually did. She even allowed Joy to go in and say hello to Beans, but cut the visit shorter than normal.

But she no longer went out of her way to see Nate between sessions. There were no invitations to lunch or supper, no taking Joy by to visit with Beans, no looking for chance opportunities to bump into him.

On Wednesday, when Verity delivered her latest millinery creation, Hazel confronted her. "Something's changed between you and Mr. Cooper. What happened?"

Now, what had brought that on? Verity wasn't even aware that Hazel had seen them together since Sunday, much less had an opportunity to watch them interact with each other. "I'm sure you're imagining things. Mr. Cooper and I are just what we've always been— friends. Nothing more, nothing less."

"You might fool everyone else, Verity Magdalena Leggett, but not me. You and Mr. Cooper were well on your way to being something more interesting than friends up until this week. Now it seems like the two of you are merely colleagues." Then her gaze sharpened. "Did he do something to you?"

"No!" Verity was shocked that anyone would think such a thing of Nate. Then she took a breath and elaborated more calmly. "I admit I was temporarily taken with Mr. Cooper, perhaps even imagined myself developing tender feelings for him. After all, he saved Joy's life and he is an attractive man. But that's all it was—a passing fancy. One doesn't build a lasting relationship on such surface things."

Hazel crossed her arms. "I would hardly call his saving Joy a surface thing."

"Of course not. But you know what I mean. He's a nice man, but *if* I were to ever marry again, it would be to a man of unquestionable character and integrity. A man who is steadfast and dependable. A man like—"

"Mercy me, Verity, you already had all of that with Arthur. Don't you want some excitement and romance in your life?"

Verity felt the tug of those words on her heart, but resolutely tamped it down. "We're not all like you, Hazel. Some people prefer to live quieter, more conservative lives."

"Some people, perhaps, but you'll never convince

me that in your heart of hearts, that's what *you* really want."

Verity decided this was a good time to change the subject. "If you're finished trying to orchestrate my social life, there was another reason I came in here this afternoon."

"Oh?"

"I've been thinking that I might want to open my own millinery shop one of these days."

"Oh, I think that's a fabulous idea! It's something you should have done a long time ago. So what can I do to help?"

"First of all, I'm still in the thinking-about-it stage, so don't start planning my grand opening just yet."

Hazel waved a hand airily. "I make no promises on that score."

Verity rolled her eyes, then turned serious. "I've always admired your business sense. You've built a successful seamstress business here and I figure the millinery business will be similar. So, I'd like to sit down and talk to you at some point about what sorts of things I will need to plan for and what the best way to go about setting this up will be. That will give me a better handle on when, or even if, I'll be ready to get started."

"Absolutely. And I suggest you also speak to Adam Barr. He has both the financial and legal expertise to guide you in areas that I'm not so adept at." Then she gave Verity an assessing look. "Do you have a place in mind to set up your shop?"

"Not yet. As I said, I'm still in the mulling-it-over stage."

"Then I have my first piece of advice to give you—

lease a corner of my dress shop. It'll be perfect—we will basically have the same customers and I could use some help around here, someone to cover for me when I have to be elsewhere."

Verity had to admit it was a very tempting proposal. It would solve a lot of her worries about how to get started. And it would be fun to work with Hazel. At the same time, though, she didn't want to take advantage of her friend's generosity.

"That's a very magnanimous offer. But you haven't taken the time to think it through—"

Hazel waved away her concerns. "I don't need to think about it—it's the ideal solution. And I assure you I plan to get every bit as much out of this as you will."

"Then thank you. That's definitely an idea to add to the list." But if she followed through on it, she'd be certain she paid her friend a fair lease price.

"You have a list?" Hazel asked.

Verity grinned. "I plan to start one. Now, as I said, I'm not ready to do anything right this minute, so let's talk some more about it after the festival. I just thought it would be good to begin thinking about some of the possibilities and obstacles now."

Hazel shook her head. "Obstacles are no fun. I plan to concentrate my efforts on the possibilities." Then she gave Verity a pointed look. "Besides, I'm sure you'll do enough thinking about the obstacles for the both of us."

Is that how Hazel saw her, as someone always looking at the negative side of things? That wasn't truly the way she was—was it?

Sure, she preferred cautious action over the impulsive, but that was how responsible people conducted their lives. That didn't mean she didn't know how to appreciate the positive aspect of things as well, though. Just look at the work she was doing with the children's choir, for example. She hadn't let any obstacles get in her way when she'd taken on that task.

Still, Hazel's comment stuck with her long after she'd left the dress shop.

"Very good, everyone." Verity smiled at the members of the children's choir. "I think you all have the first two songs down really well. Let's take a little break, then we'll start to practice that last song."

She glanced over to where Nate sat at the piano. The final song was to be sung a cappella, so he'd be helping her with the vocals rather than at the instrument.

Hazel's words from yesterday, about her needing some excitement and romance in her life, returned unbidden. Nate had been really good about respecting her wishes since Monday. He'd been polite and helpful but hadn't pressed her for anything more than friendship. Neither of them had made any mention of that kiss they'd shared Sunday.

And now they were going to sing together again.

Perhaps now that her feelings had changed, it would be different. Because singing was as much about emotion as it was about vocal skills.

But, just as before, singing with him was an incredibly moving experience. His singing voice seemed to resonate perfectly with something deep inside her, to fill up the empty places there, to complement and enhance her own voice. She couldn't help but meet his gaze as they sang. It was as if everything that stood between them melted away when they sang, as if the tight control she kept on her emotions, her very heart, were not proof against him when he sang.

When they finished, the last notes of the song seemed to hang in the air for a long moment as she felt powerless to look away from his gaze.

"I don't think we can sound like that, no matter how much we practice."

Fern's words broke the spell. Verity blinked and then turned to face the children. "Nonsense. All it takes is a little bit of practice." She could still feel Nate's gaze on her, could still feel that incredible tug of *rightness* she always felt when they sang together.

Please, let him look away so I can think. "Now we're going to break up into groups, just as we did for the first song, and Mr. Cooper will work with the first two groups and I will work with the other two groups. So find your corners."

She turned a bright, impersonal smile his way. "Mr. Cooper, let's plan to get everyone back together in about thirty minutes."

He nodded and turned away. And at last she felt free to breathe normally again.

Nate took Beans out for a walk after children's choir practice that afternoon. While the dog happily sniffed out various scents and fearlessly treed squirrels, Nate's thoughts turned to the subject that always seemed to be on his mind lately—Verity.

She had kept her word to consider him a friend— at least outwardly. He didn't imagine the casual observer would suspect anything had changed between them—including that kiss they'd shared, another thing he couldn't seem to get out of his mind.

Was Verity softening toward him? There'd been a moment, when they were singing together, that he'd seen something in her eyes when she looked at him. But it could just as easily have been his imagination.

The thing was, he couldn't blame her. After what he'd done, and how he'd let down his sister, he couldn't really expect a woman like Verity, or any good woman for that matter, to want him as part of her family.

But he was determined now to stay here and fight for his place in this community. He might have lost his chance to win her affection, but he could still find a home for himself here.

And if that was the best he could do, then it was much more than he'd had just a few months ago.

Besides, there *was* one woman he could help.

Calling Beans back to his side, he directed his steps toward the boardinghouse.

For a change, luck was on his side. He found Belva sitting alone on the boardinghouse porch, writing what appeared to be a letter. She looked up when he started up the steps and set down her pencil.

"Nate. What an unexpected surprise."

She made as if to rise but he waved her down. "Please don't get up."

She settled back down and he leaned his hip against a nearby support column. Beans trotted over to sniff at her shoes and she reached under the table to scratch his ears.

"I suppose I can guess as to why you're here. You've made a decision about my offer."

He nodded. "While I truly feel honored that you'd trust me to handle this job for you, I'm not going to take you up on your offer."

She leaned back with a resigned expression. "I'm more than a little disappointed, but I can't say as I'm all that surprised. It's pretty obvious that you've started forming ties here. I hope Verity knows how lucky she is."

Surprised by her comment, he had to smother a grimace. He decided it would be best to just let it pass. "There *is* something else I'll do for you, however, if you like."

Her demeanor perked up. "What's that?"

"I'll travel with you to your new home when you get ready to move in, and I'll go with you to meet with the solicitors and help you take care of whatever business is entailed with claiming your inheritance. I'll also stick around to help you interview candidates for that caretaker position and I won't leave until you and I are both satisfied that you have the right man for the job."

She gave him a look that was a mix of surprise and hope. "Are you sure? That's going to take a lot of time away from your business here."

"I'm sure." It was what he would have liked for someone to have done for his sister if she'd been placed in a similar situation.

Belva grinned. "I sure as Christmas morning don't aim to talk you out of it. I accept." Then she held up a cautionary hand. "But I do have one condition."

"Which is?"

"That you let me pay you for your time."

"I don't want—"

She lifted her chin. "I insist. It would be the same wage I plan to pay the caretaker I eventually hire. As far as I'm concerned, you're temporarily serving in that capacity."

Realizing how important this was to her, he nodded. "In that case, I agree."

She offered him her hand to seal the deal.

He shook her hand, then reached down to rub Beans's head. "Have you told your aunt Eunice yet? Or are you waiting until your birthday?" She'd confided to him that, according to the terms of her aunt Imogene's will, she was to take possession of her inheritance on her twentieth birthday. And she was to tell none of her relatives about her good fortune until one month before the happy event.

Belva glanced toward the house, as if worried her aunt Eunice might suddenly appear. "I'm going to tell her right after the festival. It'll give her a couple of days to get used to the idea before my birthday rolls around."

"And how soon do you plan to leave?"

"My birthday is on Tuesday. I'd like to leave on Wednesday but can postpone it a bit if that doesn't fit your schedule."

"Assuming a replacement church pianist can be found, I can make that work." He would wait until after the children's performance on Saturday to tell Verity. Would she miss him at all? Or would she be glad to have him gone for a while?

Belva rubbed her chin. "As much as I'm looking forward to being on my own and starting fresh, I think I'm going to miss the folks here in Turnabout. Everyone has been so kind to me. It's been especially nice since I joined the choir."

He couldn't argue with her there. The town, and its residents, had lived up to everything Adam had said it would. And he had a particular fondness for the choir, as well. But he gave her a reassuring smile. "I'm sure the place you're moving to will welcome you just as warmly." Then he raised a brow. "And you can always come back to visit from time to time."

"Maybe I will," she said archly. "Especially if I had the right kind of incentive. Such as attending some-one's wedding."

He ducked his head, ostensibly to scratch Beans be-hind the ears again. Hopefully she hadn't noticed any telltale sign of just how sharply that innocent comment of hers had cut him.

If she planned to wait on a wedding invitation from him and Verity before she returned, she might never see Turnabout again.

Chapter Eighteen

"So, how has it been, working with such a young choir group?"

The Saturday afternoon tea group was gathered once again in the Blue Bottle Sweet Shop. Verity's thoughts had been drifting, thinking of Nate and how it felt like a very long time since Thursday when she'd seen him last.

In fact, she found herself eager to get done here at the Blue Bottle so that they could go on to choir practice. Which was absurd, especially given that she had no intentions of relaxing her nothing-beyond-friendship stance with Nate.

So Abigail's question about the children's choir was a welcome distraction. "Actually, it's been a lot of fun." She meant that. "And quite rewarding. I'm thinking about seeing if they want to continue on as a choir after the festival."

"You mean have a full-time children's choir?"

Verity nodded. "We could even have them sing one hymn in church each Sunday."

"What a lovely idea." Janell set her teacup down.

"There may be other schoolchildren who would want to join in once we have the play behind us."

"All would be welcome," Verity agreed. "Of course, I'd have to see how Reverend Harper feels about it. And check in with Zella, too, since it would mean extra work for her, as well."

"Perhaps, if it's too much for Zella, Mr. Cooper would consider working with you on this." Hazel's tone was just a little *too* innocent.

Before Verity could say anything, though, Janell spoke up again. "You have to admit, he's done a great job these past few weeks while Zella is out of town."

Belva nodded. "Mr. Cooper does have a way of putting a body at ease. I imagine that makes him ideal for working with the children."

Verity still hadn't quite figured out what the relationship was between Belva and Nate. Just good friends? Or was Belva looking for something more?

She shouldn't be bothered by that thought since she no longer wanted anything more than friendship for herself.

But somehow, she was.

Later, as they left the Blue Bottle, Hazel fell into step beside her. "I've been thinking about ways we could arrange your hats in the fashion emporium to their best advantage," she said enthusiastically. "I'm picturing a set of deep shelves along the back wall, maybe three rows high, running two-thirds of the length. Depending on the size of your hats, you should be able to display around two dozen. What do you think?"

"I think you're being premature." But it did sound

very appealing. "I told you we'd sit down and discuss it after the festival."

"It doesn't hurt to think about it some ahead of time, does it?" She gave Verity a pointed look. "It also doesn't hurt to let you know I don't plan to drop the subject."

Verity rolled her eyes. "I never thought you would. But again, let's save this for *after* the festival."

Perhaps she would mention it to Nate, though, just to get his input. From a purely business perspective, of course. After all, he had recently opened a business of his own, so he might have some relevant insights.

The fact that it would give her an excuse to stay after practice and speak to him was just a pleasant side benefit.

Nate put his music away as the choir members drifted out after practice. Belva had paused just a minute to chat with him but then hurried off, saying she'd promised her aunt Eunice to lend her a hand with supper this evening.

It wasn't until he moved away from the piano that he realized Verity had remained behind when the others left. Was she actually going out of her way to see him?

"Do you have a minute?"

Apparently she was. "Of course. Is there something about one of the choirs we need to discuss?"

"Actually, I did want to ask you something about our practice sessions with the children this coming week."

Would she have anything to do with him once he was through acting as Zella Ford's stand-in? "I'm listening."

"We've got only two practice sessions left before the festival kicks off Friday night. They're doing well, but

I thought it might be a good idea to have this week's sessions run for ninety minutes each rather than an hour. What do you think?"

He rubbed his chin. "That sounds like a good idea to me. The more practice they get in, the more confident they will be the day of the performance." And he wasn't averse to spending a little extra time with her, as well.

"And it won't be a problem for you?"

"I think I can manage the extra thirty minutes without any problem."

She smiled and gave his arm a quick, light touch. "Thank you."

Emboldened by that touch, he nodded toward the door. "May I walk you home?"

"You can walk me as far as your shop."

At least she hadn't refused altogether.

"There was one other thing I wanted to discuss with you," she said as they fell into step together.

"More choir business?" He had to physically restrain himself from taking her arm. She wanted nothing more than a neighborly kind of friendship.

"No, this is of a more personal nature."

His attention quickened at that. Discussing things other than choir was a step in the right direction.

"Remember I mentioned once that I'd like to open a millinery shop someday?"

"Of course."

"Well, I've been thinking that I should at least look into what all will be involved in such an undertaking so I'll know when, or even if, I'll be in a position to give it a go."

That sounded so like her. Careful to a fault. But at

least she appeared to be moving forward. "That seems like a prudent approach."

"I thought so." There was just a hint of smugness in her voice. "Anyway, I mentioned this to Hazel and she's offered to lease me part of her dress shop to display and sell my hats whenever I get ready. I was wondering what you thought of that plan."

He was encouraged by the fact that his opinion still seemed to matter to her. "Actually, I can see a lot of really great advantages for you in such a setup. You'd have a place that was ready to move into with very little setup work required. The location is one that many of your potential customers already frequent. You and Miss Andrews could share the staffing duties, covering for each other as needed." He nodded. "It's ideal, really."

"So you don't see any negatives associated with going this route?"

It seemed that she was still looking for reasons *not* to follow through on her dream. "Well, I suppose there is always some potential for problems. For instance, if you and Miss Andrews had a falling out, things could get mighty awkward for your respective businesses. And you would need to make certain you both had the same understanding of how the money would be handled, how the floor space and display space should be divided and what the on-site responsibilities of each of you would be, especially in regards to each other's wares."

"Oh, my, that's a lot to think about."

"It is. But there's a way to manage the risk. You can save both of you a lot of headaches, and heartaches, by getting all of this down in a contract that you both sign. That way there won't be any misunderstandings down the road."

She sighed. "There's so much to consider. I hadn't thought of any of that. What if I miss some other key problem areas?"

He shook his head. "Verity, you're never going to be able to account for every possible catastrophe. There's just not much in life that comes with guarantees. But if you never step out in faith, you never have the chance to grab hold of the blessing."

She gave him a curious look. "Is that what you did, step out in faith?"

"Well, I'll admit that what I was stepping away from wasn't something I wanted to hold on to, so it was easier for me. I guess what you need to decide is, is that dream you have of having your millinery shop worth fighting for, worth facing the possibility of failure for? And you're the only one who can answer that question."

"I never thought of it that way." She was quiet for a long moment, then she met his gaze again. "I guess one of the things I'm struggling with is trying to decide how I will know when the time is right. Maybe I should wait until I have more money saved up."

He raised a brow. "Is that really what's holding you back? Money? Or is it fear?"

He could tell that remark hit home. They'd reached his shop by now and were standing outside it. He tried one more time to make her understand what he was trying to say. "I know you like to use a slow, well-thought-out approach to making decisions, Verity, but there is such a thing as overthinking a problem. At some point you have to act. If not, that's a decision in and of itself, isn't it?"

She gave her purse strings a little tug. "Thank you for your input—it has certainly given me something to think about. If you'll excuse me, it's time I headed home."

He watched her leave, fairly certain he'd made no dent at all in her examine-things-exhaustively approach to decision making.

And he certainly hadn't done anything to further his relationship with her at all.

Verity walked away, mulling over Nate's words. What he'd said sounded an awful lot like what Hazel had told her a few days ago. Both seemed to imply that she was overly cautious. To her way of thinking, there was no such thing—either one was cautious or not, it was a simple as that.

Yet there was a nagging little voice in her head telling her she was missing something, something important.

This was something she needed to think on more. Step out in faith, he'd said. Was that the something she was lacking—faith?

Perhaps her problem was that she thought too much. And perhaps didn't pray enough.

Chapter Nineteen

Nate arrived at the Tuesday practice session to find Verity already there ahead of him. She greeted him the same as always, without any apparent rancor from their previous conversation. Did that mean she had decided to take his advice? Or merely ignore it and move on?

The practice session went well. The children were able to run through all three of the songs with only a few missteps on the last one. It was great to see how well they were coming together, how eager they were to do a good job and how proud they were to have a part in the program.

At the end of the session, Miss Andrews came by with the smocks she'd made, and she and Verity helped the children try them on over their clothing.

Verity had them all line up side by side with the smocks on and made a big show of telling them how wonderful they looked. He saw several of the children stand a little taller under her praise.

When they were done, Verity collected the smocks from each of them, telling the children she would keep them safe and pass them out again the day of the performance.

Dismissing the choir members, Verity turned to him. "If you have a minute, there's something I'd like to discuss with you."

"Of course." Was she wanting to continue their last conversation?

"The children have been working so hard, I've been thinking I'd like to do something to reward them."

Of course she would. "Did you have something particular in mind?"

"Well, because many of the festival activities will take place on the school grounds, the town has canceled classes for Friday. I was thinking we could take advantage of that and have a group picnic down by Mercer's Pond that day. We could invite the members of the choir along with their families. What do you think?"

She certainly didn't mind making plans or undertaking large projects when it was for someone else. Why couldn't she show that same kind of spirit when it came to her own dreams?

But that wasn't what she'd asked him. "Wouldn't it be better to do that *after* the performance?"

She nodded. "I thought about that. But if we waited, that would mean doing it after church on Sunday, when everyone is likely to be tired from the prior day's festivities. Or waiting until the following Saturday, which feels like it would be too much of a delay." She grinned. "And besides, doing it on Friday lets the children know I'm rewarding their effort, not their performance."

That statement was so like her. She didn't just concern herself with teaching these kids how to do things, she concerned herself with their hearts and their spirits, as well. It was one of the many things he admired about her.

"Can I count on you to be there?"

He gave a short bow. "Of course. I'd never pass up a chance to attend a picnic." Or to spend some time with her. "What do you want me to do?"

"Just be there to help us keep an eye on the children. If everyone comes, there'll be a lot of them there. The Tucker family alone has ten children. And I don't imagine many of the dads will be available to come."

"I can certainly do that." He started to tease her about protecting her from spiders as well, but just in time he remembered where that had landed them last time, and thought better of it.

"Oh, and feel free to bring Beans," she added. "The children, especially one in particular, will enjoy having him there to play with."

He wondered if that soft smile that teased at her lips was due to her thoughts of her daughter or if perhaps she was beginning to warm toward him once more.

Friday dawned bright and sunshiny—the perfect day for a picnic. Verity had a large hamper filled to the brim with sliced ham, fresh-baked bread, cheese, apples, cucumber pickles, boiled eggs and a buttermilk pie. There was also a jar of lemonade. No one would go away hungry today if she could help it.

The children had all been enthusiastic at the idea of a picnic when she first announced it. She had also talked to the mothers, and every one of them had agreed to join in. They were going to have quite a nice turnout for their outing.

As planned, Nate collected her uncle's buggy from the livery and pulled up in front of the house to pick up her and Joy. When he arrived, he hopped down to take the hamper from her, then whistled. "This is mighty heavy for just one meal."

Verity laughed. "I have a feeling it will be quite empty by the time we head home this afternoon."

"Bringing a big appetite with you, are you?"

She laughed again. "There's a lot of sharing that goes along with these picnics. We won't be the only ones eating from this basket."

He hefted it into the back of the buggy. "Then I guess I'd better be sure to get my share early."

He took the blanket Joy was carrying and tossed it behind the seat with the hamper. Then he took the little girl by the waist and swung her up in a wide arc, making her giggle and Verity wince.

Then he turned to hand her in. There was a moment's awkwardness as she remembered the last time they'd rode in this buggy. She could tell from the slight tightening of his jaw that he was remembering, too. But then she lifted her chin, smiled and offered him her hand. She refused to let anything spoil this outing. She and Nate had called a truce and she was ready to leave the past in the past. They were friends now, and as friends, could enjoy each other's company.

In a matter of seconds she was perched on the seat next to Joy.

Nate climbed up on the other side of her daughter and they were off.

With Joy sitting between them, holding Beans and Lulu in her lap, the remaining wisps of that momentary awkwardness disappeared. The little girl's happy chatter not only entertained them during the trip, but it successfully filled any of the silences that might have popped up between the adults.

They were the first ones to arrive, just as Verity had hoped. She spread their blanket in a prime spot that was in the shade of a large cottonwood tree and what she considered a safe distance from the pond itself. Then she spread a second blanket nearby.

Nate looked at the arrangement and then raised a brow in her direction. "Expecting company?"

She smiled and shook her head. "No, that's the community 'table.' Everyone will place the contents of their baskets there and then when it's time to eat, you can choose whatever items catch your eye."

"I see." He eyed the arrangement skeptically. "But it looks like that could get a bit messy."

She laughed, enjoying the chance to introduce him to their traditions. "Trust me. We've done this lots of times. Not everyone serves themselves. Three or four of the ladies will be in charge of filling plates— you just have to let them know what you want." She grinned. "This also takes care of the problem of some of the kids who have eyes bigger than their stomachs."

As she was speaking she'd moved her hamper to the community blanket. She wouldn't set the contents out until much closer to mealtime—no point in feeding the flies and ants.

Other families began arriving almost immediately. The children scattered to play while the adults staked a claim on a patch of ground to spread their cloths. They chose patches close together to make it easier for everyone to chat and visit with each other.

As Verity had predicted, Nate was one of the few

men who had come. Most of the fathers were working or helping to get things set up in town for the festival. In fact, the only other man there was Stuart Draper, Harriett and Susie's grandfather.

Mr. Draper had walked with a pronounced limp ever since he'd gotten hurt in an accident over ten years ago. But he had a skill that didn't require the use of his legs and that endeared him to children. He was an expert at carving whistles and simple flutes from scraps of wood. At her urging, he had brought a couple of his creations for the children to play with, and also some materials to carve new ones on the spot.

In addition, several of the children had brought kites and there were balls and bats as well.

Once the picnic blankets were all arranged to everyone's satisfaction, the women were soon busy chattering away, comparing hamper contents, swapping news and generally socializing. While they visited, the children ran with great abandon around the meadow. Verity kept Joy in sight, making sure she didn't get too close to the pond, and not letting her stray too far from the adults.

Beans was also a big hit with the children. The dog was alternating his time between exploring, racing around the meadow with the children and letting himself be petted into a blissful stupor.

Nate seemed to take his role as a protector for the children quite seriously. Several times she saw him counting noses, and on the occasions when the count was not to his satisfaction, he'd march over to a section of the meadow that curved around the pond and then become hidden by trees. Sure enough, he'd reappear shortly with one or more kids in tow and send them back to safer—or at least more visible—ground. Apparently there were turtles and minnows to be found in the shallows there, and the children found it an irresistible attraction.

But he was more than a disciplinarian. He took time to play with them, as well. She saw him give one group lessons on how to skip stones, he played horseshoes with another group and worked to untangle a kite string for a teary-eyed youngster.

He even talked her into taking one end of a jump rope while he took the other, and together they turned the rope for nearly thirty minutes as the girls took turns jumping. It was so endearing—heartwarming really—to see him with the children.

When it was lunchtime, Mr. Draper blew on his loudest whistle, one that made a sound so shrill it actually startled a number of birds from the trees. But it served the purpose of getting everyone's attention, and the children came scurrying in from all directions. When everyone was accounted for and had gathered on the individual family picnic blankets, Mr. Draper offered up the blessing on behalf of the group.

Then it was momentary pandemonium as everyone tried to make food selections. But at last all the plates were served and things quieted in the meadow while everyone partook of the delicious food.

Nate, naturally, shared her and Joy's picnic blanket. She smiled as she watched Joy laugh at something he'd said to her. And then he casually slipped Beans a sliver of meat. It felt nice to have him there with them. It felt like…family.

Verity sat up straighter, trying to shake off that unexpected thought. Where was her resolve, her caution?

The trouble was, she was having trouble remembering why all that mattered. He *was* a good man, deep down she knew that. As for the rest, maybe he and Hazel had been right. Perhaps it *was* time she stepped out in faith.

Nate looked up just then and caught her staring at him. Something of what she was feeling must have shown in her face, because his expression shifted from amusement to first uncertainty, and then something much warmer and deeper. They held each other's gaze without speaking, without moving, for three heartbeats.

And then Joy spoke up, asking for another piece of corn bread, and broke the spell.

Verity blinked and turned to her daughter. "I'm sorry, pumpkin, what did you say?"

Joy held up her plate. "I'd like another piece of corn bread, please."

Nate stood. "I'll get it." He looked down at Verity, his expression still warm and rather mysterious. "Can I get you anything while I'm up?"

She shook her head, and with a nod he walked away.

As she watched him saunter over to the food blanket, she began second-guessing herself. Should she have looked away? What message had he read in her gaze? What had she wanted him to see there?

Then she remembered they weren't alone. Had anyone else noticed anything untoward passing between them? Verity did her best to surreptitiously look around the gathering. As far as she could tell, no one was paying the least bit of attention to them.

Nate returned, the requested slice of corn bread wrapped in a cloth napkin. "Here you go," he said, handing it to Joy.

When he settled back down on the blanket, she felt a new tension strumming in him, something that seemed to tug at her, as well. It was almost like when they sang together—something inside him speaking to her and vice versa.

It was so real it amazed her that no one else could feel it.

Nate stood with his back against an oak and his arms crossed over his chest. Beans lay in the grass at his feet, panting. The dog had had a busy morning trying to keep up with the children and seemed to be happy just to stay with him for now.

From here Nate had a fairly unobstructed view of the meadow. Their picnic meal had ended a few minutes ago and, like Beans, everyone appeared to be moving at a much slower pace than earlier.

Several picnic blankets had been spread in an overlapping line under the shade of a nearby tree and many of the toddlers and younger children had been put down for their naps. Mr. Draper was keeping an eye on them, freeing the mothers to help with the cleanup or to take advantage of their temporary freedom to just visit.

Some of the older children were playing with the ball and bat well away from the picnic area, while several of the girls had claimed one of the blankets as a place to play with their dolls.

He spotted Verity among a cluster of women who were cleaning up and reorganizing all the leftovers. As if she felt his gaze on her, she looked up, smiled and then went back to work.

He was still trying to decide what to make of the

look they'd shared earlier. The message in her eyes had been unmistakable. She felt something for him, something more than friendship. But was that emotion real and of the lasting variety this time? At least now he didn't have to worry about what would happen if she found out his secrets—she already knew them all.

It was frustrating that he couldn't do anything to resolve this right now, couldn't have a meaningful conversation with her among this crowd. And taking a walk alone together was also out of the question—she'd never leave Joy unattended, even among this crowd of motherly types. Perhaps, though, when he brought her and Joy home this evening, they could find some time to talk in private. It was definitely something to look forward to.

He saw Joy race up to tug on Verity's skirt, her trademark "can I please" expression in evidence. He pushed away from the tree, deciding to drift closer to the pair to see what was going on.

"But Mama, please," he heard Joy plead, "I want to see the bunny."

Verity shook her head. "I told you, pumpkin, I'm too busy to go with you right now. And besides, the bunny is probably long gone."

"You don't know. He might still be there."

"What's this about a bunny?" Nate inquired once he was close enough to join in.

Joy whirled around at the sound of his voice, a hopeful expression on her face. "Mr. Cooper, will you take me to see the bunny?"

Before he could answer, Verity spoke up. "Joy, I've already told you, you need to stay close to me."

Nate saw the mutinous expression form on Joy's

face, and spoke up quickly. "I don't mind going for a walk with her. I've been meaning to take Beans out for a bit of exploring anyway."

Verity looked from him to her daughter. "I don't know. Joy, maybe you should just stay here and keep me company while Mr. Cooper walks Beans."

"But what about the bunny?"

"Let her go." Nate tried to cajole a smile from Verity with one of his own. "I promise to keep a close watch on her. And we'll definitely stay away from the edge of the pond."

She held out for a moment longer, and then finally gave in with a loud huff of breath. "Oh, very well. I suppose it'll be all right. But Joy, see that you mind Mr. Cooper. No running off on your own."

"Yes, ma'am. Come on, Beans, let's go find the bunny."

Nate matched his steps to those of the little girl and dog at his side. He was so proud of Verity for overcoming her fears and letting Joy out of her sight in this setting. He knew it had been a big step for her. And it felt very good to know that it was putting her trust in him that had allowed her to loosen the reins.

"So tell me about this bunny," he said to Joy.

"Molly told me they saw a bunny last time they were out here."

"Is that right?" So this wasn't a recent sighting. No wonder Verity had expressed doubt that it would be nearby.

Joy nodded. "Molly said she got close enough to almost pet it before it hopped away." The wistful gleam in her eyes was sweet to see.

He needed to temper her expectations, but there

was no point in dashing her hopes completely. "We'll certainly keep a look out. But bunnies are *very* shy. There's so many people here right now that I really don't think a bunny will come out of hiding today."

"But he might," she insisted stubbornly.

"I suppose." He couldn't bring himself to express any stronger doubt. "But I tell you what. If we don't see a bunny today, we'll come back another day with just me and you and your mother and see if we have better luck."

"Okay. But let's try to find him today."

Nate nodded in solemn agreement. They were reaching the section of meadow that wrapped around the pond and formed a pocket out of sight of the picnic area. He'd intended to turn back when they got to this point, knowing Verity would want to be able to keep Joy in sight. But he heard a ruckus coming from around the point and he could tell it was some of the kids from their party.

And they sounded as if they were in trouble.

When he rounded the corner, sure enough, three kids were standing at the edge of the pond. Well, two of them were, anyway. The third was actually in the pond and seemed to be in some kind of trouble. Nate didn't recognize any of them from the choir—they must be some of the family members.

"What's going on here?" he called out.

All three started and turned to face him.

"It's Davey," one of the boys said as he waved toward the kid in the water. "He's got his foot caught on something and we can't get him out."

The boy, Davey, stood in waist-deep water right beside a tree trunk that had fallen over the pond.

"It's starting to hurt something awful," Davey added.

Nate could tell the boy was trying not to cry but was right on the verge. His foot was probably caught on some kind of rope or net that was down in the silt or lodged in the underwater part of the tree trunk.

He glanced down at the little girl whose hand he held and realized he had a problem. Verity wouldn't want him taking Joy that close to the water's edge, especially if he was going to have to focus his attention on someone else. He could take her back first, but he wasn't sure how badly hurt Davey's leg might be.

He quickly took off his jacket and spread it on the ground. "Joy, I need to go over there and help Davey. I want you to sit right here on this coat and not get up until I return. Do you understand?" Hopefully the jacket would serve as an anchor for her.

"Yes, sir. But then can we go look for the bunny some more?"

"I promise."

As soon as he reached the waterline, he turned to see how Joy was doing. She still sat where he'd left her, hugging her knees. She waved when she saw him looking and he waved back, then turned to the two boys who were unencumbered.

"What's your name?" he asked the largest of the pair.

"JJ."

"JJ, you see that little girl sitting over there?"

JJ nodded.

"I want you to keep an eye on her for me. Let me know if she tries to go anywhere."

The boy nodded, but Nate wasn't satisfied. He didn't

completely trust Joy not to forget her promise if she saw some critter that she wanted to get close to.

He held JJ's gaze a moment longer. "It's very important that you watch her. Understand?"

The boy nodded again. Then Nate turned to the other boy. "And you are?"

"Irvin."

"Irvin, I want you to go back to the picnic area and very calmly ask Mrs. Leggett to come down here. Tell her not to worry, but that Mr. Cooper needs her help with something. Do you understand?"

The boy nodded, but before he could take off, Nate grabbed his arm. "Remember, be sure to tell her not to worry." He wanted her here because of her medical experience if something should be wrong with the boy's foot. But he didn't want her jumping to the conclusion that something had happened to Joy.

When the boy nodded this time, Nate let him go. Deciding he'd covered all contingencies as best he could, Nate gingerly waded into the pond beside the trapped Davey. Then he very carefully felt under the water around the boy's foot. Sure enough, he found Davey's foot was tangled in a knotted length of rope that had wrapped itself around a limb under the water.

"I've found the problem, but it's going to take me a few minutes to get you free. Just hold on."

Nate tried loosening the rope, but it was too slippery to get a grip firm enough to work the knots.

Davey shifted position and let out a yell.

"Easy now. There are some jagged bits of wood down there." There was a real danger the boy could do himself serious injury if he wasn't careful. "Here, lean on me if you need to." Nate held out his arm, elbow bent, and the boy latched on. He let him balance like that for a minute and then helped him transfer most of his weight to the body of the tree.

That done, Nate reached for his pocketknife. Careful to position the knife in such a way as to not harm the boy, he went to work sawing on the rope. It was thick so it took several minutes, but at last it was done. As soon as the rope separated, Nate lifted the boy bodily, intending to carry him out of the pond.

"What's going on out here?"

Nate turned to see Verity striding toward them.

"You're just in time. Davey here had a little accident."

"So I see." Then she looked around. "Where's Joy?"

Nate's gaze flew to the spot where he'd left the little girl and his heart thudded in his chest.

Joy was no longer sitting on his coat.

Chapter Twenty

Nate looked around the area frantically but there was no sign of the child. He glanced toward JJ but the boy had hung his head and wouldn't meet his gaze. Obviously JJ had fallen down on the job.

He quickly set Davey down on the bank then turned back to Verity, remorse for what he had let happen, for what it would do to the woman he loved, nearly suffocating him. "She was just here. She couldn't have gone far."

He saw the blood drain from her face, saw the fear in her eyes. "What do you mean, you don't know? You promised me you would watch her."

Her words hit him like a knife to his chest. "I turned away to help Davey and when I looked back, she was gone. But I'm going to find her."

She glanced at the water with fear-filled eyes and he made a sharp movement.

"No! She didn't go near the pond—I would have seen her. She must have wandered into the woods, but she wouldn't have gotten far."

"I'm going with you to look for her."

"No. You need to stay here and check on Davey. Besides, if she slips past me in the woods and comes back here, you need to be waiting for her."

He turned to JJ. He knew the boy was feeling miserable for his lapse of attention. The kid needed a chance to redeem himself. "JJ, I need you to do something for me."

The boy looked up, finally meeting his gaze, guilt radiating from him.

"Go on back to the group and tell them what happened with Davey and with Joy. And then borrow that very loud whistle from Mr. Draper and bring it back here to Mrs. Leggett."

He turned to Verity. "If Joy does come out of the woods without me, blow that whistle and I'll know to stop my search and come back."

She nodded.

Without another word, he strode quickly into the woods. He called for Joy as he went, listening closely each time for a response. The longer it went without a response, the deeper the dread lodged in his chest. If something had happened to that precious little girl, he would never forgive himself.

Twenty minutes later he finally spotted her, curled up on the ground with her eyes closed. Was she breathing? He rushed over and dropped down beside her. The sweetest sight he ever saw was the sight of her eyelids fluttering open.

"Oh, hello, Mr. Cooper. You founded me." She lifted her arms up to him.

He pulled her into his lap, and struggled to get his voice under control. "Hello, Joy. Are you okay?"

"Uh-huh. But the bunny ran away."

He offered up silent prayers of thanksgiving that she was unharmed. Then he gave her a bear hug. "Everyone has been very worried about you. Especially your mother."

Joy wrapped her arms around his neck. "Is Mama mad at me?"

It was much more likely that it was him Verity was angry with, and he couldn't blame her. "Right now she just wants to know that you're all right."

When they finally cleared the trees, Verity was there, pacing. Her face was white and drawn and she was rubbing her arms. Several of the other women were there with her, keeping her company.

As soon as she saw the two of them step from the woods, she raced over and took Joy from his arms.

"She's okay," he said quickly.

"No thanks to you." Anger and betrayal blazed from her eyes.

"I'm sorry." It was inadequate, but what else could he say?

"I trusted you, trusted your word that you wouldn't let her out of your sight."

Her voice was low and controlled, but it thrummed with emotion, all of it sharp, all of it aimed at him.

"Please don't be angry, Mama." Joy wrapped her arms around her mother's neck. "He tolded me to stay on his coat but I saw a bunny."

Verity stroked her daughter's hair and he saw how her fingers trembled. "I'm not angry with you, pumpkin."

But the eyes-blazing look she shot his way let him know *he* wasn't so lucky.

It was going to be a very long carriage ride back to town.

Chapter Twenty-One

The children took their places in line inside the church, fidgeting nervously as they waited for the signal to take the stage. Their performance would take place in just a few short minutes—all of their hours of practice and preparation coming down to this.

Verity went down the line, talking to each child in turn, doing what she could to ease their nervous fears, letting them know how very proud she was of each and every one of them. All the time the back of her neck tingled uncomfortably with the knowledge that Nate was behind her at the piano, watching her.

The children were to perform on the church steps and they were lined up down the center aisle, waiting for their cue to file out. The church doors and windows were all thrown wide open so that the music from the piano could clearly be heard by performers and audience alike. Which meant for the first two songs on the program, Nate would be inside the church, heard but not seen.

Which was all right by Verity. She still hadn't been able to forgive him for not keeping a better watch over Joy yesterday. When she thought about her baby, alone in the woods for nearly half an hour, it just tied her stomach in knots. So many things could have happened—snakes, falls, even her finding her way back to the water's edge.

Even if Nate had been focused on helping Davey, he should have set one of the other children who was present to watch her.

No, the man was not to be trusted. He might have the best intentions in the world—trying to help his sister all those years ago, helping Davey yesterday—but his judgment was far from sound. If she'd needed a sign that he was not the kind of man she should try to build a life with, she'd gotten it loud and clear yesterday. And just in the nick of time.

Hazel finally stepped inside, signaling it was time. Verity pulled her focus back to the children and the program they were about to perform.

She led the group out the open doors and into the sunlight. They looked so cheery and hopeful in their bright green smocks. The children lined up in two rows, just as they had practiced, without any missteps.

Hazel stayed inside the church and positioned herself where she could see both Verity and Nate. She would relay any signals that needed to pass from one to the other.

Verity tried to maintain her composure as she turned to face the audience. By now, most of the town knew what had happened yesterday, and how she had reacted to it. Hazel had tried to talk to her, to tell her Nate deserved another chance. But Verity had simply walked away from her. She was done with giving him chances.

She could have forgiven him, maybe, if what he had done had endangered her. But not her baby—that she could not forgive.

Pulling her thoughts away from her anger one more time, she gave the children a broad smile and then turned to the audience.

"Welcome, everyone, to the very first performance of Turnabout's new children's choir. They've all been working very hard these past few weeks, and once you've heard their performance, I think you'll agree that it hasn't been in vain. And now, without further ado, I present to you the Turnabout Children's Choir."

There was a small smattering of applause as Verity turned back to face the children. She raised her hands, then nodded to Hazel. The music started almost immediately.

Using the hand signals the children were now accustomed to, Verity counted the beats and the four youngest children stepped down one stair right on cue and started the song. They were a bit wobbly at first, but they gathered confidence as they went and by the end of their assigned verse they were singing with vigor. All the children chimed in on the chorus and then it was time for the next four to step down and sing their verse.

At the end of the number, the audience erupted in applause and Verity was happy to see the wide smiles on the faces of her choir. Once the applause died down, she signaled that they were to resume their positions, and they did so with only minor scrambling. Again she held up a hand to bring them to attention, then signaled Hazel. This time, when it was time to sing, the group sang out all together. There were two children who had their timing slightly off, but they caught up quickly and on the whole, that number was a success, as well.

The third song was the one Nate had taught her, the one that would be sung a cappella. The original plan had been for Nate to come on out here and help her direct it. But after waiting a few minutes, Verity realized he was not going to make an appearance.

She had a slight pang over that since he had worked as hard as she on this program and deserved some recognition for his efforts. But part of her was relieved as well that she would not have to face him in front of her neighbors.

Smiling at the children, she gave them the count. This time, when the younger group stepped forward to sing the first verse, she sang softly with them, helping them to carry the tune without the piano for help.

When the final note had been sung, the applause was louder than before and lasted longer. Verity had the whole group step down and take a bow.

And then it was done.

Most of the children raced off to join their parents, and several folks came up to offer Verity congratulations on how well the program had come off. Again she felt that slight pang of conscience that Nate was not present to get his share of the praise.

At one point, Joy tugged on Verity's skirt. "Why didn't Mr. Cooper come out to be with us on the last song like we practiced?"

"I don't know, pumpkin. Perhaps he was feeling a little shy. But you all still did a wonderful job."

"Is he going to walk with us through the festival? He told me yesterday at the picnic that he would and that Beans could come, too."

"Oh, pumpkin, I don't think so."

Joy gave her a solemn look. "Are you still mad at him because I got losted?"

"That's between Mr. Cooper and me." Despite her feelings, she didn't want to taint Joy's feelings toward Nate. She knew his fondness for her daughter was genuine.

She quickly changed the subject. "Why don't we go see what we can find at the festival? I hear they have a talking parrot that you can see."

That was sufficient to distract her daughter, and away they went. Verity did her best to see that Joy had a good time. They watched the other schoolchildren perform the play. They cheered for the contestants in the three-legged race and wheelbarrow race. They did indeed get to see the talking parrot, which Joy considered interesting but not very cuddly.

But Verity was just going through the motions. She wasn't able to lose herself in the spirit of the event. Twice she caught herself looking for Nate, without success, among the crowd, and she despised herself for it.

More than anything else, she felt a deep sense of loss and betrayal. And she wasn't sure which hurt the most.

Zella, who had returned to town on Friday, was back at the piano on Sunday. Verity looked for Nate and saw him sitting near the back of the church. Next to Belva.

Nate strode down the sidewalk toward the clinic, Beans at his heels. He'd done a lot of thinking, and a lot of praying, since the incident at the picnic four days ago. And he'd reached one significant conclusion. He couldn't—wouldn't—let things go on the way they were.

It was time he moved on.

He climbed the front porch steps to the Pratt home and rapped on the door. It was the doctor's wife who answered his knock. To his relief, the look she gave him held more sympathy than animosity.

"Hello, Mr. Cooper. Are you here to see Verity?"

He removed his hat. "Yes, ma'am. If you don't mind, please let her know that I don't plan to take up much of her time."

"She and Joy are out back, working in the garden." The doctor's wife pointed to her left. "Just follow the house around that way and you'll see it." She gave him a look that was almost conspiratorial. "If you need time alone with my niece, just tell Joy I said she could bring Beans inside to feed him some scraps I have."

"Yes, ma'am, thank you." It seems he had at least one ally in this household.

Nate followed Mrs. Pratt's directions and found the garden easily enough. Verity was on her knees with her back to him, pulling weeds. Joy was nearby, rather inexpertly weaving a daisy chain. As soon as Beans spotted them he gave a yip of recognition and raced forward. Joy scrambled to her feet and met him halfway.

Verity was slower to react, though he thought he detected a certain stiffening of her back. When she stood and turned to face him, there was a guarded expression on her face.

"Hello, Mr. Cooper," Joy said. "I looked for you at the festival but couldn't find you."

"I'm sorry I missed all the fun, but I wasn't feeling

up to it." Before the little girl could press further, he delivered Mrs. Pratt's message. "Your aunt Betty told me she has some food you can feed Beans if you want to take him to the kitchen."

"Yes, sir. Come on, Beans."

And with that, child and dog were off.

Verity watched her daughter go, ignoring him, until he heard the back door spring closed. Then she turned to him. "What are you doing here?"

Not exactly a warm welcome. "I came to let you know I'm going out of town for a while."

There was a flicker of something in her expression, but he couldn't tell if it was relief, surprise or curiosity. It certainly couldn't be regret.

When she didn't say anything, he continued. "I was wondering if you would allow Joy to take care of Beans for me while I'm away."

"I don't know—"

"Look, I know you're angry with me. And I probably deserve it."

"Probably—"

He held a hand up. "I'm not here to debate that point with you. But just because you no longer trust me is no reason to punish Joy and Beans. I'd like to know that someone who cares for the animal as much as I do, someone like Joy, will be looking out for him."

"How long will you be gone?"

He slid his fingers along the brim of his hat. "I'm not sure. Perhaps a month or more."

"That's quite a lot of time to be gone from your business."

Did she seem so disapproving because of the commitment she'd have to make with Beans, or was there another reason?

She hadn't asked for an explanation, at least not outright, but he decided to give her one, anyway. "I'm going to help Belva to get settled into her new place and to deal with some staffing issues. I'm not sure how long that will take, but I've committed to not leave her until I'm satisfied everything is running smoothly." The news about Belva's inheritance and her moving to her newly acquired estate had broke yesterday, so he wasn't betraying any confidences.

"I see." She tilted her head, studying him almost analytically. "But you *are* coming back?"

He saw no indication of whether she was hoping for a yes or no answer from him. "I am." That was part of the thinking he'd done these past few days. He'd come very close to telling Belva he'd take her up on her offer after all.

But in the end he'd decided he wasn't going to run away. Not from Verity. And not from his past. "But don't worry, I will make very sure that our paths don't cross any more than they must. You have no need to fear you will receive any unwanted attentions from me. You've made it clear you want me out of your and Joy's lives and I plan to honor that wish."

It hurt that she felt this way, but he couldn't let it define his life, who he was. He'd dealt with loss before. This was just a different kind of loss.

He felt his jaw tighten and he deliberately relaxed it. "I just have one last thing I want to say. I've made a lot of mistakes in my life, some of them really big mistakes. Those mistakes have been costly, to me and to those around me. I regret what happened Friday, and the pain it cost you, more deeply than you will ever know."

He put his hat back on. "Tell Joy goodbye for me. I'll come by to retrieve Beans when I return." With that he turned and walked away.

Verity watched him depart and tried to sort out the emotions she was feeling, without much success.

Deciding she needed a walk to clear her mind, she went inside to clean up. When she told Joy about Nate leaving Beans in her care, her daughter wasn't as excited as she'd thought she would be.

"But Beans will be sad that Mr. Cooper is gone," her daughter said. "And I will be, too."

"He won't be gone forever. He's coming back whenever his business is finished."

"But you said he would be gone for *weeks*. That's a long time. Me and Beans are going to miss him."

"I'm afraid it can't be helped." And with that unhelpful answer, she headed to her room before her daughter could press further.

As Verity changed clothes, she remembered what Mr. Barr had said, something along the lines of children giving their heart only to those who are deserving.

Verity had intended to take a nice long walk, but somehow she found herself standing in the doorway to Hazel's shop.

Hazel looked up and gave her a broad, welcoming smile. "Hi there, come on in. Have you heard the news about Belva? It's all anyone is talking about."

Verity joined her at the counter and nodded. "I have. I'm happy for her."

"You should have seen Eunice this morning at the mercantile. The poor woman couldn't decide if she was more happy for her niece or irritated that Belva had kept the whole thing secret from her. I, for one, have a new respect for Belva. Anyone who can keep a secret from a busybody like Eunice, while living under the same roof with her no less, is one clever, resourceful person."

Verity was able to smile at that. "It seems she was able to keep it a secret from everyone, not just Eunice."

"Except perhaps Mr. Cooper."

"Mr. Cooper?" Funny how she couldn't seem to get away from him.

"Yes." Hazel was obviously enjoying being privy to something Verity wasn't. "Haven't you heard? He's going to go with her to help her deal with the solicitors and make sure she gets settled in okay."

"I heard."

"Well, I imagine she gave him more than a few hours' notice when she asked him—don't you?"

Of course. So that was the bond the two of them shared—Belva had trusted him with her secret.

Hazel, apparently tired of waiting for a response from her, tried a slight change of subject. "I hear he went to see you this morning."

Verity grimaced. "Word certainly travels fast around here."

"Well? Was it just to let you know he was leaving?"

"That, and he asked us to watch over Beans while he was away."

"I hope this means the two of you have made up."

"Made up." Verity couldn't control the note of anger in her voice. "Hazel, we didn't have a lover's spat. He

put Joy's life in danger. That's not something I can easily forgive."

"I know, but—"

"The subject is closed. Besides, there was something altogether different I came here to discuss with you."

Hazel didn't seem at all happy with her change of subject, but she didn't argue. "And what might that be?"

"I've decided that I'm not ready to open a millinery shop right now after all, so there's no point in us discussing it."

"If it's the money, I can—"

"It's not that." She grimaced. "Well, it's not *just* that. I've decided I want to spend more time with Joy. Setting up a millinery shop, even if I did it here with you, would take away from that. Maybe, once she starts school in the fall, we can talk about it again."

Hazel's lips were pursed in disapproval and her hands were crossed over her chest. "And when fall arrives you'll have some other excuse."

Verity was taken aback by her friend's directness. "You don't know that—"

"Oh, but I do." She waved a hand. "It's what you do. Any time, *any* time, you get close to achieving some long-held dream, you find a reason to back away. Like you're doing with your millinery-shop dream. And with the way you're pushing Mr. Cooper away."

Verity took exception to that. "Pushing Mr. Cooper away has *nothing* to do with anything but his trustworthiness. He promised to keep an eye on Joy, and because he broke that promise she wandered off. It ended well, but that was no thanks to him."

"Actually, according to what I heard, it was he who actually found her."

Verity made an impatient movement with her hands. "Yes, of course. But she was missing for twenty minutes. So many things could have happened to her."

"But they didn't. And what did he do to earn your wrath—he turned his back for just a few minutes in order to help one of the other children."

She couldn't believe Hazel was actually taking his side in this. "With a child Joy's age, a few minutes is all it takes."

"You mean like that day a few weeks ago when she ended up in the street in front of my shop."

Verity felt as if she'd been slapped in the face. "I don't… It's not the same…"

Hazel's expression softened. "I wasn't trying to imply that you're not a good mother, Verity. I just wanted to help you see that it can happen to anyone, even the most vigilant of guardians. Even *you* can't keep your eyes on Joy every hour of every day."

Verity shook her head, refusing to accept that.

But Hazel wasn't ready to let it drop. "Yes, something could happen when you're not looking. Like with Arthur. And with your parents. But you've got to trust that God is in control."

Then Hazel straightened. "But, back to my original complaint. You've become quite adept at giving up before you reach the finish line. I'm not sure what it is you're scared of—failing, achieving your dream but being disappointed by it, or something else. Whatever it is, you need to take a really good, honest look at yourself and see what kind of example you're setting for Joy."

What did she mean by that? Surely—

Hazel stepped forward and wrapped her arms around Verity. "I love you like you were my sister. But it's a sister's job to say the things to you that no one else will."

Unsure how to respond to that, Verity merely nodded and took her leave.

Not wanting to pass in front of Nate's shop, she turned in the opposite direction. Then turned on Schoolhouse Road. She wasn't ready to return home yet. She needed to be alone and do some prayerful thinking about what Hazel had just said to her. And there was a nice quiet spot in an open field just past the schoolyard that was perfect for that.

How could Hazel, her very best friend, have said such things to her? That she was being too hard on Nate. That she was setting a bad example for Joy. That—

"Mrs. Leggett?"

She stopped walking and found herself confronted by a young boy. She realized now that she had been passing the schoolyard and all the children were out at recess, which must be where he had come from.

Taking a closer look at the student, she recognized him as one of the boys who'd been involved in Nate's rescue of Davey.

"Hello, JJ. Is there something I can do for you?"

"I just wanted to say how really sorry I am for what happened with your little girl on Friday."

His words caught her by surprise, but she smiled down at him. "Thank you for your concern, JJ, but Joy is fine now."

The boy swallowed, something obviously still on

his mind. "But I've been feeling real guilty about what happened, and I just wanted you to know."

"Guilty? JJ, I know you were there when Joy went missing, but none of this is your fault."

"Yes, it is." The boy's Adam's apple bobbed twice, then he drew his shoulders back. "Mr. Cooper, he asked me to keep an eye on Joy while he was helping Davey. I was supposed to let him know if she tried to get up. But I was just so worried about Davey, and then he yelled real loud and I just forgot all about watching her. I'm just so, so sorry."

Nate had assigned someone to watch Joy? Why hadn't he told her? Then the explanation jumped out at her—because he was trying to sparc JJ's feelings, of course.

She put a hand on the boy's shoulder. "Thank you for telling me, JJ, and for your apology. It takes a really brave person to own up to something like that."

Some of the tension seemed to leave the boy and he offered her a shaky smile. "I just thought you ought to know, it wasn't Mr. Cooper's fault." And with that, he rushed back onto the schoolyard.

Verity slowly continued on her way, her head spinning with everything she'd heard today.

What if Nate had told her about JJ's role? Would it have made a difference? Or would she have railed at him, anyway? Was she, like Hazel said, afraid of achieving her dreams, to the extent that she looked for reasons not to reach for them?

What had she become?

And what had it cost her?

The next morning, Verity approached the saddle shop with some trepidation. She'd spent much of yesterday searching her heart and praying for both clarity and guidance.

So many things had come clear to her now, not the least of which was that she had been hiding behind this cautious, indecisive attitude for most of her life, and it had kept her from enjoying so many of the blessings God had in store for her. And even worse than that, she had been well on her way to doing that to Joy, as well.

She had also realized, with absolute clarity, that she loved Nate, had loved him for a while now, and that she had been doing just as Hazel said, pushing him away out of fear.

But no more. She was ready to reach for that dream—even if she was too late, it was worth risking that disappointment to have a chance at that kind of happiness.

But some of her old fears returned as she wondered if she'd taken too long to come to her senses. He'd said yesterday that he was ready to let her go. Had he meant it?

She reached his shop door only to find it locked. The Closed sign hung in the window and all the shades were drawn. Well, that was to be expected since he'd be leaving today. But surely he hadn't actually gone to the station yet—the train didn't leave for another hour and a half.

Taking a deep breath, she knocked on the door.

Nothing. No light, no sound of movement.

Had she missed him after all?

She knocked again, louder this time. Still no response.

She couldn't let him go off for goodness knows how long without letting him know how she truly felt. She'd prefer to have that discussion in private, but if she had to have it at the train depot, or in the middle of Main Street for that matter, she intended to have her say.

From the corner of her eye, Verity saw that she had attracted some attention from a few passersby on the sidewalk. She also spotted Hazel standing in the doorway of her shop, giving her an approving grin.

Titling her chin up defiantly, Verity ignored her audience, raised her fist, and this time she pounded the door for all she was worth.

Chapter Twenty-Two

Nate had his bag packed and was ready to head to the train station. Trouble was, it was ninety minutes until the train was scheduled to pull in.

So what did he do with himself in the meantime?

If he had a piano here he could lose himself in music. If Beans were here, he could take him for a walk.

But since neither of those things was true, he was left to his own thoughts. And he'd had just about enough of his own thoughts lately.

An unexpected sound caught his attention. Was someone knocking at his shop door?

He considered ignoring it—after all, he was leaving town, so he wasn't available to do any repair or commission work right now. But then he thought better of it. Perhaps whoever it was wanted one of his stock pieces. Besides, it was a distraction, and that's just what he needed right now.

As he headed down the stairs, the knock came again, this time louder, more insistent. That didn't sound like a customer. He quickened his pace, making it to the door in record time. He turned the knob and yanked the door open, then froze as he saw Verity standing there, poised to knock again.

"Hello," she said feebly, looking suddenly shy and uncertain.

"Is something wrong? Is it Beans?"

She waved a hand in a feeble gesture. "No, no, nothing like that. I just needed to speak to you before you leave."

What was going on? When he'd met with her yesterday she'd hardly said anything at all, and what words she *had* uttered had been hard, unforgiving. He wasn't sure he could stand much more of that right now.

Then she looked at him with a vulnerability that snagged at his heart. "May I come in? I promise I won't keep you long."

Without a word he stepped aside to allow her to enter.

She walked to the center of the room, then turned to face him.

Whatever she had to say, she was being uncharacteristically dramatic about it.

"I made a couple of decisions last night," she said by way of opening. "Well, this morning, really, since it was well after midnight."

Where was she going with this? "Making decisions is a good thing," he said mildly.

She nodded. "I decided I'm going to take Hazel up on her offer and go into business with her."

Despite the tension between them, he was proud of her. He knew how much she hated taking risks, and this was a big one. This time he was able to give her a genuine smile. "So you're finally ready to reach out and try to catch your dream. I know it seems scary, but if there's anything I can do to help, from a purely business perspective of course, let me know."

"Thank you." The smile she gave him was every bit as warm as those she'd given him during that ill-fated berry-picking expedition. Was her excitement over her newfound business decision spilling over into other parts of her life?

Then he shut down that train of thought. He'd let himself be fooled by her softening attitude in the past. He couldn't let it happen again. So he pasted on a polite smile. "I'm almost disappointed that I'm going to be away while you're getting everything up and running."

"So am I."

It was getting harder and harder to ignore those wistful looks she was giving him. "Talk to Adam. He can help you get your business off on the right foot."

"I will."

She stood there silently, but he could tell there was something else she had left to say. Then he remembered she'd said she'd made two decisions. "Was there anything else?"

"Yes." She straightened and met his gaze with a straight-from-the-heart directness. "I couldn't let you go away without telling you how I feel."

Everything inside him stilled, waiting to hear what she'd say next.

"I've been a fool and a coward. You have an adventurer's heart—you're impulsive, you're willing to try new things, and you know how to make a game out of most anything. You're not afraid to take charge when necessary, but you can follow just as well. When you see someone who needs help or something that needs doing, you find a way to get it done. And you have the biggest heart of anyone I've ever met."

His pulse, traitor that it was, was ignoring his resolve to not read too much into her words. She could just be apologizing, nothing more.

But she wasn't through talking. "Yet, knowing all that, I ignored what my heart was telling me and looked for ways to push you away. Because you're not the kind of man I wanted to fall in love with—you're not predictable, deliberate or particularly cautious."

She took a step closer. "But as I said, my heart has a mind of its own, and it finally got through to me. I love you. You're not a safe choice, but you're the person I want to spend my life with. I know you have no reason to trust me, to return those feelings, but I had to say it to you because you deserved to know."

She loved him? Did she really mean that? Or would she turn on him the next time he failed her? "What happened with Joy—"

"Was no more your fault than her nearly getting run over by a wagon was mine." Her expression held regret and something else. "You could have thrown that back at me all the time I was blaming you, but you didn't."

"I couldn't. You already felt so guilty—"

Her smile wavered. "There you go, being all noble again, making me love you even more."

He still couldn't wrap his mind around those words, couldn't believe after her coldness of the past few days that she could mean those words.

Then he saw her expression shift, saw the hurt and disappointment behind the overly bright smile she pasted on her lips. "Well, I've said what I had to say. And as I said, I don't really expect you to return those feelings after all I put you through. I hope you and Belva have a nice trip."

She made as if to pass him and he stepped in front of her. "Verity, please don't say those words unless you mean them." The words felt as if they'd been torn from someplace deep inside him. "Because I do love you— deeply, completely, eternally. And I love Joy as if she were my own daughter. But I will never be those things you say you want. I will never be the safe choice. So it would be far better for you to never say those words to me again than to say them lightly."

She lifted a hand to stroke the side of his cheek. "You are the man I want—not some list of traits. I love you, not because you're a hero—which you are, by the way. But I love you because of the man you are. I love *you*. Today and forever."

Those beautiful words, the love shining from her eyes, the soft caress of her hand on his face all combined to erase the last of his doubts. His hand snaked up to close over hers and he gave her palm a quick kiss, his gaze never leaving hers. But he'd much prefer to kiss those sweet lips of hers. And when she lifted her face to him, it was all the encouragement he needed.

He pressed his lips to hers. And once more was lost.

Verity wrapped her arms around Nate's neck. Because of all they'd been through, and all they'd just promised each other, this kiss was much sweeter than the last one. Her heart was so full she thought it would burst from her chest.

And this time when the kiss ended, it was with mutual sighs. He held her against his chest a moment, stroking her hair, both of them comfortable with the silence, knowing that there would be time enough later to speak of the future they would build together.

For now she reveled in his closeness, in having his arms around her, in knowing he'd forgiven her and returned her love.

Why had she ever feared this?

Finally she pushed back, resting her hands on his chest. "You still have a train to catch."

He grimaced. "I wish now that I'd never agreed to go."

"You wouldn't be the man I love if you hadn't. Belva needs you right now."

He bent down and dropped a kiss on her forehead. "I expect you to be planning a wedding while I'm gone. Because I'll be wanting to walk you down the aisle when I get back."

She raised a brow and put a hand to her heart. "Why, Mr. Cooper, is that a proposal?"

Nate frowned. "Did I skip over that part?"

"I do believe you did."

He placed a finger under her chin and tilted it up. His beautifully intense blue eyes were filled with an emotion that set her heart aflutter all over again.

"Verity Leggett, will you do me the very great honor of agreeing to be my wife?"

She threw her arms around his neck again. "I thought you'd never ask."

Epilogue

Verity stood at the back of the church, accompanied by her uncle, her daughter and her best friend.

"Hazel, stop fussing with my dress. It's fine."

Her friend ignored her plea. "Hold still. I just want to make sure this bow is perfectly even." Hazel stepped back and then sighed. "You make an absolutely radiant bride."

"Thank you." And Verity felt radiant. And blessed. And so marvelously happy.

It was her wedding day.

It had seemed as if this day would never come. Nate had been gone for five very long weeks. They'd exchanged letters during that time, but it hadn't been the same as seeing him. Hearing his voice. Holding his hand. Kissing his lips.

He'd finally returned to Turnabout just three days ago and today they were getting married. Within the hour she would become Mrs. Nathaniel Edward Cooper. She definitely liked the sound of that.

Joy glanced up at her. "Mama, how come your bouquet is so much bigger than mine?"

She smiled at her ever-curious daughter. "Because I'm the bride and you're the flower girl."

Joy seemed to think about that for a moment. Then she looked up again. "Well, then, why can't I be the bride and you be the flower girl?"

"Because you're not old enough to be a bride yet." She gave her daughter a serious, conspiratorial look. "Besides, I have to be the bride so Mr. Cooper can become your new daddy."

That seemed to make everything okay for Joy. Her demeanor lightened and she nodded in satisfaction. "Oh, okay."

Verity turned to her uncle, stepping forward to adjust his tie. "Uncle Grover, did I ever tell you and Aunt Betty how much I appreciate you taking me into your home all those years ago, and how very much I love you?"

Her uncle patted her hand, gazing at her fondly. "It was our pleasure, my dear. You have brought so much joy into our lives." He glanced at the little girl standing nearby. "Both literally and figuratively."

There was to be a grand reception at her aunt and uncle's home after the wedding. Verity had tried to dissuade them but they had insisted.

She stood on tiptoe and kissed her uncle on the cheek. "Thank you for making me feel loved."

Piano music signaled the beginning of the ceremony and Verity's pulse jumped in anticipation. Hazel opened the door and signaled Joy to lead the way. Verity smiled as she saw that Joy had managed to slip Lulu among the flowers in her basket.

The little girl, her flower basket on her arm, headed

down the aisle with her head held high, leading the way to where Nate waited for them both.

Then it was Verity's turn. She slid her hand onto her uncle's arm and together they walked through the door and into the church proper.

And there he was, standing tall and proud at the front of the church, watching her with those amazing blue eyes, waiting for her to join him.

His gaze was focused on her with enough love and pride to make her feel like the luckiest woman on earth. She was so blessed to have this man in her life.

Joy stood beside him, holding on to his right hand. The little girl's face was beaming with happiness. The sight of the two of them together, obviously already connected by a beautiful father-daughter love for each other, made her happiness complete.

When they finally reached the front of the church, Uncle Grover turned and kissed her cheek, then placed her hand in Nate's free one. In a completely impulsive, unplanned gesture, she reached down and placed her bouquet in Joy's flower basket then took her free hand. For a moment they stood in a circle there at the front of the church, the three of them joined together, a symbolic sign of the life they were embarking on today.

Nate smiled into Verity's eyes, loving that she was learning to be impulsive, learning to figure out when it was okay to follow her instincts.

He gave her hand a squeeze and she squeezed right back. Then Verity bent down to kiss her daughter on the cheek and released her hand. Nate, with great formality, escorted the little girl to the front pew, where Verity's aunt and uncle sat. He, too, kissed her cheek, and then seated her, bowed and turned to return to Verity's side.

His oh-so-wonderful wife-to-be welcomed him back with a smile that held love and the promise of wonderful things to come.

He couldn't believe this woman, this sweet, intelligent, sometimes frustrating but always loving woman, was finally going to be his—his to cherish, to protect, to share his life with. She knew about all his scars, his dark secrets, his weaknesses, and she loved him anyway.

He had truly been blessed when God brought her—and the little girl he already loved as a daughter—into his life, a blessing he would spend the rest of his days thanking God for.

Then together, he and Verity turned to face Reverend Harper, ready to speak the vows that would bind their lives together from this day forward.

Vowing to love and cherish, for the rest of his life, the woman standing before him with the sweetest smile and eyes brimmed with love for him was the easiest promise he'd ever had to make. His "I do" was said loudly and with absolute conviction.

Hearing her speak those same vows in her beautiful voice and with that steady, unwavering gaze that was focused on only him both humbled him and filled him with pride.

At last he had found the place he belonged—right here at the side of the woman he loved.

* * * * *

Dear Reader,

Thank you so much for picking up a copy of Verity and Nate's story. Verity first popped up in the previous Texas Grooms book, *Her Holiday Family*. She had a very minor role in that book, but when she agreed not once but twice to put her own life on hold to answer Simon's call for help with the orphan children, I knew I wanted to dig deeper into who this woman was—she had to have a book of her own.

It was as I was doing that digging, and figuring out how her husband had died, that the character of Nate Cooper began to take form. But Nate was a bit stubborn and it took a little while for him to reveal all of his secrets. The character who finally emerged, however, was one I absolutely fell in love with. I hope you did, as well.

If you enjoyed this book, I hope you'll look for the next in the series, which will feature the town's schoolteacher, Janell Whitman. Janell and Hank's story will hit the shelves in December 2015. For more information on this and other books set in Turnabout, please visit my website at www.winniegriggs.com or follow me on Facebook at www.facebook.com/WinnieGriggs.Author.

And as always, I love to hear from readers. Feel free to contact me at winnie@winniegriggs.com with your thoughts on this or any other of my books.

Wishing you a life abounding with love and blessings.

Winnie Griggs

COMING NEXT MONTH FROM
Love Inspired® Historical

Available June 2, 2015

WAGON TRAIN PROPOSAL
Journey West
by Renee Ryan

When Tristan McCullough's intended wagon train bride chooses someone else, Rachel Hewitt accepts a position as his children's caretaker—not as his wife. She'll only marry for love...yet perhaps the McCulloughs are the family she's always wanted.

HER CONVENIENT COWBOY
Wyoming Legacy
by Lacy Williams

When cowboy Davy White discovers a widowed soon-to-be-mother in his cabin, he immediately offers her shelter from the blizzard. As their friendship grows, so does Rose Evans's belief that Davy is her wish come true for a family by Christmas.

THE TEXAN'S TWIN BLESSINGS
by Rhonda Gibson

Emily Jane Rodgers dreams of opening her own bakery, not falling in love. Then she meets William Barns and his adorable twin nieces, and soon the ready-made family is chipping away at Emily Jane's guarded heart and changing her mind about marriage and happily-ever-afters!

FAMILY OF HER DREAMS
by Keli Gwyn

As a railroad stationmaster and recent widower, Spencer Abbott needs help raising his young children. He's surprised when Tess Grimsby fits so well with his family—maybe she's meant to be more than a nanny to his children...

LIHCNM0515

REQUEST YOUR FREE BOOKS!

2 FREE INSPIRATIONAL NOVELS
PLUS 2 FREE MYSTERY GIFTS

Love Inspired® HISTORICAL

Rachel Hewitt survived the journey to Oregon, but arriving in her new home brings new challenges—like three adorable girls who need a nanny, and their sheriff father, who needs a second chance at love…

Read on for a sneak preview of Renee Ryan's WAGON TRAIN PROPOSAL, the heartwarming conclusion of the series JOURNEY WEST.

"Are you my new mommy?"

Rachel blinked in stunned silence at the child staring back at her. She saw a lot of herself in the precocious six-year-old. In the determined angle of her tiny shoulders. In the bold tilt of her head. In the desperate hope simmering in her big, sorrowful blue eyes.

For a dangerous moment, Rachel had a powerful urge to tug the little girl into her arms and give her the answer she so clearly wanted.

Careful, she warned herself. *Think before you speak.*

"Well?" Hands still perched on her hips, Daisy's small mouth turned down at the corners. "Are you my new mommy or not?"

"I'm sorry, Daisy, no. I'm not your new mommy. However, I am your new neighbor, and I'll certainly see you often, perhaps even daily."

Tristan cut in then, touching his daughter's shoulder to gain her attention. "Daisy, my darling girl, we've talked about this before. You cannot go around asking every woman you meet if she's your mommy."

"But, Da—" the little girl's lower lip jutted out "—you said you were bringing us back a new mommy when you got home."

"No, baby." He pulled his hand away from her shoulder then shoved it into his pocket. "I said I *might* bring you home a new mommy."

When tears formed in the little girl's eyes, Rachel found herself interceding. "I may not be your new mommy," she began, taming a stray wisp of the child's hair behind her ear, "but I can be your very good friend."

The little girl's eyes lit up and she plopped into Rachel's lap. No longer able to resist, Rachel wrapped her arms around the child and hugged her close. Lily attempted to join her sister on Rachel's lap. When Daisy refused to budge, the little girl settled for pulling on Rachel's sleeve. "You don't want to be our new mommy?"

The poor child sounded so despondent Rachel's heart twisted. "Oh, Lily, it's not a matter of want. You see, I'm already committed to—"

She cut off her own words, realizing she had no other commitments now that her brother was married. He didn't need her to run his household. *No one* needed her. Except, maybe, this tiny family.

Don't miss
WAGON TRAIN PROPOSAL
by Renee Ryan,
available June 2015 wherever
Love Inspired® Historical books and ebooks are sold.

Can a widow and widower ever leave their grief in the past and forge a new future—and a family—together?

Read on for a sneak preview of
THE AMISH WIDOW'S SECRET.

"Wait, before you go. I have an important question to ask you."

Sarah nodded her head and sat back down.

"I stayed up until late last night, thinking about your situation and mine. I prayed, and *Gott* kept pushing this thought at me." He took a deep breath. "I wonder, would you consider becoming my *frau*?"

Sarah held up her hand, as if to stop his words. "I…"

"Before you speak, let me explain." Mose took another deep breath. "I know you still love Joseph, just as I still love my Greta. But I have *kinder* who need a mother to guide and love them. Now that Joseph's gone and the farm's being sold, you need a place to call home, people who care about you, a family. We can join forces and help each other." He saw a panicked expression forming in her eyes. "It would only be a marriage of convenience. The girls need a loving mother and you've already proven you can be that. What do you say, Sarah Nolt? Will you be my wife?"

Sarah sat silent, her face turned away. She looked into Mose's eyes. "You'd do this for me? But…you don't know me."

"I'd do this for us," Mose corrected, and smiled.

The tips of Sarah's fingers nervously pleated and unpleated a scrap of her skirt. "But we hardly know each other. What would people think? They will say I took advantage of your good nature."

Mose smiled. "So, let them talk. They'd be wrong and we'd know it. I want this marriage for both of us, for the *kinder*. We can't let others decide what is best for our lives. I believe this marriage is *Gott*'s plan for us."

Sarah's face cleared and she seemed to come to a decision. She smoothed out the fabric of her skirt and tidied her hair, then finally took Mose's outstretched hand with a smile. "You're right. This is our life. I accept your proposal, Mose Fisher. I will be your *frau* and your *kinder*'s mother."

Don't miss
THE AMISH WIDOW'S SECRET
by Cheryl Williford,
available June 2015 wherever
Love Inspired® books and ebooks are sold.

*Could an intruder at the White House be the break the
Capitol K-9 Unit needs to track down a killer?*

*Read on for a sneak preview of
SECURITY BREACH,
the fourth book in the exciting new series
CAPITOL K-9 UNIT.*

Nicholas Cole hurried toward the White House special in-
house security chief's office in the West Wing, gripping the
leash for his K-9 partner, Max. General Margaret Meyer
stood behind her oak desk, a fierce expression on her face.

The general moved from behind her desk. "This office
has been searched."

He came to attention in front of his boss, having a hard
time shaking his military training as a navy SEAL. "Anything missing?"

"No, but someone had searched through the Jeffries
file, and it would be easy to take pictures of the papers
and evidence the team has uncovered so far."

"What do you want me to do, ma'am?" Nicholas knew
the murder of Michael Jeffries, son of the prominent
congressman Harland Jeffries, was important to the
general as well as his unit captain, Gavin McCord.

"I want to know who was in my office. It could be
the break we've needed on this case. With the Easter Egg
Roll today, the White House has been crawling with visitors since early this morning, so it won't be easy." She

shook her head. "Especially with the Oval Office and the Situation Room here in the West Wing being used for the festivities. If you discover anything, find me right away."

"Yes, ma'am." Nicholas exited the West Wing by the West Colonnade and cut across the Rose Garden toward where the Easter Egg Roll was taking place.

He scanned the people gathered. His survey came to rest upon Selena Barrow, the White House tour director, who was responsible for planning this event. Even from a distance, Selena commanded a person's attention. She was tall and slender with long, wavy brown hair and the bluest eyes, but what drew him to Selena was her air of integrity and compassion.

Selena would have an updated list of the people who were invited to the party. It might save him a trip to the front gate if he asked her for it. And it would give him a reason to talk to her.

Don't miss
SECURITY BREACH by Margaret Daley,
available June 2015 wherever
Love Inspired® Suspense books and ebooks are sold.